Maddie fought the lust zinging through her body...

...her sensible side telling her to get rid of him. Her sensible side rarely won in situations like this. "Talk?"

"Yeah, you know. The thing you're doing with your mouth."

Her mind flashed to him kissing her. "I like what you do with your mouth."

She held his gaze, willing him to come out of the shell of sarcasm and bad attitude he crawled into whenever she was near.

"Don't," he said, slamming his hand against the table. "Don't fuck with my head."

Her chest heaved. He was so close. She knew how he could be when he was mad. Knew how he'd take her. Nobody could make her feel what MJ made her feel when he was cloaked in darkness trying to break free.

"It's not your head I have in mind," she said, easing forward.

His lips tightened, eyes narrowed. He grabbed her and pushed her down onto her back on top of the table. His hands fisted in the hem of her shirt. She wrapped her legs around his waist and pressed her hips into him.

He groaned. "You just don't know."

Acclaim for *Taken by Storm*

"This book hooked me from the very beginning and glued me to every page. MJ stole my heart and quickly became one of my new favorite leading men. Loved it."

—Michelle Valentine, *New York Times*
Bestselling Author of *Rock the Heart*

"*Taken by Storm* is a passionate love story that grips you by the heart from the first page and doesn't let go. MJ and Maddie's love is soul-deep. Maine has written a masterpiece!"

—Kristen Proby, Bestselling Author of the
With Me in Seattle series

"If it were even possible for another Rocha man to seduce and beguile me, MJ delivers from the very first page. With his father's DNA and dimples, he's every woman's dream in and out of the bedroom. Maine has crafted another fast-paced, passionate love story."

—Katie Ashley, *New York Times*
Bestselling Author of *The Proposition*

"Sexy, beautifully written, and just plain HOT, *Taken by Storm* stole me away for hours and is a read I plan to take in again and again. Sorry Hubby, MJ is officially my new book boyfriend!"

—Emily Snow, *New York Times* and *USA Today*
Bestselling Author of *Devoured* and *Tidal*

Taken by Storm

BY KELLI MAINE

FOREVER

NEW YORK   BOSTON

Copyright © 2013 by Kelli Maine

Excerpt from *Taken* copyright © 2012 by Kelli Maine

Excerpt from *No Takebacks* copyright © 2012 by Kelli Maine

All rights reserved. In accordance with the U.S. Copyright Act of 1976, the scanning, uploading, and electronic sharing of any part of this book without the permission of the publisher is unlawful piracy and theft of the author's intellectual property. If you would like to use material from the book (other than for review purposes), prior written permission must be obtained by contacting the publisher at permissions@hbgusa.com. Thank you for your support of the author's rights.

Forever

Hachette Book Group

237 Park Avenue

New York, NY 10017

www.HachetteBookGroup.com

Printed in the United States of America

Originally published as an e-book in April 2013

First trade edition: June 2013

10 9 8 7 6 5 4 3 2 1

RRD-C

Forever is an imprint of Grand Central Publishing.

The Forever name and logo are trademarks of Hachette Book Group, Inc.

The Hachette Speakers Bureau provides a wide range of authors for speaking events. To find out more, go to www.hachettespeakersbureau.com or call (866) 376-6591.

The publisher is not responsible for websites (or their content) that are not owned by the publisher.

ISBN: 9781455598991

Dedicated to The One.

Acknowledgments

Introducing MJ and Maddie into Merrick and Rachael's lives and love story was incredibly fun for me, but no easy task. From front to back cover and everything in between, the support, encouragement and combined literary brain power of Emmanuelle Morgen, Lauren Plude and Amy Pierpont was invaluable in bringing *Taken by Storm* together. Jessica Bromberg started introducing *Taken by Storm* to readers before the story was even finished, and the Grand Central Forever art department went beyond my wildest expectations.

I'm not sure where I'd be today in my writing career if it weren't for a group of exceptional women who I've had the good fortune of talking and sharing my work with daily for the past five years. Michelle Valentine, Emily Snow and Katie Ashley, let's face it—you guys are family, and Kristen Proby, our newest cousin, you make every day brighter with your kindness and humor. Ava Black, you're an inspiration. From maps of islands to family trees, you always take on my projects—and you're next!

Melanie Kramer Santiago, Jennifer Wood, Chanelle Gray, and all the LitBitches, you're a force of raw talent to be reckoned with. I look forward to many more celebrations and triumphs with you in years to come.

Maureen Mayer has been supportive of *Taken* and Rachael and Merrick from the beginning. Thank you for suggesting the name Nadia. It's perfect! Scott Mosley, I'm glad we were introduced, mate! You look handsome on the cover. Neda Amini, Maryse Black, Cris Soriaga Hadarly, Holly Malgieri, Kim Box Person and all the book bloggers who are too many to name, you're more than exceptionally giving of your time, you're friends to authors and I'm so glad I got to know you.

I would be amiss to not mention one person who was stuck listening to me drone on and on about writing every weekday for years. Many of my author friends know him as Co-worker Dan. Dan listening to me through the best and worst of times and being there to bounce plot ideas off of has meant the world to me.

Over the past five years, my kids have grown to know that Mom doesn't leave her laptop for long. For them and my husband, whose patience is constantly tested being married to me, I strive to be the best author I can be so not one minute of the time I spend away from them is wasted.

Thank you to you all. I appreciate you!

One

The soles of MJ's boots echoing off the concrete driveway sounded like drum beats in his head. A raging, metal death band soundtrack to his shit life. He reached his car—a black '68 Camaro convertible bought with blood money from his grandfather—and tossed his duffel bag in the backseat.

"Don't tell me you're running away again."

Her voice sparked chills up his back. MJ turned and looked, but could only see a cloud of cigarette smoke lingering under the garage light. "Stay out of my business," he said into the darkness.

Her deep, sultry chuckle sank inside his ears and made him close his eyes. That laugh. So many nights...that laugh in the dark, under the sheets. God, how he'd ached for her when she left.

"I thought you quit smoking," he said, despite himself. Why could he never walk away from her?

Maddie slipped around the corner from the side of the garage and leaned against the door. He could just make out the faint red shine of her lips. Her dark hair loose around her shoulders. The predatory gleam in her eye. "Old habits die hard."

MJ let out a sharp laugh. "Not all of them." He opened

the car door and got behind the wheel. There was no way he'd stay and get lured into her bed again. No way he'd go through that kind of torture when she took off on him.

Never again.

Maddie had been his addiction, his drug, and he intended to stay clean. Clean, but not sober. The only place he wanted to be was at the bottom of a bottle of Jack Daniel's.

He fumbled with his keys, giving her one too many seconds to cross the driveway and reach his car. "The first time you ran away," she said, laying her hands on top of his car door, "you got as far as Coach's house. That time it was my fault because I spent two weeks of our summer at sleep-away camp and abandoned you here alone. Is it my fault this time too?"

Jesus, she was wearing that perfume—the one that smelled like vanilla and spice.

He remembered that summer. Two whole weeks without Maddie. She was the only bright spot in his life back then. His best friend, before she became even more.

His grandfather, Enzo Rocha, The Puppet Master, had kept MJ under his care and his thumb since he was born. MJ had been shipped from nanny to private boarding school, then another boarding school and another when he got kicked out for fighting, but he was never wanted under *this* roof—his grandfather's roof—this fucking mansion of a house where his grandfather would never even have had to see his face if he didn't want to. MJ's stays had been limited to short visits during summer and winter breaks.

And Maddie had always been there. The house manager's daughter. Four years older and wiser. Four years more experienced—a college girl when he was in high school. It was Maddie who had taken his virginity and his heart. It was Maddie who had destroyed his trust and ruined him for any other girl.

MJ's eyes roamed her face and down her body. The body that used to belong to him. His palms tingled with flesh memories of holding her breasts in his hands. The image of her naked was seared into his mind like it had been branded there. The way he made her sigh. The way he made her moan and whimper his name. His mouth watered, knowing exactly how she would taste, her lips, her skin, her...he had to stop himself. She wasn't his. She'd broken her promise. She'd left him.

"Where are you going?" Maddie asked him. "Can I come along?"

"My life is none of your business." MJ shot her a stony glare. "Why are you even here?" He threw up a hand to stop her from answering. "You know what? Never mind. I don't even care."

He shoved the key into the ignition and fired up the engine. When she didn't step back from the car, he glanced up at her to find her staring down at him. He tried to look away, but couldn't. She'd always had a way of seeing inside him to the pain and hurt. She could always make it go away, and damn it, he needed her to. So he kept his eyes glued to hers like she was a fucking life-line until he felt something shift and crack inside him.

Fucking Maddie.

"You're not doing this to me again." He put the car in reverse knowing, it was too late, his words were a lie.

❀

Maddie slowly strolled into the backyard. She hated hurting MJ. The hurt in his eyes, mixed with anger and something close to loathing...it was more than she could bear.

She wrapped her arms around her stomach and took a few deep breaths to calm her nerves. She should've found somewhere else to go.

Maddie laughed silently to herself. She'd asked MJ if he was running away, but she was the one doing the running. She fingered the diamond ring under her shirt hanging on the chain around her neck and felt the familiar sting of anxiety shoot up from her stomach to her throat. Talan had been so understanding when she told him she needed time to think. She wasn't sure she deserved it.

The night he gave her the ring, the city skyline in the sunset took Maddie's breath away. Across the table from her, Talan's hazel eyes didn't leave her face. His expression held so much love and sincerity. She had a feeling she knew what the special night was about, why he brought her to Coach Insignia all the way up on the seventy-second floor of the Renaissance Center. A romantic, sunset dinner at the most expensive restaurant in town could only mean one thing.

They'd finished their dinners, and Maddie's dessert sat

half-eaten on the plate in front of her. She couldn't eat one more bite.

She knew it was now or never.

Then the waiter approached their table with a bottle of chilled champagne and two flutes.

Maddie swallowed. Hard. Was this really happening?

She wasn't ready to be married. She wasn't ready to be with Talan for the rest of her life. Was she?

Purposely avoiding looking at Talan, Maddie watched the waiter walk away.

"Maddie?" Talan said.

She turned to him. He balanced a black ring box in the palm of his hand. She held her breath and studied his warm face, a sprinkle of freckles across his nose, amber flecks in his eyes, auburn hair to match the sunset outside the windows.

Talan was everything a woman wanted.

He was everything Maddie should want.

So, why was she so afraid?

He opened the box. A beautiful, platinum diamond ring sat on the cushion. "Will you do me the honor of being my wife?"

It felt like a porcupine crawled through her stomach. Yes. No. Her mind whirled. "I—I want to say yes, but I need some time to think."

Talan sat the ring box on the table and nodded, discouraged. "You don't want to be with me?"

"No! I do want to be with you." Maddie reached across and took his hand. "We haven't even been together a year yet. What's the rush?"

Talan frowned and rubbed his forehead. "No rush. It just felt like the right time."

Maddie's heart sank. How could she do this to him? She loved Talan and it wasn't like she'd never thought of marrying him over the last few months. They were clearly heading in that direction.

"This was a total surprise," she said. "I just need to think about it, that's all. Okay?"

Talan took a deep breath. "Maddie, maybe we need to take a break. Keep the ring and think about it." He opened her hand and sat the ring box on her palm.

It was heavier than she'd imagined it would be. "A break?"

She could tell he was disappointed and maybe even a little angry, but he wanted to break up?

"I love you, Maddie. Whatever you decide, it won't change that. But, I can't make you want to marry me. Take some time away from me to figure out how you feel. Do whatever you need to do to make your decision. When you're ready to be with me or let me go, tell me."

It had only been a couple days. The emotions the memory spurred in Maddie were still so strong, they knocked the breath out of her. She had no idea how to make this decision.

Maddie had wandered inside her father's apartment over the garage while reliving the night Talan proposed. Now, she paced the floor in her dad's living room. He should've been home from the big house by now. It wasn't that she was worried. She knew where he was, but she wanted him here. He was too old to be staying out so late. She wished he didn't need this job. The last person she wanted him working for was Enzo Rocha, the Old Man, as she and MJ liked to call him. But her dad had come to think of the Old Man as a good friend over the years he'd worked for him. She just hoped her dad hadn't mentioned the fact that she was back.

The Old Man had run her off a year and a half ago, but this time it was different. She was here for a good reason. A reason that had nothing to do with MJ.

Maddie sat on the end of the couch and dug her chain out from under her shirt. Her ring really was beautiful, a full carat emerald cut diamond set in a platinum band. It sparkled and shot rainbows up onto the ceiling.

She knew Talan would be at home, sitting up in bed with his electronic tablet wearing his black-framed glasses, no shirt and pajama pants. He'd have ESPN on the TV, but he wouldn't be paying any attention to it.

Contentment settled over her thinking about how warm it would be snuggled next to him. How he'd still smell faintly of cologne and play with her hair.

She'd been so lucky to meet Talan. After graduating from Michigan State and coming home to Sandy Springs for what she thought was forever, only to be run off by Enzo Roach, she was devastated when she moved back to East Lansing. She and Talan hadn't started dating right away. She told him about MJ, about how she'd had to break up with him, although she didn't dare tell Talan—or anyone—why she left Sandy Springs.

They became great friends first, then slowly, their relationship developed into more. He was perfect. Loving and loyal, caring, hard-working. She never had to worry about the ground shifting under her feet with him. He was stable and their relationship was what good marriages were based on.

Maddie curled up on the couch with her head on the armrest. She even liked Talan's family, and from what she knew from her married friends, that never happened.

Clearly, there were more pros than cons when it came to her decision. Any sane woman would jump at the chance to marry a man like Talan. So, what was she doing wasting time back in Sandy Springs, Georgia, at the Rocha Estate?

Don't answer that question, she told herself. It was of the rhetorical variety that had plagued her mind on repeat for the past year and a half. Every question came down to the same, one-word, one-name answer.

MJ.

❀

He hit the door of the Third Base Lounge with both hands, making it bounce back off the wall as he stepped inside. His first priority was a drink or five, then he'd move on to a distraction. Glancing around, he didn't see the female distraction he'd been getting around to knowing better. Carnally better. Too bad. Tonight would've been a night for her to remember.

He was glad Paul was behind the bar tonight and not

the new guy Coach had hired who tried to card MJ two nights ago. He settled in on a bar stool and ordered a double of Jack. This was home and Coach Harting, the owner, was as close to a father as he'd ever had. MJ had grown up eating peanuts and watching cartoons with Maddie in the bar's back office while Coach balanced his books.

Coach Harting had coached every summer Little League team MJ had ever been on and sponsored them with Third Base Lounge jerseys. He was the reason MJ made it onto the GSU baseball team at all after Maddie left.

Those first few months after she'd left, MJ had been a mess. He got drunk and passed out every night, dropped most of his classes his first semester, and started fighting with anyone who wouldn't back down. Coach wouldn't give up on him though, said MJ had too much talent to let a woman destroy his dreams. Coach met with the GSU baseball coach and personally vouched for MJ, said he'd kick MJ's ass if he didn't shape up. Somehow, the GSU coach believed him and let him on the team.

Now Coach owed MJ an ass whooping.

MJ took the shot glass from the bartender. "Keep these coming." He tossed the fiery whiskey down his throat and slammed the glass down onto the bar.

"Bad day?" Paul asked, whisking the empty away and replacing it with another.

MJ rolled his head back and forth from shoulder to shoulder. The Jack warmed his stomach and dulled his senses. "You wouldn't believe the day I've had."

Paul braced his hands against the bar. "A chick?"

MJ took a deep sip of his double shot, nodding. "Kicked me square in the balls." He swallowed and winced. No need to mention his daddy issues. That situation was too fucked up to even try to explain.

Paul dropped his hands. "Sorry, man."

"Yeah. Whatever. We haven't been together for over a year anyway."

Paul leaned in, resting his forearms on the bar. "Wait. You mean Maddie? Is she back?"

MJ exhaled sharply through his nose and downed the rest of his shot.

That was all the answer Paul needed. He gave MJ a friendly punch to the arm and shook his head before striding to the other end of the bar where he was being flagged down for a beer.

Someone ran into MJ from behind, jolting him sideways on his stool. Instantly enraged, he swung his fist around, connecting with the back of the guy's head. It was one of the idiots playing pool. "Watch yourself."

The guy grabbed the front of MJ's shirt and threw him back into his stool where he lost his balance and fell off onto his ass on the floor. "Want to try that again?"

Drunk and stumbling, it took a second for MJ to get onto his feet and start swinging. The dull, dark pounding in his head was a tribal drum beat spurring his anger. The man became every guy he'd ever imagined Maddie with in Michigan and MJ threw every punch harder than the last, determined to take back what was his. He wouldn't be denied any longer. MJ slammed his fist into the side of the man's head, making him shuffle sideways against the bar. MJ rushed forward, eager to finish this asshole.

With another punch to the man's gut, the man became MJ's father, and a surge of animosity crackled under MJ's skin. He would be heard. Seen. Acknowledged. His fists jabbed hard and fast against the man's face and abdomen. The cracks of fist against skin urged MJ on again and again. Thanks to his trusty friend, Jack Daniel's, he didn't even feel the hits he took.

A pair of hands grabbed him from behind, and as he was being dragged backward, he saw Paul had a hand on the other guy's chest pushing him back.

"You've got way to much piss and vinegar in you, Son," Coach said from behind him. "Let's get you back to the office and sobered up."

Looking up into Coach's face, etched with disappointment, MJ wished he'd make good on his promise and kick his ass. He deserved it.

Two

"Y our boy's drunk off his ass, Peach. Got in a fight. Come get him."

From his spot lying in the old, battered booth inside Coach's office, MJ heard Coach's words spinning around in his head. Peach. Maddie's nickname. "I'm not her boy," he mumbled, incoherently. "I'm not her boy," he said again, to make sure it was understood.

His bottom lip throbbed, and when he swiped it with his thumb, he realized it was split open and bleeding. One punch was all he let the other guy have. Or maybe it was the only one he remembered.

"Paul says you been in here talkin' about her all night," Coach said, putting a hand over the receiver to talk to MJ. "I've known you both too long to fool me, kid."

MJ could only imagine what Maddie must be thinking, must be saying on the other side of that phone conversation. The last thing she wanted was for him to be her boy. She'd made that perfectly clear.

MJ grabbed the sides of his head. Jesus, why did she have to come back? Thinking about her sent a freight train loose inside his head. Off the tracks. Derailed. Combusted into a million flaming pieces. Or was it the music blaring on the other side of the wall, and the crack of billiard balls breaking his brain in half?

Fuck, he was dizzy. And his stomach hurt like hell.

"Thanks, Peach. The kid owes you one." Coach hung up the phone and loomed over him, glaring down into the booth. "Your woman will be here in ten. Get your drunk ass out of that booth."

MJ grabbed the top of the booth and pulled himself up. "You know she's not my woman."

Coach cocked a gray, hairy eyebrow. "She's back, ain't she?"

MJ couldn't help but smirk. She *was* back. He didn't know why that made him feel like grinning like an idiot while facing Coach. Maybe because he couldn't hide anything from the man. Maybe because he was drunk off his ass.

"Make her stay this time." Coach smacked him on the back, sending spots flashing in front of his eyes and the room spinning.

Coach grabbed a bowl of peanuts off his desk and slid into the booth across from MJ. "You didn't come in here hell-bent on oblivion just because of her." He rested his arm across the back of the booth. "Tell me what's eatin' you."

How could he tell Coach what he'd come to the bar to drown? How could he admit that his father found out he existed and bolted without a word? Didn't even talk to him on the phone.

This fucking day. Why was he still conscious? "Same

old shit, Coach. Just wasting time until classes start again. Had to get out of the Old Man's house for a while." His words slurred in his ears. Slurred or not, they didn't sound convincing.

Chuckling and chewing peanuts, Coach shook his head. "Nah. You've been tame all summer long. All the sudden you get ants in your pants about getting out of that house, get shitfaced and start a fight in my bar? Who do you think you're talkin' to, boy? Something's got you riled up tonight, and it's not just that pretty Peach coming back."

"Peach," MJ muttered. Coach had started calling Maddie Peach when MJ was in fourth grade and addicted to playing Mario Bros. video games. Coach said MJ was Mario, the Italian stallion, and Maddie was Peach, his pretty princess— even though she could field a ball better than him back then.

MJ patted the scratched tabletop with his palm. "Really, it's cool. Sorry about the fight."

Coach narrowed his eyes but didn't press him. "I'm risking my business serving you underage you know. Don't start pulling this getting into fights shit and get the cops on my ass."

MJ patted the table again. "A few more months, and I'm legal. I'll keep it straight until then."

He laid his forehead on the table. The room had just stopped rotating when the door flew open and banged against the wall. The sound was like a nail being driven into the back of his skull.

"What the hell, MJ?" He didn't think Maddie would be

happy with the call to come haul his ass home, but he didn't expect her to be this livid.

He turned his head and willed his eyes to focus on her. "Hey, Mads. S'up?" Might as well stoke that fire. He could tell by her tight, drawn-in expression she was already in flames.

She stormed over to him and shoved his shoulder. It was all he could do to keep from falling over in the booth. "Don't s'up me! You come here, get drunk and start a fight? Who are you?"

Her eyes were bright and wet with unshed tears. Her eyebrows, dark tilted strips making a crease above her nose. That look made him want to crawl under the table. "Don't act all concerned. You've been back all of what? An hour?" He scoffed and shook his head. "Go back to Michigan and stay the fuck away from me."

He didn't look at her face, but by the way her shoulders sagged and her fists unclenched and fell to her sides, he'd gotten a punch in on her tonight, too.

Good. She'd beat the hell out of him without ever laying a finger on him. She couldn't come back and pretend they could be...whatever she wanted from him now. Friends? Not hardly. They couldn't turn back time.

Shit, all he wanted to do is slide his hands up her bare arms and rest them on her shoulders. Kiss her pouty lips until she smiled. Would she smile if he kissed her? Who the hell knew anymore. She'd probably smack the shit out of him.

Coach cracked him on the back of his head. "Don't talk

to Peach like that. Now, get out of my bar and sober up." He grabbed MJ by the upper arm and yanked him onto his feet. "Call me tomorrow and let me know you're alive."

MJ stumbled toward the door. Maddie followed behind him. "I'm parked on the street."

"Whatever."

"Why did I even come? I should've just left you here. Don't you have anyone else to bother at..." she pulled her phone out of her back pocket and glanced at the time, "quarter 'til one in the morning?"

No. He didn't. Is that what she wanted to hear? That he'd shoved away everyone who might want to get close enough to leave him flattened like road kill, exactly like she had? "Screw you. I'm not the one who called you."

"Fine!" She shoved past him out the front door. "Call the Old Man to come pick your ass up. I'm out of here."

She strode across the street, her hips twitching back and forth in tight jeans and that little black tank top...ugh. Damn. It. "Wait!" He jogged to catch up with her at her car.

"What?" She snapped around to face him. "I'm good enough for a ride when the only other option is your grand-father?"

Those dark blue eyes of hers flashed with rage. God, she was hot, and he hated it when she was mad at him.

"Screw you?" she shouted. "That's how you talk to me now? Well, no. Screw. You. MJ." She drove home each word with a sharp poke of her index finger to his chest.

He grabbed her finger and wouldn't let go when she

tried to tug it free. He held her eyes, praying to feel her open him up again and climb inside. He needed her there. Needed someone to care as much as she used to. "Don't leave me, Mads."

He saw her anger melt away, like a wave that had crashed on the shore and rushed back out into the ocean. She sighed. "Just get in."

She had her window rolled down, and the whole way home the wind blew her intoxicating scent right in his face. There was no escaping the memories of them together that flooded his senses. The ones he'd buried so deep, he was surprised they could surface so easily.

The feel of her hair twisted in his fingers.

Her soft sighs against his neck.

The salty-sweet taste of her skin.

Jesus. The basketball-sized knot in his stomach twisted and pulled tighter. He had to get out of this car.

MJ rolled his window down and stuck his head out. There. Now he couldn't smell her spicy-sweet whatever it was.

"What are you doing?" Maddie asked. "You're not going to puke are you?"

"No. Just getting some air." He glanced over at her and watched her eyes dart from him to the road and back again.

When she'd first gotten her license, he was only twelve. She'd taken him everywhere with her that summer when he came home from boarding school. He'd still been like a little brother to her. That hadn't changed until the summer after high school. That summer was the best three months of his life. She'd just graduated college and was home again to stay. She said they'd get an apartment right off GSU's campus. They didn't though. She left. Gone back to Michigan, practically a thousand goddamn miles away from him.

"What?" she asked. MJ hadn't realized he'd been staring at her.

"Nothing." He turned his face back out the window and took a deep breath. Nothing. Nothing would ever be like that summer again. He'd never been so close to having a home with someone he loved. She offered it up like a dream and tore it away like his worst nightmare come true.

He wished she'd talk about something—anything—instead of leaving him sitting there brooding in silence.

"How's baseball?" she asked.

That wasn't what he wanted to talk about. "Over."

"When does practice start for next season?"

"It doesn't." She needed to stop asking him personal questions. It only led to things he didn't want to discuss.

She stopped at a red light. "What are you talking about?" Her fingers gripped the wheel tighter, like she was preparing to hear him say something terrible.

She knew him too well.

"Got kicked off the team for fighting." MJ propped his elbow in the window and leaned his head on his hand. He studied her face, but it didn't budge. Stone-faced Mads. It was the expression he hated the most. The one that said he'd pushed her right over the edge, and she'd erected a mental wall between them.

He wanted to kick that fucking wall down and never see it again. How many times could she shut him out? It must've been the Jack Daniel's that made him grab her wrist. "Don't do that."

She jerked her arm away. "Do what?"

The light turned green, and she slammed her foot down on the accelerator making his head snap back against the seat. Her hair blew wild around her face. He wanted to reach over and ball it in his hands.

"Do what?" she repeated.

"Doesn't matter." MJ stared straight ahead and let the lights from the other cars on the road blur and double in his drunken vision.

❀

For the rest of the drive back to the Rocha Estate, Maddie tried to force the words out that she should've said over a year ago.

I'm sorry.

What did those words mean anyway? They couldn't take back what she'd done. They couldn't make MJ forgive her. Why bother saying them when they were meaningless?

She couldn't change the past. Leaving was the only option she'd been given. She had to protect him from getting hurt. Maddie knew hurt all too well, and she'd always stand between MJ and pain if she could.

She'd never let him feel the twinge of fiery anguish that hit her in the heart every time her mother was mentioned.

Every time she fingered the smooth silver angel pendant crammed in the very back of her jewelry box that her mom left behind. Over the past sixteen years, Maddie had relived the day her mom left a million times in her head.

The pain was still raw even after all the time that had passed. Driving down the road so many years later, it still felt like her mom had walked out on her only yesterday.

"Watch it!" MJ shouted and grabbed the wheel. "You almost hit that light post."

"I did not! You're so drunk, you can't even see straight. Let go!"

He let his hand drop to his lap. Sitting beside her, MJ was painfully close. She could almost feel his body heat pulsing off his skin into hers. Or maybe she imagined it. Manifested it because it was what she wanted to feel so badly. Being so close to him and not being able to reach out and touch him drove her crazy.

But it shouldn't. Not anymore.

Maddie glanced at MJ out of the corner of her eye. When had he become so cynical? Had she done that to him? Caused him to be so jaded and cold?

That fucking Old Man was going to pay if she couldn't figure out how to reach MJ, how to bridge the gaping hole between them that she'd ripped open when Enzo made her leave the Rocha Estate.

She pulled into the long driveway and parked in front of the garage. MJ had his car door open before her foot was off the brake. "Thanks for the ride."

She scrambled out of her car, not willing to let him get away from her that easily. "Are you okay? Do you need help getting inside?" She placed a hand on his arm and felt his muscle flex under her touch.

He stepped away breaking their contact. "I'm fine."

His tone made it clear that he didn't need her. Didn't want her. So much for making things better with him—getting back to being like brother and sister.

Like that could ever happen. What a dumb, desperate idea anyway. "Okay. Goodnight."

She watched him walk away. His footsteps echoed as he walked to the back entrance of the big house. When he reached for the door handle, he stumbled and almost fell, knelt down and caught himself on the cement sidewalk. "You're not fine," she said, rushing to his side as he stood and wobbled from foot to foot. "I'll help you to your room."

"I don't want your help," he said, his tone less than convincing.

"Too bad." She hooked her arm around his waist and opened the back door. "Come on."

They stumbled into the dark back entryway. Maddie glanced down the hallway running off to the right. The double wooden doors to the Old Man's office at the end were closed. Light poured out from the crack underneath.

She had to get MJ upstairs quickly and not run into Enzo.

The two of them walked like they were in a drunken sack race down the hallway to the front staircase. MJ raised his foot and missed the first step, then busted out laughing.

"Shut up!" Maddie hissed, jerking her head back behind them to watch for the Old Man. "Hurry." She nudged him in the back with her knuckles and he jolted forward, laughing again. "You're a terrible drunk." Maddie skittered up the first few steps, taking his hands and hauling him up after her. "How do you get home on your own when you're like this?"

"Carefully."

They were finally at the top. Maddie let go of his hands and pushed her hair back out of her face. "Tell me you don't drive like this. You'll kill yourself or someone else."

He took a step toward her, brushed her cheek with his fingertips and frowned. His dark-as-midnight eyes radiated hurt. "I don't have anything left."

A sharp pain hit her in the chest. "Don't say that." She let out a huge, shaky breath and felt the sting of tears in her eyes.

It was too much. She should've stayed away.

She thought she'd done the right thing. She'd left, kept the secret, and she hadn't hurt MJ by revealing the truth. She moved on with her life. She might think of MJ and cry every single day for the rest of her life, but she couldn't be with him and not tell him what she knew. She hated keeping secrets from him, but she could never hurt him with the truth.

So, she did the only thing she could. She resigned herself to a life without him.

MJ walked by her and opened his bedroom door. With

his hand still on the knob, he looked back at her. "My dad found out about me today."

A second jolt rocked her chest like an electric shock. He'd waited so long for his dad to find out about him—that he even existed—and she hadn't been there for him when it finally happened.

But she was here now.

Before she could speak, he turned away and shuffled into his room, collapsing on the bed. Maddie followed and shut the door behind them. "MJ, what did he say?"

"Nothing," he mumbled into his pillow. "The Old Man got my dad's girlfriend to come here so he could break the news to her, use her as the messenger. She told my dad about me and he took off. She doesn't even know where he went."

This was the worst possible outcome, and over the years she and MJ had considered them all.

"What if he finds out about me and doesn't want anything to do with me?" MJ asked, sitting on the branch beside her, high up in the willow tree beside the lake.

Maddie watched their feet dangle and sway, side-by-side. It was the summer after eighth grade for her. She'd be a freshman in high school in the fall. She knew everything, or thought she did. "Of course he'll want to be your dad. Why wouldn't he?"

MJ shrugged his boney, ten-year-old shoulders. "What if he doesn't, Mads?"

She elbowed him in the side, making him laugh. "Then I'll kick his butt."

He elbowed her back. "Like you could."

She swung an arm over his shoulder. "For you, I would." She squeezed him against her. "I promise."

❀

Maddie walked over to the head of MJ's bed. She reached out to brush a hand over his hair, but drew it back. "Want me to find him and kick his butt? I did promise after all."

She heard him sigh into his pillow. "You made a lot of promises."

Maddie let herself fall onto the bed beside him. Sitting at his side, she put a hand on his back. He was warm under the soft cotton T-shirt. She wanted nothing more than to snuggle up against him and make him forgive her.

She longed to tell him the truth. He couldn't think she honestly wanted to leave him. It wasn't fair.

But this wasn't about her. And it wasn't the time for secrets to come out. "What can I do?" She rubbed her hand in circles, hoping to give him some comfort.

With his head still turned away in his pillow, he reached for her and pulled her down next to him. He didn't say a word, just kept his arm tucked around her waist.

Maddie slid her left leg over his right and laid her head on his back where her hand made small circles.

He was drunk. Maddie knew this would never be happening if he was sober, but she'd take it.

She stared at the full moon glowing between the slats in the blind covering his window. The repetitive motion of her hand and the friction of his shirt against her palm lulled her into a trance. For the first time in forever, she wasn't searching for some answer inside herself. She was just feeling and breathing and living for each second as it came.

MJ's steady breathing slowed and she thought he'd gone to sleep. Reluctantly, she slid out from under his arm and stood. It was time to leave, or she'd stay all night, sleep in his arms and wake to those eyes and that smile in the morning—it wasn't like that between them anymore.

Maddie tugged his shoes off and pulled a blanket up over him. "It wasn't a promise I wanted to break," she whispered.

Three

"I knew you didn't come back to visit *me*."

Maddie wiped her eyes and turned to her father's teasing tone. She'd just left MJ sleeping and was taking a few minutes to gather her thoughts, steady her mind.

Her dad's strides were slow due to his limp, coming toward her from the big house. "Hi, Daddy."

"Hi, Peach." Everyone but MJ called her Peach. "I'm guessing you spent some time with MJ?"

She sighed and crossed her arms. "He got drunk at Coach's place and needed a ride home."

Her dad squeezed her shoulder. "He's lucky he's had you to depend on all these years."

She leaned into her dad, breathing in the familiar scent of his aftershave and relishing the reassurance of his arm around her shoulders. It had only been about eight months since he visited her in Michigan, but his face was more wrinkled than the last time she'd seen him, his gray hair thinner, but his frame was as solid as ever as he held her steady. "He'll never forgive me."

She knew she'd always been the one person MJ depended upon. The one and only person he trusted. Until she left. She'd broken his trust, and he might never give her the chance to earn it back.

"What's to forgive? You're both young. This rift is only temporary. You two will work it out." He turned her around in his arms to face him. His eyes were as blue as hers behind his glasses. "Don't you remember how you two fought when you were young? Always bickering and picking at each other. That's what you do." He gave her a little shake, smiling. "Do you trust me, Peach?"

She felt the corners of her lips tilt up, and she nodded.

"Good. You'll get past this. Give it time." He kissed her forehead and let her go.

Her dad's confidence never wavered, and it gave her hope that maybe he was right. Maybe she was just too close and too emotional to see her situation with MJ objectively.

"How'd he take the news?" He tapped her ring under her shirt.

"There is no news. I haven't decided. That's why I'm here, remember?" She tapped his forehead.

He laughed. "I know why you're here."

She shook her head, but didn't ask him what he meant. She knew. He thought she was there for MJ. Maybe she was. Maybe she couldn't make this decision without fixing things with him first.

"Have you spoken to Talan since you've been here? I'm not blind, Peach. I know you were just crying. You can't think clearly around MJ. That boy pushes your buttons like nobody else ever could."

Maybe it was the accusing look in his eye more than his question that had the guilt in her heart rearing its head.

"No, I haven't talked to Talan. We're on a break, remember? That means I don't talk to him until I figure out if I want to marry him."

He nodded slowly. "I think a break is an excellent idea. Why the rush?"

Maddie took his hand in both of hers. "He said it felt like the right time, and it was, except I panicked. He's incredible. I couldn't ask for a better man to marry. Really." It was the truth and Maddie hoped her dad could see the conviction in her eyes. "He loves me so much, Dad, and he makes me happy. He'll take care of me."

Much to her chagrin, her dad frowned. "But do you love him? Will you take care of him? It goes both ways, Peach. I can tell you from experience it doesn't work when your marriage is housed on a one-way street."

"Yes. Of course I do." She did. She knew in her heart it was love she felt for Talan. A warm, kind, and caring love— not a love that would burn her to the ground and leave her in ashes. It was the responsible kind of love that people based marriages on. "Yes," she said again.

Her dad smiled, pacified, and kissed her cheek. "I know you'll make the right decision, Peach."

They walked side-by-side to the patio behind the garage. Maddie hooked her arm through her dad's. "You shouldn't stay up so late. I expected you to be in bed by now."

"Who's the parent here anyway?" He tweaked her nose, and they started up the stairs to the apartment. "Enzo had a lot on his mind tonight. A lot to discuss."

"It's after one in the morning! That's excessive, don't you think?"

"I know I'm no spring chicken, but I'm not dead yet." He opened the door and ushered her in before him. "Besides, I can't sleep more than a few hours anymore anyway. Might as well have some company."

A twinge of guilt sank into her chest for not being around to help her aging father. Another man she loved and let down by leaving him alone.

"Get that look off your face," her dad said, picking up a throw from the back of the couch that she'd wrinkled earlier and re-folding it. "I'm more than fine here by myself. I don't need you around here worrying about me. I'm a grown man, Peach."

She rolled her eyes at him. "Obviously. But I do worry. You should be retired, lounging on a beach somewhere or a golf course."

"Enzo and I went golfing three days ago. It's not like he has me digging ditches."

"I know."

He kissed her forehead. "But it is time for these old bones to crawl into bed. Don't stay up too late."

"Already have." She rose on tip-toe and kissed his cheek. "See you in the morning."

"'Night, Peach."

Restless after her dad went to bed, Maddie bounded down the stairs and out onto the patio. She felt like lighting up another cigarette, but knew the only reason she was smoking again was because she was back home and completely stressed out. She'd hate herself if she got hooked again. It took forever to quit.

Plus, her dad would smell the smoke on her.

One of these days she'd stop worrying about what he thought. She wasn't a kid anymore, and she'd left all of her teenage fantasies behind over a year ago.

❀

MJ stood at his window peering through the slats in the shade. When Maddie pulled his shoes off, she'd woken him.

She hadn't wanted to break her promise, she'd said.

But she had, and that was what put them here now—apart.

Maddie had been sitting on the patio sofa under the blinding full moon for at least twenty minutes. He couldn't tell if she'd fallen asleep with her head tilted back or not. If she had, she'd have one hell of a sore neck when she woke up.

He thought about going down and finding out, but hated himself for even considering it. Hated himself for standing there watching her like some love-sick high-school boy.

Shit, she wasn't his to think about like that anymore. He had to get out of here. If she was staying, then the sooner he left the better.

The house he rented with two roommates was only for the school year. The problem was that they were teammates, or had been before he got booted off the baseball team. Now he didn't know if they'd welcome him back or if he'd have to find somewhere else to crash. He only had a couple weeks to figure it out.

With one last look, he stepped back from the window. She'd shaken him. From the minute he heard her voice tonight, he'd been out of his mind. His sanity had already been hanging by a thread since Rachael, his dad's girl-friend, had shown up, before Maddie had strutted into the driveway and back into his life.

MJ crashed down on his bed and squeezed his eyes shut tight so the room wasn't spinning. From outside his bedroom door, he heard his grandfather, the only other person in the house, pad down the hall. He didn't think the man ever slept, probably thought sleeping was a waste of time when he could be scheming how to ruin someone's life. The man was sadistic, worthy of being the evil dictator of a third-word country.

MJ shucked off his jeans and yanked his T-shirt over his head. He was hot from drinking and wondered what temperature the cheap Old Man had the AC set to. Didn't help that thinking of Maddie made him sweat.

He ran his hand over his chest and stopped above his heart where a black tattoo of an ornate skeleton key was inked on his skin.

She had its other half—a lock in the shape of a heart with a keyhole in the center—tattooed on her lower stomach beside her right hip bone. Laying on top of her, he'd slide down to kiss her breasts and their two tattoos would come together. Lock and key.

God.

He ran his hands over his face, roughly.

He had to stop thinking about her. She wasn't his and never would be again.

His pillows shifted and the sheet tangled around his legs as he rolled over and buried his head. Sleep. He just needed sleep. Everything would look better in the morning.

❀

Sometime during the night, MJ's lip had swollen to double its normal size. It throbbed like it had its own heartbeat. So did his head.

Hungover and feeling the aftereffects of his night of heavy drinking, he stumbled out of bed and staggered to the adjoining bathroom.

Why did he have to be so stupid?

After taking the hottest shower he could stand, he dressed and headed down to the kitchen to find food. The greasier the better. He smelled bacon and his stomach growled.

He rounded the corner into the kitchen and stopped dead in his tracks. Rachael sat on a stool at the breakfast bar jabbing a text message into her phone. Yesterday he'd been hesitant and a little nervous when she arrived. Now he just wanted her gone.

She looked up and saw him standing there like an idiot. "Morning," he said.

"Morning." Her eyes had dark bags under them. "What happened to your lip?" she asked.

"Nothing." He spotted a plate of bacon and some toast on the counter and helped himself to it, clamping his teeth down on a slice of toast and tearing a piece off.

"Right." He could feel her eyes boring into his forehead. Her phone chimed and she struggled to keep back a smile that tugged at the corners of her lips as she read the message on her screen.

"Merrick?" he blurted without thinking. Damn if he didn't sound anxious for it to be his dad she was texting.

Her eyes darted up to his, dark brown and guilty as hell. "No," she said, and flickered her eyes back to her phone. "Sorry."

Bullshit. MJ knew something was going on.

Rachael tucked her phone into her back pocket. "So, are you coming to Turtle Tear with me to visit with your aunt and uncle and meet your cousins, Holly and Sam?" She patted her pocket with the phone. "That was, um, Beck, the pilot. He wants a time to meet at the airport."

Beck the pilot, huh? "I don't think I'm going with you. I'm going to pretend none of this ever happened after you leave."

Rachael smirked, silently calling bullshit on *him*. "Do what you have to do."

MJ's grandfather slipped into the kitchen. "Why are you eating in here? We have a dining room." He put a hand on Rachael's back. MJ watched her flinch. "How are you this morning, dear? Have you heard from my son?"

Enzo Rocha, always on his game. MJ laughed silently to

himself. He knew his grandfather's strategy. First he took Merrick's son, then his property, and finally he'd turn his girlfriend against him. If the Old Man had his way, Rachael would leave here wondering why Merrick was such a terrible son, why he couldn't see that his father was doing everything for his family's best interest.

If only MJ could figure out why Enzo had to make Merrick out to be the bad guy. Why was it so important that the Old Man come across as the hero?

Maybe Merrick was a bad guy, but MJ knew Enzo was one too.

He didn't want anything to do with either of them.

Rachael squeezed her lips into a thin line and shook her head. "I haven't heard from him."

MJ almost spit out the sip of coffee he'd just taken. Rachael was a terrible liar. A poker face she *did not* have. She'd heard from Merrick, all right.

His grandfather made a *tsk tsk* sound. "He'll come around."

MJ tossed his toast back onto the plate. He wasn't going to stick around and listen to false promises that his asshole father would come around. He strode past his grandfather, but the Old Man caught him by the arm. "Hold on a minute. I'd like to talk to both of you in my office in an hour."

"I have plans." MJ tried to free his arm, but his grandfather held tight.

MJ clenched his teeth and smiled. He knew not to press his luck with his grandfather, but if he could take one swing…it would only take one and the years of held back aggression would take the Old Man down.

"Your plans can wait." The look he gave MJ was like a dare and a promise all in one narrow-eyed glance. It said, *I'm the reason you're not on the street. You'll do as I say or you will be.*

MJ jerked his arm hard, freeing it. "Yeah. One hour. Got ya."

Four

Maddie stopped the golf cart beside the lake at the back of the Rocha property. She walked a fine line by being there. More memories of her and MJ than she cared to remember lingered in the water and the blowing limbs of the moss-covered trees. She wasn't sure she could hold them at bay, or the tears they would inevitably bring with them.

She picked up a long stick and rounded the lake, batting the tall grass in front of her as she went. Startling unseen things—turtles and frogs—with each footfall, they splashed into the lake making the water ripple and sparkle in the morning sunlight. Mixed with the heady scent of dry grass and wildflowers, it was almost too much for her to take.

She ached to be young again, swimming in the lake and playing truth or dare with her best friend in the world. How much longer could she keep his grandfather's secret? Keeping it for MJ's own good was tearing her apart.

"Don't crush it!" she yelled at MJ, and tried to save the lightning bug in his cupped hands.

MJ twisted away from her. "Todd Calabreeze said if you squash it and rub its stuff all over your hands, they glow."

"Don't you dare." Maddie wondered why nine-year-old boys had to be so dumb. And gross. "I'll tell my dad if you do and he won't be happy."

If there was one person MJ would listen to, Maddie knew it was her dad.

"Fine." MJ opened his hands and shook them. The bug blinked a few times and flew into the air. "Happy?"

He stomped off and stood at the edge of the lake. Maddie followed. She hated it when he was mad at her. They didn't have much time together, and the weeks he was home on breaks she didn't want to spend fighting.

She plucked a cattail from the bank and whacked him in the head with it.

"What the heck, Mads?" He pulled a cattail of his own out of the ground and batted her back. She ducked and it hit her shoulder.

They were both laughing now and sword fighting with their cattails, chasing each other along the bank of the lake. Maddie hit a patch of mud and slid. Shrieking, she reached back and grabbed MJ's arm. Both of them toppled into the lake.

❦

The memory made Maddie laugh. They'd walked home in the dark, wet and covered in mud. "You should've let me squash the lightning bug," MJ had said.

Walking through the side yard of the original Rocha Estate, a small stone cottage from the eighteen hundreds that now served as a guest house, Maddie reached the tree line behind the lake and easily found the trail that headed toward the Rocha family cemetery. There had once been a split-rail fence at the entrance through the trees, but all that remained of it was rotted wooden posts. Over the years, the path had been marked by a stepping-stone in the shape of a cross.

Dead leaves crunched and twigs snapped under her feet. She knew it wasn't far. Just over a small hill. She trudged forward, up the incline and stopped at the top.

There it was, directly to the right of the ancient, crumbling Rocha mausoleum. The square, pink marble grave marker with the angel statue on top. The angel that haunted MJ, just as Maddie's angel pendant haunted her. Who knew angels could bring such demons into the lives of two little kids?

Nothing's forever. Sometimes not even death.

Maddie jogged down the slope and stopped in front of the stone that read *Gina Renee Montgomery, Beloved Daughter.*

She traced her fingers across the letters. MJ never questioned why his mother was buried back here, but to her it had always been strange since no one in the Rocha family had been buried in the cemetery for a hundred years.

She and MJ used to bring candy and soda here, and he would leave some on her grave. Maddie bet if she looked around hard enough, she'd find soda cans buried in the dirt, tall grass and leaves. Dr Pepper was always his favorite.

They were so young and naive. Maddie never expected the lengths she learned Enzo went to in the name of keeping up appearances. That's what he was doing. It had nothing to do with caring for any member of his family. He was a man obsessed with wealth and power, and wealth and power came from manipulating people. He couldn't manipulate people who didn't fear or respect him.

She glanced up at the sky between the tree branches. *What do I do*, she asked anyone up there who might have an answer. She waited for a few minutes, but an answer never came. Maybe it was one of those things you had to listen for in your heart.

Giving up, she made her way back to the lake. She slipped off her shoes, sat on the bank and stuck her feet in the cool water. Mud squished between her toes, but she didn't care. The sensation was familiar and comforting. At least some things never changed.

She startled when a rock skipped across the water and jerked her head toward the direction it came from. MJ slid his hands into his pockets and rocked up on his toes. "I thought I might find you here." He scratched the back of his head and turned his dark eyes out over the lake. "I need a ride to the bar to get my car."

So, she'd been relegated to the position of taxi service in his life. She guessed that was a start toward forgiveness. She stood and brushed off her shorts, wiped the mud from her feet on the grass. "Does your grandfather know I'm here?"

He shrugged one broad shoulder. "I don't know. Why?"

Standing there with his wavy dark hair, T-shirt that shifted with his lean muscles, and long legs in worn, faded jeans, she hated how much she wanted him. She wondered if she begged him, if he'd throw her down on the grass and take her right here beside the lake. God, how she missed the feel of his hands on her, his body and lips pressed against hers.

She clenched her fists and dug her nails into her palms. She wanted to run away from her own mind, her own thoughts and memories. There was no escaping them here, and definitely not with him standing in front of her.

"Maddie?"

She blinked a few times, making eye contact with him—here—now, in the present where he still hated her. "Sorry. I just wondered if he knew. I haven't seen him since I've been back."

He crossed his arms over his chest. "I don't talk about you."

The sharpness of his words sliced through her chest. "No. Of course not." She blinked a few more times hiding her devastation while putting on her shoes.

They hopped in the golf cart, and as she drove them back to the house, she noticed him running his fingers across his swollen bottom lip. Despite her efforts to not think about his lips, she wished she could kiss it. "Does it hurt?" she asked instead.

He made a noncommittal sound and shrugged. "Had worse."

Dark stubble lined his jaw, and she knew exactly how it would feel against her cheek. Her face and chest grew warm thinking about it.

If they were any other two people, the silence would be filled with questions like: How've you been? How were classes last semester? Have you seen that movie that just came out?

But, they weren't two other people and they were so far beyond small talk, they couldn't even pretend. She might as well stick with the sore subjects then. "Where were you going to stay last night? You had a duffel bag with you."

He contemplated his answer. His gaze dropped to his lap before he spoke. "With this girl I know."

Her throat constricted. She inhaled a shallow breath and kept her face forward. He couldn't know he'd just killed her.

Maddie hadn't thought for a second that MJ had been mourning her in celibacy for the past year and a half. He was a college baseball player. Girls were probably all over him constantly. But, she hadn't allowed herself to think about him with someone else. Now here it was—the truth—right in her face, in his own words.

Words that killed her. Twisted her into knots inside. Her heart rioted and writhed in pain, but she'd never let on. "Your girlfriend?" The question came out small and quiet. She hated how it sounded.

"You want to talk about this?" he asked in a pissed off rush of words. "Should we dig it all out and talk about our feelings, Maddie? Is that really what you want to do? Maybe you should start by finally telling me why you left."

MJ would never understand unless she told him why she left. How his grandfather confronted her. How he'd threatened to fire her dad if she didn't leave.

"No," she whispered. "I don't want to talk about it." She slammed the golf cart to a stop behind the garage.

MJ grabbed her wrist before she could jump out. His lips were drawn tight. His brows knit. "Don't make me say things that will hurt you." His gaze dropped to her lips then back up. He closed his eyes and shook his head slightly. She pulled her wrist from his grasp and slid out of the cart.

"I have to get my car keys." Maddie took the stairs up to her dad's apartment as fast as she could. She had to get away from him and collect her thoughts, control her emotions. Inside it was dark and cool with the curtains pulled shut. She wanted to collapse onto her bed, hide under the covers and never come out. Instead, she grabbed her purse off her dresser, dug her keys out of the front pocket and headed back outside.

MJ waited on the passenger side of her car. She clicked the key fob to unlock the doors, and they both climbed in. The leather seat was scorching hot and burned the back of her legs. She jumped and practically landed in his lap.

They fumbled trying to get distance between each other, but her hair was tangled in his watchband. She'd given him the watch on his birthday two years ago. "Don't move!" she yelled. "You're pulling my hair out." Her head tilted awkwardly to the side.

"Why did you jump like that?" His fingers frantically worked to free her hair.

"The seat's too hot." She bobbed her knees trying to keep the heat off the backs of her thighs.

He gave up and took his watch off. "Here. You can get it out easier than I can."

She took his watch and slid back behind the wheel, immediately feeling a sense of loss from being so close to him. She unwound most of her hair then gave up and yanked the watch free. Her scalp stung for a second, but she didn't care. This torturous moment needed to be over. "Here." She handed the watch back to him, and he shoved it in his pocket.

Maddie wished the drive was longer than the five minutes it took them to get to the Third Base Lounge. Neither of them said one word on the way.

MJ's car was the only one in the lot. With the top down, he was lucky it was a good neighborhood or it might not have been sitting there still. He'd never been this careless before. This reckless.

"Thanks," he said, getting out of the car.

His door slammed closed before she muttered, "Welcome." So, she rolled down the passenger side window and shouted, "You're welcome!"

He stopped and looked back over his shoulder with a smirk on his face that made her heart fall into her stomach. It was the dimple she saw in his cheek that did it.

❊

MJ pulled into the driveway right behind her. By the time she'd gotten out of her car, he was already halfway to the back door. A woman was strolling toward her with her eyes locked onto her phone while she was texting.

"Hey," Maddie said, reaching out and grasping the woman's shoulders. "You better watch where you're walking. The neighbor's Great Dane likes to wander over and leave presents in the yard sometimes. That dog's the bane of my dad's existence."

The woman gazed at the grass around her, then examined the soles of each of her shoes. "I'm good. Thanks for the warning."

The two of them stared at each other for a moment. "I'm Maddie. The house manager, Mr. Simcoe's daughter."

"Nice to meet you. I'm Rachael DeSalvo, Merrick Rocha's girlfriend."

This was MJ's dad's girlfriend. "Nice to meet you. Were you heading somewhere, or just wandering?"

"Wandering."

Maddie walked with Rachael down the driveway toward the front of the house. "Don't take this the wrong way," Maddie said, almost unable to breathe with her disbelief building by the second. "But, why are you still here? MJ told me his dad wanted nothing to do with him." Enzo Rocha and his son, Merrick, hated each other. Nobody ever even spoke Merrick's name at the Rocha Estate. Maddie knew there was some lawsuit going on between the two of them over Rocha Enterprises, Merrick's company that Enzo held some rights to or something. She wasn't too clear on the details, and neither was MJ, as far as she knew.

Rachael let out a sharp laugh and let her head drop back. "I've been asking myself that question all day." She turned toward Maddie. "I woke up yesterday morning in paradise and ended up here. Enzo Rocha asked me to come so he could tell me Merrick has a son he didn't ever know about. I got to be the one to break the news to him." Rachael rubbed both hands over her face. She looked exhausted.

They settled onto a white, iron bench with a scrolled back under an enormous oak tree. Irritation bubbled inside Maddie. "MJ told me his dad didn't want anything to do with him when he found out, that he took off. Have you heard from him?"

"No," Rachael said, but her eyes skittered around the yard, and Maddie had the feeling her answer wasn't exactly the truth. "But that doesn't mean he doesn't want anything to do with MJ." She let out an exasperated groan. "I can only imagine now that he knows he has a son, he's off to put some insane scheme into motion thinking it's going to fix everything."

Maddie glanced out to the high pines that hid the brick wall around the estate and the street beyond. She felt her annoyance dissipate. Maybe Merrick could find a way to fix everything, but more than anything, MJ just wanted his dad in his life. "I hope he knows all he has to do is be around for MJ now. That will fix it."

Rachael nodded. They sat in silence for a moment, and Maddie was just about to excuse herself when Rachael spoke again.

"It's funny," she said, her hand running back and forth over the smooth iron bench seat between them. I haven't lived there long, but I really miss Turtle Tear. It's a hotel on an island in the Everglades that Merrick and I renovated a few months ago." Rachael held her phone tight. Watching her, Maddie inferred her unspoken words—Rachael missed Merrick even more.

"I'm sure you miss it. You probably can't wait to get back home."

"I can't." Rachael leaned forward and stuck her phone in her back pocket. "Do you like living here?"

Maddie gestured behind them to the apartment where her dad lived over the enormous four-car garage. "I don't live here anymore. I live in Michigan. I grew up here though."

"Oh. So, you grew up with MJ?" Rachael asked. "Tell me about him."

Maddie folded her hands in her lap and squeezed them together tight. Rachael's penetrating gaze was impossible to avoid, and the last thing Maddie wanted to do was talk about MJ. "He went to boarding school, but he came home during the summer and on breaks. He was like a little brother to me."

The thought almost made Maddie laugh. Then cry. He'd been her family. The one person other than her dad who she could always count on. That was before they became more. Much, much more, and it all imploded.

Rachael was still staring at her, expectantly.

"I haven't seen him very much over the past year," Maddie said. "But MJ's…" She sighed. "If you take the most impossible route to anywhere and make it a thousand times more complicated, that's the way MJ goes through life."

Rachael laughed. "Sounds like Merrick. He's his own biggest obstacle."

Maddie shook her head, smiling. "Like father, like son, I guess." She really hoped MJ and his dad would get to know each other, that they would go to baseball games like MJ always wanted to do with his dad.

A pang of regret struck her heart, realizing she wouldn't be around to see it happen. She wouldn't even get to hear the stories.

Maddie fingered the engagement ring under her shirt. It was better this way.

"Were you and MJ always just friends?" Rachael asked. "I'm sorry. It's none of my business. You just looked a little wistful when you talked about him."

Maddie clutched the edge of the bench. "We were more once, but we weren't good together."

"Why were you bad together?" Rachael asked. The look on her face made Maddie wonder if Rachael had deliberated the good and bad about Merrick the way Maddie had—and still did—with MJ.

Maddie hadn't told a soul the real reason she'd left MJ. It had been eating away at her for over a year. She wanted to tell someone so badly, but the words were locked deep inside.

"We just were. What we had wasn't a get-married-and-grow-old-together kind of love. It's the kind that burns too fast and explodes. It was too intense." Maddie leaned back and looked up at the sky. "It was young love and not a real, adult relationship that takes into account jobs and futures and goals and the gritty, everyday things that couples face." Maddie sighed. "It was kids' play."

Five

Bullshit.

MJ stood listening at the library window. Listening and seething.

"Kids' play my ass," he muttered. She was afraid. He didn't know why, but he'd make her face her fear.

There was no way she could ever find an *adult* relationship even close to as all-consuming and mind-blowing as what she had with him.

No fucking way.

He'd let her stay away for too long. Now she had these crazy-ass thoughts in her head.

But that was about to change.

Maddie was his.

Always had been. Always would be.

"I need to get inside," Rachael said. "Enzo wanted to meet with me and MJ about something."

The two women stood and MJ stepped away from the window. He ran his hands through his hair in a futile attempt to get his mind off of Maddie before it got screwed over by the Old Man. He'd yet to go to a meeting with Enzo that didn't leave his head fucked six ways to Sunday.

The one thing he knew for certain was that he could never trust the Old Man to tell him the truth. He took nothing his grandfather said at face value. There was always an ulterior motive lurking under his tongue with every word he spoke.

Sitting beside Rachael in the black leather chairs in front of his grandfather's desk, MJ twirled the silky hair stuck in his watchband around his finger. His mind raced. He had to get out of this office and get to Maddie.

He knew he was in a riptide being pulled under while he fought to get back to shore and keep his footing. With her, it was a competition to see who would drown the other faster. He wouldn't lose this time.

She would always be what he wanted. If she was near, he'd want to hear her laugh, watch her full lips quirk into that slightly off-center smile, be the one to put that hazy, needful look in her eyes when he kissed her.

"Do you understand what I'm telling you?" His grandfather pounded on his desk.

MJ hadn't heard one word the Old Man had said. "I understand."

"It's not your fault your father doesn't want to see you. He's always felt guilty about Gina's death. He thought you died, too. I'm sure he's carried an enormous burden. You'd be nothing to him but a reminder."

Rachael shot forward in her chair. "Your mother's dead? Merrick knew there was a baby, but thought you'd died?"

MJ could only stare at her. "He didn't tell you?"

His grandfather let out a sarcastic chuckle. "Of course he didn't tell her. My son is nothing if not self-gratifying. He'd never tell the truth if it could be avoided."

Rachael's eyes met MJ's. "He gave the impression... I didn't think he knew about you at all. How did your mother die?"

MJ felt his mouth open, but no words would come out.

"In childbirth," his grandfather said, filling in the blank. "My son took the news hard, blaming himself for her death and the baby's."

"It wasn't his fault," Rachael said, shifting nervously in her chair. "How could he think it was his fault?"

MJ felt the words form like a ball of fire and erupt from his throat. "He didn't keep his dick in his pants and knocked her up. If he would've, she'd be alive."

"And *you* wouldn't be here!" Rachael's eyes blazed. Her nostrils flared. Her hands gripped the armrests like she was afraid if she let go she'd strangle him. "What happened between them was as much your mom's doing as it was Merrick's. It was consensual!"

"Was it?" his grandfather said, steepling his fingers and cocking an eyebrow.

"What?" Rachael's eyes widened, and she eased back in her chair. "What are you saying?"

"I'm saying," his grandfather stood and came around to lean against the front of his desk, "that I spent an enormous sum of money to keep a family quiet. Gina was never forthcoming about the details."

"But what did *your son* say?" Rachael's face was void of color. Even her lips were faded to a dull pink. "Did you even ask him?"

MJ's grandfather grinned, but his eyes remained hard and humorless. "A pubescent boy who needed the comfort of a woman after the loss of his mother isn't someone you trust to tell the truth."

"You trust your *son* to tell the truth." Her voice was cracked ice, smooth and cold with jagged edges.

Enzo threw his hands in the air. "Either way. She's dead. My son has taken the burden of her death on his shoulders for twenty years." His eyes shifted to MJ. "I'm sorry. I thought maybe if he knew you were alive, he'd come to terms with it." A smile slinked across his lips. "He still might. But if not, I've made certain that your future is secure."

All business again, MJ's grandfather hustled back around to his desk chair, sat and perched his glasses on the bridge of his nose. "Rachael, I wanted you here to witness this so my son will know I haven't stolen his fortune out from under him for no good reason." He tapped a file folder and turned his eyes on MJ. "Merrick Enzo Rocha, Junior, I'm offering you full control of Rocha Enterprises upon your twenty-second birthday. *If* you graduate college, and after you graduate you're able to successfully manage as the company's president, all properties and holdings will be signed over to you."

The use of his full name was something MJ had never heard uttered by his grandfather—or anyone else for that matter. He figured it was being used now to convince him of the sincerity of his grandfather's offer.

It didn't work.

Everything in Enzo Rocha's world came with strings attached.

"Well?" the Old Man said, flicking his thumbs, questioning a response.

MJ figured it was best to go all-in at this point and try to pry out his grandfather's true motives. "What if I don't want it?"

The Old Man threw his head back and howled with laughter. He tugged his glasses off by one arm and rubbed his eyes with his thumb and forefinger. "What if you don't want it." He chuckled some more. "That's priceless, MJ. Priceless. What else do you plan to do with your life? MMA fighter perhaps?"

"Yeah. Maybe." He was more cut out to be an MMA fighter than the president of Rocha Enterprises.

"What's your definition of successfully managing the company?" Rachael asked, uncrossing and re-crossing her legs.

MJ realized he'd pegged her right. She was someone who would go right for the kill every time. He bit back the urge to tell her to mind her own business. It was the question he'd been circling in his mind.

Enzo flatted his palms on the file folder and spread his fingers. "I'm a fair man, Rachael. MJ and I will do a full evaluation of each property and determine goals we mutually agree upon."

"I'm sure you will," she said. She shot Enzo a shrewd look. "Who will train him? You haven't been running Rocha Enterprises."

The Old Man licked his lips and steepled his fingers again. "Are you suggesting your *boyfriend* train him? If you find him, you can ask him of course, but I wouldn't hold my breath if I were you."

MJ watched Rachael's chin jut forward. She'd soon learn obstinacy didn't get you anywhere with his grandfather. You couldn't affect someone who didn't give a shit.

"I'll let you know," MJ said. "I need to think about it."

The corner of his grandfather's mouth twitched. "While you're thinking about it, think about finding a permanent residence somewhere near. A corporate president doesn't live with his granddad."

Granddad? MJ had never once called him that. And the permanent residence was just a way to get him out of this house under the guise of looking and acting like a *corporate president*. He'd never been welcome here, and the Old Man couldn't send him away to boarding school anymore.

Not that it mattered. MJ didn't want to be here anymore than his grandfather wanted him to be. He should've found a lease that went through the summer.

MJ stood and smoothed the legs of his jeans. "That it?"

"That's it." His grandfather pushed his chair out from the desk.

"Wait." Rachael stood and stepped up to Enzo's desk. "Why now? After twenty years, why tell Merrick about him now?"

Enzo braced both hands on his desk. "As I said, I spent a lot of money keeping Gina's family quiet. They agreed on one condition: Keeping Merrick out of MJ's life. Once he was eighteen though it was out of my hands. MJ's a man, as is his father, and men need to deal with the truth. I should've told him two years ago."

MJ studied Rachael's face. She wasn't buying it. Good for her. It was all bullshit. Everything out of Enzo Rocha's mouth was bullshit, MJ had learned that early on.

Rachael lifted her chin slightly higher and let her stony stare linger on Enzo for a moment longer. "Your son is nothing that you make him out to be," she said, and strode out of the office ahead of MJ.

He caught up with her in the hallway. "Hey, don't worry about any of that. I've known him long enough to not become one of his minions."

Rachael's gaze darted over his shoulder to the closed office door at the end of the hall. "Minion, huh? What do you think he has up his sleeve?"

MJ glanced behind him. Within the Old Man's earshot was not the place to discuss Enzo's motives. He took her by the elbow, led her through the house and out the back door to the patio. "I think you and I both know there's no chance of me successfully managing Rocha Enterprises. Even if there were, I don't want it. When I fail, he's free to own everything with a clear conscience and not look like the bad guy. Keeping up appearances is as vital as air to the Old Man."

Rachael shot one hip out and tapped her foot. "So, this is all a ploy to keep control of the company himself. I see."

She yanked her cell phone out of her pocket and started jabbing buttons sending a text message. "He better get his ass here," she muttered.

"My...Merrick?" MJ couldn't bring himself to say dad.

"Yes. I can't fight this battle by myself. He needs to face this. And *why* wouldn't he tell me your mother was dead and he thought you were too? God, that man!" She shook her head and poked the SEND button. "I'm sorry, by the way," she said, looking up at him, "about your mom."

He smiled, wanting to put her at ease. "It's okay. I never knew her."

She eased her phone back into her pocket and crossed her arms appraising him. "What do you want to do if not run Rocha Enterprises?"

His throat burned knowing he'd have to admit he was a total fuckup, and he ran his hands through the back of his hair. "I did want to be a scout for probaseball."

"Not anymore?" She rocked from foot to foot.

"I don't think it's an option for me at this point." Getting kicked off the team was probably not a step in the direction of his dreams. No pro team would touch a guy who wasn't a team player on and off the field.

Rachael tilted her head. "What are you going to do then?"

He chuckled. She was unbelievable. Why couldn't she let it go? "It's undetermined."

He noticed her hand press against the phone in her pocket, as if anticipating a return message from his dad. What kind of asshole lets his girlfriend walk into this fucked-up mess and disappear when she needs him most? "You deserve better," he said, nodding to her pocket.

She shook her head. "It's fine. I can handle him." Her phone chimed as if on cue. Her face lit. "See?" She tugged her phone out of her pocket, and MJ watched her lips move as she read. "He says he's taking care of some business that has to do with you." She shoved her phone back in her pocket. "Once you understand him, you'll realize he has to circle a problem for a while before he rushes in and tackles it. Then watch out."

"All hell breaks loose?" MJ fought the curiosity to ask her more about Merrick. He didn't want to know anything more about a man he might never meet.

Rachael smirked. "Yeah, all hell frequently breaks loose when Merrick's involved."

She might be the most loyal person MJ had ever met. Or blinded by love. All of the fire and fight and stubbornness inside her reminded him of Maddie.

Except Maddie hadn't fought for him.

Maddie had left him.

Six

Standing a few yards behind MJ, Maddie kept silent. She'd been sitting outside getting some sun while browsing the job boards on her laptop when he and Rachael exited from the big house. Something serious was going down, and call her nosey, but where MJ was concerned, she wanted to have details.

"Hey, Maddie!" Rachael said, spotting her and taking a few steps toward her.

She saw MJ's back stiffen before he turned to her with a half-cocked smirk.

"Hey," she said, sensing a shifting in the air between her and MJ that made her uneasy.

"Why don't you guys come to lunch with me?" Rachael said. "My treat." She placed a hand on MJ's forearm. "I could use some company to get my mind off things."

MJ kept his eyes glued to Maddie's. This was some kind of test, and they both knew it, but only he knew the rules and she had the distinct impression she was about to fail.

Her nerves thrummed under her skin as he stared at her with those practically black eyes that never faltered. Who would look away first? Was he doing this on purpose? Searching to find an answer inside of her somewhere?

He licked his lips and blinked, turning his gaze to Rachael. "I'll drive," he said.

He headed toward the driveway. Maddie and Rachael followed. "What was that about?" Rachael whispered in her ear.

"I'm not sure," Maddie whispered back.

"Intense," Rachael murmured.

Exactly. MJ was the definition of intensity. There was never a moment when he was at peace and calm in his own skin. Something was always brewing inside him, like a storm ready to drench the world.

It was that drive and focus that made Maddie believe in him. MJ could do anything he put his mind to. And that's what scared her to death.

If he set his mind on having her back, she could never resist him. She didn't think that was a possibility until now.

Opening the passenger door, she touched the ring under her shirt. Talan was so different. He was a shelter, a safe harbor, not a destructive storm that would crash down on top of her.

❀

The three of them sat outside Café Gelato at a round wrought-iron table on the sidewalk. Lunch had been deli sandwiches and chips. Now they indulged in dessert. When Maddie ordered tiramisu flavored gelato, she caught MJ smiling before he realized and became stoic once more. What game was he playing bringing them here for lunch?

Maddie stood in front of the freezer case at Café Gelato trying to decide which flavor to order.

"Just try it," MJ said, holding out a little plastic spoon.

"I don't like coffee flavored ice cream," she said, wrinkling her nose.

"You'll love it." He ran the spoonful of tiramisu flavored gelato across her lips, leaving a cold, sticky-sweet trail. "Trust me."

Maddie licked her lips. It was delicious. She smiled and grabbed his spoon, licking the rest off.

MJ laughed. "I told you." He leaned in and kissed her. She'd never get used to the feel of his kisses—like they were meant just for her. Like the reason her mom left and she ended up at the Rocha Estate with her dad was so the universe could bring the two of them together.

When he pulled away and gazed into her eyes, it was perfectly understood. He was hers and she was his. It had been that way every summer and winter break since they were little, and this summer she'd seen him with different eyes. It had been hard to tell him she wanted to be more than friends, but she couldn't resist her feelings.

She rose on tip-toe and kissed him a second time. The girl behind the counter drummed her fingers on top of the freezer case. "I'll have the same," Maddie told her.

She and MJ took their gelato out to the little patio tables and sat down. They'd been here almost every night since he got home for the summer a week ago. Now that he was headed to college, they'd have all the time in the world to be together. Not just during his boarding school breaks.

When they were finished, they hopped in her dad's vin-

tage Torino convertible. Her dad's love of muscle cars had spread to MJ long ago. She let MJ drive while she stuck an old Eagles cassette tape in the tape deck and turned the volume up. It was her dad's favorite, so they both knew all the words and sang along, loudly to Hotel California the whole ride home.

"Make it to go," MJ said to the waiter.

"In a hurry?" Rachael asked. "Got a hot date?"

Maddie's insides jolted. Please no, don't let him have a date. She instantly felt guilty for wanting him to be alone. How selfish could she be? She had Talan's ring around her neck after all.

But, she and Talan were on a break, and maybe…

No. She couldn't start anything with MJ that she'd have to call quits again. It wasn't fair to either of them.

He tapped the table and shot Maddie a look like he wanted to eat her alive. "Just ready to get back."

Maddie felt her entire body flush, from her toes to her hairline. MJ had given her heated looks before, but nothing like the one she was getting from him now.

He wet his bottom lip with his tongue. The pulse points in her neck hammered with her rapid heart rate.

The server brought their plastic dishes of gelato, breaking the tension, and the three of them piled back into MJ's car. He turned the radio up loud on the way back so none of them could hear each other to talk.

There was something about him so inherently dominant, but at times, he fell vulnerable and needy. MJ's moods had always shifted from hot to cold faster than Maddie could catch her breath.

MJ parked his car in the driveway and turned to her. "I need to talk to you. Alone."

She froze with her hand on the door handle and his eyes on hers, searching again like she had all the answers.

She did have the answers, she just never allowed herself to give them to him.

Maddie pushed her door open and hopped out so Rachael could climb out of the backseat. "Thanks for lunch. It was fun."

"You're welcome. Thanks for coming with me."

Maddie smiled and watched her stride toward the house.

MJ got out and stood beside his door while Maddie rounded the car. "What do you need?" she asked, almost afraid of the answer. He'd been so cocky this afternoon, God only knew what would come out of his mouth.

"Follow me."

She hated the emotionless, monotone, monosyllabic way he spoke to her. Skeptical, she narrowed her eyes, but followed behind as he led her around the garage and through the door to the stairway up to her dad's apartment.

"If there's a problem," she said, halting at the bottom.

MJ grasped her wrists and pinned them above her head, pushing her against the wall before she could finish her thought. His lips claimed hers in a hard, possessive kiss.

At first, she fought against the flame igniting in her belly and stayed unresponsive and tense. She had to push MJ away. She should *want* to push him away. But she couldn't stop her lips from moving against his, and finally her entire body gave in to his demands. Fighting her feelings for MJ was as futile as attempting to make time run backward.

He teased her bottom lip with his tongue and cupped her breast with one hand, the other wove through her hair, pulling her even closer. Her mouth opened in response. She quickly grabbed her ring and ran it along the chain behind her neck and let it dangle between her shoulder blades.

He couldn't see it. Not like this.

His tongue met hers, and she sighed relief into his mouth, running her hand up over his shoulder to the back of his neck.

She'd wanted him for so long. It was wrong, but at the same time, he was the only thing that had ever felt completely right in her life.

The little plastic cup of gelato in her hand fell between them. Breathless and dizzy, she barely registered the icy-cold wetness dripping down the neck of her shirt. The cup clattered to the floor, and his went with it as his hand clenched her hip.

His mouth left hers, and when their eyes met, she saw a spark of regret in his. But, instead of backing away from her, he dipped his head and ran his tongue down the sticky-sweet path of melted gelato. He nibbled and kissed her before setting her down, letting her go and leaving her breathless as he walked back out the door.

Seven

*J*esus. What the fuck had he been thinking? That he could take what he wanted and keep enough control to make her go crazy without becoming invested in being with her? Really? This was Maddie, and he was an idiot for even trying.

MJ tore his hands through his hair and paced around in the back hallway inside the big house. He wanted to get out and go to Coach's bar, but getting drunk and fighting again would only get him kicked out and piss off Coach.

There was nowhere to run. Staying felt like being a rat trapped in a maze, but this rat knew where the cheese was. He'd just tasted it and ran like hell. That cheese had poisoned him before. You'd think he'd learn his lesson. He'd make one dumbass rat.

He cracked his knuckles then pounded his fists against his forehead. He could smell her perfume on him. It made him want to crawl back to her and beg her to never leave him again.

MJ took a deep breath and blew it out hard. He had to take a cold shower and forget this ever happened.

Like that was possible.

Shit, the whimpers and sighs she made and the look

on her face. "Ugh." He scrubbed his eyes with the heels of his hands and focused on not getting hard.

There was no running away from this. No matter where he went, his memory would remind him of her just like it had for the past year. Her voice would come to him in a crowd and he'd look around expecting to see her, but she was never there. The wound she left never healed. He'd been bleeding for her since the day she took off.

"Everything okay, young man?" MJ spun around to face Mr. Simcoe, Maddie's dad. Just the person he needed to be standing in front of right now.

"Fine. Thanks." He mustered a smile and tried not to look guilty for the images of Maddie running rampant through his brain.

Mr. Simcoe folded his arms and smiled back. "Maddie was glad to see you again. It's been a while since the two of you spent time together."

"Yeah. It's good to see her again." And to kiss her and press her up against a wall.

He placed a hand on MJ's shoulder. "You mean a lot to her. I don't know what went on between the two of you, but whatever it was I hope you can get past it."

MJ clenched his jaw holding back a slur of words that would, no doubt, make Maddie's dad punch him in the mouth. He wanted to shout, tell him how Maddie promised the world—the fucking *world*—and bolted from him for no reason.

There hadn't been a fight or an argument, only plans and dreams. So many fucking dreams. He hated her for that. Why didn't she tell him it was all lies? Why lie to him in the first place? He wasn't some kid to be screwed with.

God, Maddie was the last person who would've screwed with his head.

Then why? Why did she?

"I've got to go," MJ muttered and brushed past Maddie's dad.

❀

MJ sat in the corner of the shower and let the hot water beat down on his skin washing her away. He could stay there forever in the steam and silence and never see her again.

He had to get away from this fucking house, and everyone in it.

Start over somewhere new.

But, where the hell did he have to go?

He lifted his face into the water. He knew where. He'd go with Rachael. She'd already mentioned it to him. He could take her up on her offer to go to Turtle Tear and be gone from this place.

He'd also get to meet his cousins he was never allowed to know because they're little kids and little kids can't keep their mouths shut. One of them would've outted MJ to Merrick, and Enzo couldn't have that.

He stood and turned the water off, dripped onto the

bathroom floor and padded out into his bedroom in search of a towel. Out his window, he caught the back of Mr. Simcoe's golf cart heading toward the lake. Maddie's hair blew out behind her as she drove away.

Why was she spending so much time out there? It killed him to spend time at the lake where they spent their summers when they were young, where they made love for the first time in the dark with lightning bugs blinking around them in the tall grass. Where she told him she wanted to be more and kissed him for the first time.

MJ loved being home on break and he hated it. Hated being where his grandfather didn't want him, but loved being with Maddie. Now high school was over and he'd start college in the fall. No more being hidden away at boarding school. He could do what he wanted, when he wanted and nobody could stop him. He hoped that included spending a lot more time with Maddie.

She looked incredible tonight, like always. Her skin was tan, her shorts were very short, and her dark hair hung loose and wild around her bare shoulders. Those shoulders in a tank top did something to him. He wanted to touch them. Taste and nibble them with his teeth.

"Don't you think?" she said, laughing.

He had no idea what she'd said, but agreed anyway. "Yeah. Sure."

She pulled the top of a fat, white wildflower off of its stem and set it in the water. They watched it float. "I have to tell you something," she said, suddenly serious.

"What?" Her blue eyes grabbed his and held on. It was like being punched in the stomach. "What?" he asked again.

"I...um..." She blew out a big breath and shoved her hair away from her face. "Why is this so hard?"

"I don't know. Just tell me." Playfully, he punched her arm and smirked. "It's me."

She smiled and bit her lip. "It is you. That's the thing. I don't feel like your friend anymore."

No. No, no, no. He couldn't lose Maddie.

He gripped her arms and held her tight. "What are you talking about? You're more than a friend to me, Mads. You know that."

She could barely look him in the eye. "What if I want to be a lot more?"

It took him a minute to understand what she was saying, then he thought he'd misunderstood. He'd been in love with Maddie for as long as he could remember, but she never thought of him like that. He was her best friend. Her younger brother.

Wasn't he?

"More, how?" he asked. The question sounded stupid, but he didn't know what else to say. He needed to be certain.

Maddie looked up at him and saw right through him as always. She took his face in her hands, rose up on her toes and kissed him.

His arms immediately found their way around her and held her to his chest.

Finally.

He never thought it would happen, but now that it was, he wondered why it had taken so long. It was obvious they belonged together. Nobody knew her like he did, and nobody knew him like Maddie.

His Maddie.

❀

How could he think he could seduce her and get her back? Did he forget how addicted he was to being with her like that? With her breathless and ready to bend to his will? Jesus, it was all he could do to keep control of himself, and he wouldn't take her unless she was his. Not again.

Never again.

MJ shook his head and turned away from the window. He had to find Rachael and figure out what the plan was. He had to get the hell away from here.

After throwing on a pair of worn jeans and a blue GSU T-shirt with holes in it, MJ wandered downstairs. Rachael had to be there somewhere. She didn't answer his knock on the guest bedroom door, and she didn't have a car to get around. He knew she wasn't with Enzo, because his grandfather was locked away alone in his office.

He passed the living room. It was empty, the TV dark on the wall above the fireplace. She wasn't in the library or the sunroom either. Heading to the kitchen, he figured he'd check outside. That's when he heard her voice.

"Shannon, it's not like that. You don't understand." Hearing Rachael's words edged with temper, MJ peered around the corner into the kitchen. She stood against the counter with her back to him. "I never should've told you, I guess. I thought you'd understand." She gripped the edge of the counter with one hand. "No. I'm not coming back." She shook her head fiercely. "Because, Turtle Tear *is* my home now."

MJ waited until she hung up her phone before entering the kitchen. "Hey, Rach. Hear any more from my dad?" He almost choked on the word. It sounded awkward, but he'd gotten it out.

Rachael's eyes darted around the kitchen as she tip-toed to the entryway and glanced down the hall. She turned back to him with a small, secretive smile. "Yes. He's in Miami wrapping up some business. He doesn't want you with Enzo for one more second than you have to be. Have you thought about coming to Turtle Tear with me?"

This was perfect. He wanted out and Rachael would take him. MJ put a huge smile onto his face, making his dimples—his dad's dimples from what he'd been told his entire life—dent his cheeks. "Consider me there, Rach. Thanks." He hooked an arm around her shoulders and gave her a squeeze.

Eight

Maddie's heart lunged to her feet when she saw MJ's car missing from the driveway. She'd spent all day at the lake and at the grave in the woods steeling her emotions and trying to figure out if she should talk to MJ and tell him everything, or just let him go. Either way, she had to face him. Now, after finally mustering the courage to find him, he wasn't around.

She sat in the manicured grass and slipped off her shoes, reveling in the feel of the slick, cool blades prickling her toes.

She should call Talan. Not because she was guilty for what went on between her and MJ. She and Talan were on a break, so she shouldn't feel guilty. Still, she should call him because... well, because she wanted to hear his voice.

Maddie took her phone from her pocket and hesitated before dialing his number. When her thumb came down on the call button, it wasn't Talan she dialed.

"Maddie? Is everything okay?" Her roommate—now ex-roommate since she'd gotten married last weekend—always worried like a mother hen. She knew Maddie had avoided going home to see her dad since last Christmas, she just didn't know why.

"I'm fine, Mrs. Kara Bridges. I'm sorry for interrupting

your honeymoon. Is it everything you ever dreamed it would be?"

Kara laughed. "Oh, definitely. Steven's sunburnt and peeling everywhere. I can't even touch him without him batting my hands away. It's quite the lover's getaway."

Her laugh sent a wave of warmth through Maddie. "Good thing you two covered that ground before you were married."

Kara sighed. "I'm afraid it's already a well-worn path, my friend. We're beyond the sexy lingerie phase and stuck in yoga pants and stained T-shirts."

"Don't forget the granny panties." Maddie laughed with Kara and wound blades of grass around her pinkie finger.

"How's home? Is your dad thrilled to see his little Peach?" Kara always used her nickname against her, like it was the most embarrassing name Maddie could be called. When they were out with friends, Kara would let the nickname slip and Maddie would have to tell everyone how she became Peach and MJ was Mario.

Everyone always thought it was adorable.

"Of course he's happy I'm here."

"Have you come to your senses and told Talan yes?" Kara's wedding planning bug was still in a feeding frenzy. She couldn't wait to get Maddie in a bridal shop.

"No. I haven't decided yet." Something hard and shaped like regret shifted in her stomach.

"What did your dad say?"

Maddie squeezed her toes together, ripping out grass by the roots. "To take my time and make the right decision."

There was a pregnant pause and Maddie knew what was coming next.

"And how did *he* take the news?"

Maddie should've never told Kara about MJ. "I didn't tell him. There's nothing to tell." Maddie rubbed her throat. It was dry and getting sore.

Kara sighed. "*Yet.* Tell me what's going on between you two."

Maddie sank down onto her side. "Nothing anymore."

"Tell me anyway."

Maddie rolled to her back, rested her wrist on her forehead and gazed up at the blazing blue sky. "MJ and I..." Are explosive together. Are not meant to be. Are perfect. "He hates me." Maddie shook her head. "I left him. I promised him I'd stay, and I left. He'll never understand."

Kara was silent for a second. "Why did you leave? You never did tell me."

"I can't tell you," Maddie whispered.

"I won't tell him. You can talk to me."

"I can't tell anyone." Maddie swallowed her tears. She wanted to tell her. Needed to tell someone. But didn't have the courage. "I can't."

Enzo Rocha's strings were tied too tightly around her neck. If she breathed a word about what she knew, her father would lose his job, and he needed his job. If he didn't, he'd already be retired. After student teaching in college, Maddie found out it was the last career on earth she wanted. Since then, she'd bounced from job to job and was currently without one. She couldn't take care of herself, let alone an aging father. If something happened to her dad— if he needed to be hospitalized for some reason—Old Man Rocha would pay the bills. She couldn't lose that and risk her father's financial stability for her own love life.

But, it wasn't just her love life. It was MJ's entire life— who he was. Didn't that deserve to come first?

"Hey, Peach?" Kara said. "Don't do anything stupid. Okay?"

Maddie's mind immediately went to MJ licking gelato off of her. "Define stupid."

Kara groaned. "Do what you have to do to get him out of your system. Trust me. You're just nervous about having that ring on your finger."

"You're probably right." She couldn't imagine the ring on her finger. It was making her a nervous wreck just being around her neck. "I'll talk to you soon. Hope Steven's sunburn fades fast."

Maddie hung up feeling marginally better. She stretched in the grass under the sun like a cat. Kara was right. In a couple days, this situation would look much better. She'd get MJ out of her system, have a level head and make the best decision she could. Even if that meant being alone.

It was an option that was looking better by the second. MJ, with his crazy family and terrible temper, wasn't a good choice no matter how her body and heart responded to him. Her mind knew better. And Talan might be perfect on paper, but her heart and body failed to respond the way it should to him.

It was all wrong and backwards.

The only decision that was logical was to cut them both out of her life and strike out on her own again.

❀

MJ stuck some tokens in the pitching machine and took his stance in the batter's box. He needed to blow off steam and whacking baseballs at the batting cage was the best way he could think of without getting in trouble.

The balls came at him and he hit as hard as he could. They crushed into the back of the fenced-in cage.

Since he'd been booted off the GSU team, he had to settle for the run-down, slow-as-hell pitching machine at the mini golf course a few miles from the Rocha Estate. The group of middle school boys hanging out at the cage beside him wouldn't shut the hell up, there was a half-dried puddle of soda making the soles of his tennis shoes stick to the concrete, and the huge lights throwing a yellow glare across the entire place buzzed so loud, he couldn't concentrate.

If there was a baseball Hell, this was it.

He hit the last couple balls and took off his helmet.

"Hey! Coach MJ," one of the boys said.

MJ dropped his bat and turned around. How could he not have recognized these kids? He helped coach their team the past couple years. Two years ago, Maddie had too.

"Hey fellas, what's up?"

"Where've you been all summer?" the pudgy one asked. MJ forgot their names—had always relied on them being printed on the back of their shirts—but he knew this one. This one had a single dad who hit on Maddie every chance he got two summers ago.

"I've been around. Playing ball?"

The four boys had their fingers thread through the chain-link fence and were all staring at him. "We're playing," Pudgy said. "Coach could use some help if you ask me."

MJ gathered his bats and zipped them in his bat bag. "Coach doesn't need help. He always did fine on his own."

"He's getting old," the tall kid with glasses said. "We did better last year with you helping."

"Well, I don't have time to hang out at Little League games."

"Too busy getting in fights at Coach's bar? That's what my dad says." Pudgy was really starting to piss MJ off, just like his big-mouth dad had. He'd like to shut Pudgy's dad's mouth for him.

"Is that what he says?" MJ pushed through the door and stepped out onto the sidewalk. The boys gathered around him like he was their fucking queen bee or something.

"Yeah," Pudgy said. "Heard you got kicked off the GSU team, too."

Was it legal to kick a little kid's ass if he goaded you into it? "Are we done here?" MJ took a few steps down the sidewalk.

The tall kid stepped up beside him. "We suck. Our next practice is tomorrow, three o'clock at Butler Field. Come if you want to help us." He threw MJ a pleading glance.

"I'll think about it," MJ muttered.

He walked to his car feeling like an asshole. How did he not even think to offer to help Coach this summer? Sure, if he hadn't been kicked off the GSU team, he'd be too busy. But, that wasn't the case any longer.

God, he was so self-absorbed, he never even thought about Coach needing his help. Coach who was always bailing his ass out every time he turned around.

MJ tossed his bat bag into his trunk. Resigned, he knew where he'd be tomorrow afternoon. Driving home, he thought back two seasons ago. The last season Maddie helped out with Coach's team, the last game of their summer together.

❀

Maddie had her ponytail pulled through the back of her baseball cap. They wore powder blue and white hats and jerseys that matched the team. Coach's said COACH on the back. MJ and Maddie's said ASST COACH. The third base lounge logo of a baseball diamond with a foamy cartoon mug sitting on third base was embroidered on the front pocket.

They were nicer jerseys than the printed T-shirts Coach used to spring for when he and Maddie were on Coach's team.

Maddie stood behind the fence cheering on their team's batters, reminding each one what they'd worked on at practice the past week while MJ warmed up their pitcher for the next inning. Coach liked to stay out by first base. The three of them made one hell of a team. They were undefeated and this was the last game of the season, top of the ninth. They were up by one. If they could score a few more runs and hold the other team off when they were up-to-bat, they'd finish the season 12-0.

They'd won, took the kids for ice cream and then gathered at Coach's bar. Maddie sat next to him in a corner booth. Her hand was on his thigh. He couldn't wait to get her home. She leaned in and whispered in his ear, "I found us an apartment near GSU. I put down a deposit. We can move in next week."

He couldn't believe it was actually happening. She was moving back from Michigan. She wanted to be with him. She'd just graduated college and said she could find a job anywhere, and wanted it to be where he was.

She snuggled in to his side. "I love you, MJ."

He held her close and kissed her. For the first time in his life, he was exactly where he belonged.

❀

She was standing in the driveway under the garage light again.

"Waiting on me?" he asked.

She wasn't smoking this time. He was glad. He hated it when she smoked.

"Yeah," she said. "I want to talk to you."

She wanted to talk to him? The time to talk was that summer before she took off. "I'm helping Coach with his

Little League team tomorrow afternoon. You can come and talk to me then if you want."

First, she looked confused, then she got a little excited. "The same kids?"

"Yep." He lugged his bat bag out of his trunk. "Even the smart-mouth pudgy kid."

"Charlie," she said. "His name's Charlie."

"Whatever." MJ walked by her with his bag. "Be standing in that spot at 2:45 tomorrow if you're coming with me."

He made the mistake of glancing back at her. He wanted to kiss her so badly, his entire body ached. His tongue prickled with the need to taste her again.

He could resist.

Had to.

Instead, MJ turned and ordered his feet to keep walking away, just like she'd done to him.

Nine

After being awake half the night tossing and turning and wishing she could somehow go back a couple years and figure out a way around the Old Man, Maddie rolled out of bed a little after noon.

It had been a long time since she'd let herself sleep that late, but that's what this trip was about. Figuring herself out. Staying up into the early hours of the morning letting her mind wander qualified.

Maddie stumbled out into the living room, stretching and noticed the light on her phone lying on the kitchen counter was lit, indicating she had a text message. She picked it up and unplugged it from the charger. The text was from Talan.

Just wanted to say hello. Hope everything's good at home.

The ring hanging around her neck felt so heavy, it could pull her to the floor.

Or maybe that was her heart.

Why couldn't she just tell him yes and be happy like any normal woman would be? Talan had a great job as a design engineer at Chrysler, he was sweet and funny, and he'd be a patient and loving husband and father—no question about it.

What was this mental block in her way?

As if she needed an answer to that question. MJ was

always in her way. Him and his intensity, his inability to tell her how he felt. He'd never once told her he loved her.

Talan told her every day since the first time he'd said it. What was she doing?

Maddie slumped down into one of the chairs at the tiny kitchen table. She had to get over MJ. Past their past. On to her future. Just because he knew her inside and out didn't mean they were meant to be together.

They fought too much to be together anyway.

She got up and grabbed a paper towel and some cleaning spray to wipe up the coffee ring her dad left on the table. Her mind drifted to a fight she and MJ had over the summer when they were together. He'd been jealous of one of the single Little League dads who had stopped her to talk after practice one day. Charlie Singleton's dad.

"You're a pretty good fielder," Mr. Singleton said, helping her collect baseballs scattered behind the backstop. "Got an arm on you for a girl," he said, laughing. He winked and let his eyes roam up and down her body. "For a woman I should say."

He was good looking for a guy probably ten years older than her, but she only had interest in one man. "Thanks," she said, stuffing balls into the big, canvas ball bag.

"Charlie really likes you. Talks about you all the time. I think he might have a little crush." He came close, his arms loaded with balls. She held the bag open for him. "Not that I blame him." He dumped the balls in and ducked his head so his mouth was close to her ear. "I think I have a little crush too."

Flattered and embarrassed, Maddie stepped back, letting go of the bag. Baseballs rolled in every direction. "Oh," she said, watching the balls leave trails behind in the soft, dusty dirt.

One of the balls flew past her and hit Mr. Singleton on the leg. Maddie's eyes shot up to find MJ stalking toward them.

"Oh, I'm sorry," he said, his eyes hard, brow lowered and creased in anger. "I meant to toss that into the bag. Guess she dropped it for some reason."

"Yeah," Mr. Singleton said, brushing dirt off his jeans where the ball hit. "Good aim." He smiled, like he was joking, trying to lighten the mood, but MJ wasn't lightening up.

MJ stood beside her, feet planted apart, arms folded across his chest, glaring at Mr. Singleton.

"Don't," Maddie whispered. "Please. For Coach."

"Good practice today," Mr. Singleton said. "I was just telling Maddie how much Charlie talks about you guys. You've taught him a lot this year."

"Great," MJ said, the word sharp and pointed.

Mr. Singleton watched MJ for a moment before turning and waving them off. "See you at the game Saturday."

"Bye!" Maddie called, hoping Coach hadn't just lost his team's catcher. She pivoted on her heel to face MJ, her hands coming up to rest in fists on her hips. "What the hell was that about? You totally threw that at him intentionally."

MJ stepped toward her and leaned in, his nose almost touching hers. "You're damn right I threw it at him intentionally. One of us had to stop him before he tossed you on the ground and screwed you right here."

"Are you insane? It was no big deal. I'm not going to run off with every guy who hits on me."

He cocked his head, his own hands on his hips. "Guys hit on you all the time then, huh? That's just fucking fantastic, Maddie."

She threw her hands in the air. "Why are you mad at me? I don't ask them to!"

MJ gestured to Mr. Singleton's retreating form. "You don't stop them either!"

"Enough!" Coach stood beside them. They hadn't noticed him walk up. "You two are being stupid." He grabbed MJ's shoulder. "Especially you. Peach is a beautiful girl. Of course men are going to notice. Don't make your insecurity her problem. That's not fair to her."

MJ smirked and shook his head. "I'm not insecure."

Coach quirked an eyebrow. "You sure about that?" He patted him on the back and left them standing in the pile of spilled baseballs.

Maddie knelt and began collecting the balls. "Why are you like this?"

MJ crouched and held the bag open. "I'm not supposed to be mad when another guy hits on you in front of me?"

She sighed and pushed her hair off of her sweaty forehead. "Don't you trust me?"

He didn't stop tossing balls in the bag and didn't look at her. "Of course I trust you," he muttered.

"It doesn't seem like it."

MJ blew out a deep breath and sat back on the dirt.

"You could have anyone." He nodded toward the now empty parking lot. *"Mr. Singleton is set. He's got a good job, a house, money in the bank."*

Maddie eased down on her knees beside him. "You're right. I should go for it. I mean, isn't every twenty-two-year-old woman's dream to hook up with a divorced, single dad? Instant family. Good thing he's 'set' so I can go shopping whenever my step-kid starts driving me crazy. You know how I am with the retail therapy."

She hated shopping and he knew it. He licked his lips and fought back a smile. "It's not a joke."

"It is a joke if you think I want to be with anyone else." Maddie got up and brushed the dust off her butt. Everyone was gone. It was just the two of them at the very back field in the complex.

MJ stood and wrapped his arms around her from behind, burying his nose in her neck. "I didn't do it to piss you off. I can't stand it when men look at you like that. I wanted to tear his head off." He gently bit the curve between her neck and shoulder. "You bring out urges in me I can't control, Mads."

A shiver ran down her back, followed by the heat of his breath against her skin. She let herself relax against him. "You have a terrible temper."

MJ sucked her earlobe and groaned. "I know a better way to get this aggression out of my system." His hand snuck up her shirt and teased her breast. The other blazed a trail down over her stomach and between her legs.

Suddenly, her jeans seemed too hot, too tight and too in the way. "MJ," she whispered.

"Behind the concession stand or in the car?" His fingers teased and rubbed.

"Concession stand is closer." She ran her hand up his arm and squeezed.

MJ spun her around, picked her up over his shoulder and ran to the little wooden shack standing with its back to an open field of wildflowers. Setting her on her feet behind it, he pressed her against the wall and kissed her.

His lips opened hers and their tongues tangled, his fierce and urgent. She shut her eyes against the blinding yellow-red of the setting sun streaking the sky behind him, cloaking him in dark shadow.

With deft, fast fingers, he unbuttoned her jeans, lowered the zipper and pushed them down her legs. "Turn around." He didn't wait for her to move. He spun her around, placed her hands above her head, palms flat against the sun-warmed wood of the concession shed.

His fingers shoved inside her and she gasped, arching her back and pushing her bottom against his hand.

"How do I make you feel?" he asked, balling her hair up and pulling her back against him harder. His fingers never stopped caressing and rubbing her inside and she felt herself coming unglued.

"So good," she whispered. "I love it."

He nipped the back of her neck, then licked it, soothing her. "Nobody else gets to do this. Only me."

"Only you." He moved in and out of her faster, rocked her harder against his hand. Her body swelled, tingled, throbbed. She moaned and writhed her hips in pleasure.

"Stay still," he said, and his hands were off of her, his body taken away.

She heard his zipper and reached behind her to take him, hard and ready, in her hand.

"Jesus, Mads, you kill me. You make me crazy."

Maddie leaned her chest against the wall, arching her back and guiding him to her opening. "Please," she whispered, so close she could go mad with waiting for him to give her release.

MJ gripped her hips and drove inside her. She cried out and slammed her hands against the wall.

❀

A knock on the door made Maddie jump and pulled her out of her fantasy. She was flustered, her body heated from the memory.

She threw the paper towels away and stalked to the door. Tugging it open, she looked into the face of the shadowed man from her daydream, complete with ball cap and stubbled jaw.

Her body responded instantly, nipples puckering, slick heat between her legs.

He studied her for a moment. "What's wrong? Are you sick?" he asked, shoving his way inside. He put a hand to her forehead. "Your face is all red."

Her skin burst into flames with his touch. "No. I'm fine."

She turned from him and slammed the door. "Why are you here? It's not 2:45 yet."

MJ drummed his fingers on the table, gazing around the apartment. "You wanted to talk." His ebony eyes met hers, making her put a hand out to steady herself against the counter. "So talk," he said.

Maddie fought the lust zinging through her body, her sensible side telling her to get rid of him. Her sensible side rarely won in situations like this. "Talk?"

"Yeah, you know. The thing you're doing with your mouth."

Her mind flashed to him kissing her. "I like what you do with your mouth."

She held his gaze, willing him to come out of the shell of sarcasm and bad attitude he crawled into whenever she was near.

"Don't," he said, slamming his hand against the table. "Don't fuck with my head."

Her chest heaved. He was so close. She knew how he could be when he was mad. Knew how he'd take her. Nobody could make her feel what MJ made her feel when he was cloaked in darkness trying to break free.

"It's not your head I have in mind," she said, easing forward.

His lips tightened, eyes narrowed. He grabbed her and pushed her down onto her back on top of the table. His hands fisted in the hem of her shirt. She wrapped her legs around his waist and pressed her hips into him.

He groaned. "You just don't know."

When she dug her heels into the back of his thighs and thrust against him a second time, he tore her thin T-shirt up the front. Still in her pajamas, her chest was bare and she was all too aware of the diamond flashing on the long chain between her breasts.

MJ braced his hands on either side of her, peering down at the ring, eyes wide with disbelief. "What the fuck is *that?*"

She reached for it, but he was quicker. He snatched the ring off of her chest and squeezed it in his hand, his eyes burning into hers. "You're fucking *engaged?"*

How could she have forgotten it was there? "No. I—"

"No?" He held the ring in front of her face.

Maddie gazed through the sparkling stone between them. MJ's tilted eyes and parted lips spoke louder than anything he could say. How could she let this happen? How could she hurt him again?

"I haven't decided," she said, her voice hoarse and thick.

"You haven't decided?" He let his head drop, laughing, mocking her.

It was painful to hear. Not because she didn't deserve it, because his pain was so raw in the hollow sound.

He looked back up at her and squeezed the ring in his fist above her chest. "You *decided* to let me fuck you on your dad's kitchen table with this around your neck. That's how much I mean to you."

"No!" She grasped his face between her hands. "I—"

MJ shook her off. "Fuck this, Maddie." He yanked the

ring. With a sharp, painful, burn of metal digging into her neck, the chain broke. "You're not getting married."

She shoved him back and sat up, rubbing the back of her neck. "I haven't decided, or I wouldn't be here."

He took a few steps back and folded his arms. The chain dangled from his fist. "Why *are* you here?"

She ran her hands down her face. Her legs dangled off the edge of the table. Her shirt hung open, but she didn't try to cover herself. She was as bare now as she could be with him holding her ring in his hand. "I told him I needed time to get away and think, so we agreed to a break."

MJ threw his head back and paced into the living room and back again. He stopped in front of her and stepped between her legs. "I'll make this easy for you." He let the ring slip between his fingers, holding tight to the end of the chain. The diamond swung back and forth in front of her face, flashing in the overhead light.

He took her chin and held her still, his dark eyes fixed on hers. "When you can look me in the eye and tell me you want to marry him, I'll give it back."

He wasn't playing fair. He knew she could never do that. She would never say those words to him.

Maddie reached for the ring, but he pulled it away. "This isn't about you," she said.

He smirked and shook his head, knowing as well as she did what an enormous lie she'd just uttered.

It was always about him.

Ten

When the hell would he get a goddamn break? It wasn't bad enough that he had the shitty end of every fucking stick when it came to family, now the universe had to take a dump on him in the form of a big shiny diamond around Maddie's neck.

And here he was being the good guy and helping out Coach with his team. Was there no such thing as a good deed being rewarded in this world?

"Thought you said Peach was coming too," Coach said, standing beside MJ on the third baseline watching the boys practice batting.

"Something came up."

Yeah it did. Something came up hard and fast, and he'd almost shoved it home. Then he saw the ring, and it went right back down and hid deep inside his boxer briefs. Nothing like another guy's engagement ring to make the mood wither and die.

The bat cracked into the ball, sending it out in left field. "Good hit!" Coach yelled.

"Get under it!" MJ shouted to the left fielder who caught it. "Nice!"

Coach spit tobacco juice on the ground. "Everything good between you two?"

"What do you think?" MJ eyed the small kid in the batter's box. He remembered him from last year. He couldn't hit far, but the boy could run. "Move in!" he yelled to the infield. "He's going to bunt."

"He's actually been hitting some decent grounders," Coach said. "Boy's fast."

MJ tugged on the bill of his cap. Maddie's ring sat like a lead rock in his pocket. Knowing her, she'd sneak in the big house and snoop through his bedroom while he was gone, which was why he'd keep it in his pocket until she asked for it back.

Which she wouldn't.

Maddie was always trying to make up rules as she went along, but she never realized they just delayed the real outcome. You win a game, or you lose. There's no almost. You get engaged, or you don't. There was no taking a break to think about it.

If she didn't say yes, then the answer was no.

What kind of loser agrees to a break? Why would anyone want to marry someone who has to run away and tear you apart in her mind, weighing each piece to see if it's worth enough to be tied down to you for the rest of her life?

MJ hooked his thumbs in his pockets and scuffed his foot along the base line.

She'd run away from him, too. Guess that made him a pathetic loser who hoped she'd come back for over a year.

What had he done wrong? Yeah, he lost his head

sometimes and his temper all the time. But it wasn't like that was a surprise to her. She'd known him forever.

Maybe it was like she'd said, only kids play to her.

"All right!" Coach yelled. "Give me five laps around the diamond and you're free to go. I want you all here fifteen minutes before the game starts on Saturday. Don't be late!"

MJ realized he'd spent the whole practice lost inside his head over Maddie. "I wasn't much help," he said. "Team looks good this season."

"We're not winning many games, but they're fighters. You and Peach whipped them into shape their first year. You two make a good team. Always have though."

He could feel Coach eyeing him, but kept his gaze on the team running laps. "She was wearing an engagement ring around her neck."

Coach shuffled from foot to foot and tucked his hands in his pockets. "Not on her finger?"

MJ let out a sharp chuckle. "She and the guy are taking a break until she figures out if she's going to tell him yes or no." He turned his head to Coach. "I took it from her. The ring."

Coach's face went blank, then he slowly smiled, shaking his head. "What am I going to do with you two? You're like fire and gasoline."

"Yeah." MJ thought about earlier, with her under him on the table, how easily she could get him worked up—like tossing gas on a fire. "We are."

"Take it easy on her. I don't know why, but it seems like

she hasn't had her head on straight since you two broke up. She's got something stuck in her brain she's being stubborn about."

MJ had sensed it too, but he figured it was just him. Maddie not wanting to be around him.

He reached into his pocket and squeezed the damn ring. How long had she been with this guy? Long enough for him to be proposing?

"Good to see you helping out again," a man said beside MJ, jerking him out of his thoughts.

Mr. Singleton stood beside him. MJ's back stiffened. "Thanks."

Coach chuckled. "If you call hanging around on the baseline with his thumbs in his pockets helping out."

"No Maddie again this year?" Mr. Singleton asked. MJ wasn't sure if it was the guy's tone or his own imagination that implied more than what was on the surface of the question.

"She stayed home today," he said, smugly.

"Hope she can make it to the game this weekend. We missed her last season." He motioned for his son. "Let's go, Charlie!"

MJ squeezed the ring in his pocket again. If it wasn't Ring Man, it would be Mr. Singleton after her. He couldn't take it anymore. Being around her was torture. He couldn't get away fast enough.

❀

Pulling into the driveway after practice, MJ parked beside a black Mercedes sedan he'd never seen before. The Old Man was always having business meetings, so it wasn't like this was the first time he'd seen a strange car at the Rocha Estate. But, this one had him feeling uneasy. Too many surprises had been dropped in his lap lately—Rachael and Maddie to name two—and he didn't want to be caught off-guard again.

He walked in the back door and glanced down the hall to his grandfather's closed office door. The house was quiet, but it always was. Still, something seemed different.

"You're home," Mr. Simcoe said, bustling out of the great room. "Come with me." He took MJ by the arm, spun him around and almost had him out the door.

"Wait. Where are you taking me?" He wasn't walking into anything unprepared.

Something lit behind Mr. Simcoe's eyes. A hopefulness. Eagerness maybe? But it was shaded with uncertainty. "MJ, your dad's here."

He stared at him trying to register the words. They came into his ears and jumbled before reaching his brain. There was no way he was putting them together right. "What?"

"Merrick. He's here."

Realization slammed into him full force, like a door shut in his face.

He wanted to run, scream, flip the fuck out, but he could only stand there staring at Mr. Simcoe, struck dumb. He cocked his thumb toward Enzo's office. "Is he in there?"

Mr. Simcoe shook his head. "No. They spoke already. Very briefly. He's back at the guest house with Rachael. Maddie's in with Enzo. He wanted to make sure she knew what was going on so she could be there to support you."

"Maddie?" His brain was tearing in two. One half wondering what the fuck Enzo wanted with Maddie, the other half scared shitless to meet Merrick.

"I'd hoped she'd be out of there before you came home so she could go along to the guest house with you. I'm sure it would be nice for you to have someone familiar along."

"Familiar. Yeah. Maddie's familiar." What was this random string of words coming out of his mouth?

Mr. Simcoe patted his back. He probably thought MJ had lost his mind. "Will you wait for her?" Mr. Simcoe asked.

Should he wait for Maddie? He'd been waiting for her his whole life. A few more minutes wouldn't kill him.

And he needed her there. He didn't know if he could face Merrick alone.

"I'll wait for her." He glanced down at his old, dust-covered jeans. "I'm going to go up and change."

He took a few steps down the hall.

"MJ?" Mr. Simcoe called.

He glanced over his shoulder.

"Everything will be fine. Good even. You'll see."

MJ nodded, not sure he believed him, and headed upstairs.

Eleven

Maddie dug her fingernail into the black leather chair in front of Enzo's desk. "Leave my father out of this. He has nothing to do with it, and he's disgustingly loyal to you."

She wished she was digging her nail into his eye, especially when his smug expression didn't budge with her plea.

"No." He pushed his rolling chair back from behind his desk and stood. "You will leave today, and I will never see you back here again. Do you understand me? I will make certain of it this time."

Was he threatening her? Exactly how far would he take this?

Before she could wonder any longer, he pulled his wallet from his back pocket, opened it and handed her a wad of bills. A wad of one hundred dollar bills. "I realize your father is important to you. I should've been more...accommodating to you when I asked you to stay away from him. I plan to see that you're taken care of as well as your father. Do I make myself clear?"

"You want to pay me off to not visit my father?"

"He's free to visit you whenever he likes," he said, not

directly answering her question. "My grandson, however, is out of your life for good."

She ignored the invisible belt tightening around her chest. "Why do I have to leave today?"

He tapped his fingers against his side in agitation. "You know why."

"Because Merrick's here and you're afraid I'll spill your secret. Well, I haven't for almost two years, have I? Why would I do it now?"

Enzo let out a derisive laugh. "When would you have told MJ? It's not exactly the type of conversation to have over the phone, is it?"

Her frustration ebbed and came dangerously close to defeat, but she wouldn't be defeated by him again. "When it's your only option, maybe it is. I'm tired of lying to him. Tired of keeping a secret that shouldn't be a secret at all." She stood up and threw her shoulders back, telling herself she wasn't intimidated by this man, the Old Man who'd controlled her for too long.

He threw his hands out. "So, tell him. See what happens. Let's see how he takes this news and knowing you've been keeping it from him."

She folded her arms over her chest and glared at him. He was right. "Maybe this isn't the time, but he'll find out. This isn't something you can keep from him forever."

The corners of his mouth twitched. "I can't? Who will stop me, Maddie? You?"

She lifted her chin in defiance and held his eyes like it was a staring contest and she'd lose if she looked away or blinked first. But this wasn't a game and she didn't know how she could possibly win anyway.

The money practically burned her fingers. She wanted to throw it at him for daring to think handing her a stack of paper earned her loyalty, would keep her from MJ.

She choked back a sob of frustration and strode out of his office. The money in her fist was damp from her nervous, sweaty palm. She opened her fingers and glared at the offensive, crumpled bills in her hand. How much value did the Old Man put on her love for her father? Her history with MJ? However much, it wasn't enough. There was no amount in the world that would ever be enough.

Maddie wadded up the cash and sat it on a table against the wall in the hallway. Enzo could keep his money. She wanted her father in her life.

She wanted MJ in her life, however she could have him. Friend, acquaintance, distant stranger, she didn't care. She'd take whatever scraps he'd give her. He was a fixture in her life even if they didn't work together, and she couldn't give him up.

"Are you okay, Peach?" Her dad took her by the shoulders. She hadn't even seen him when she rushed down the hall.

"I'm fine." She made herself smile and tried to look convincing.

"Good. MJ's home and he needs you to go meet his father with him."

"I can't." No matter how brave she thought she could be, when it came down to it, she was afraid of Enzo Rocha. She didn't know his limitations or if he had any.

"Of course you can. You know how difficult this will be for him. He's been waiting his entire life for this day." He ran his knuckles over the top of her head. "What's wrong with you? You've never walked away when he's needed you."

"You don't have to." Tall and broad shouldered, MJ strutted down the hall toward them. His wavy hair was damp, and he smelled like laundry softener and the sporty deodorant he wore. Maddie liked the clean smell of him better than any cologne or aftershave. He stopped in front of her, his jaw clenched and unclenched nervously.

"I'll go," she said. Despite the gnawing voice in her head telling her Enzo would make good on his threat, the protective streak she had for MJ kicked in. There was no way she could let him face his dad alone.

MJ shrugged and walked past her, opening the back door. He could play it off, but she could practically see the tension lessening from the stiff line of his shoulders.

She followed him outside. They walked to the golf cart behind the garage in silence, MJ a step ahead and to her right. "I'm not in the best frame of mind to do this after this morning," he said, getting behind the wheel. His face was a steel trap, locking her out.

He gripped the wheel, and looked straight ahead, pressing on the accelerator and letting out a groan of frustration. "I don't know what the fuck to do about you."

Maddie's stomach tightened. She'd wanted him so badly this morning. Wanted to purge him out of her system. She couldn't think straight when he was around, and didn't trust herself to make a life-altering decision.

The golf cart bumped over a tree root and pushed through the tall grass beside the lake. The guest cottage was only about the length of a football field away. "This is going to be good," she said, sliding her hand across the seat so her pinkie finger touched his leg. "It's going to be everything you've ever wanted."

"I stopped wanting this a long time ago."

He was lying. Talking around the steel trap again. Closing out all emotion so he wouldn't get hurt. If that was what he had to do, she'd go along with it. She took a chance and squeezed his leg, expecting his muscle to tense under her hand, but he stayed relaxed when she touched him. Maybe he needed her with him after all.

Her fingers ran over a round ridge in his pocket. She traced it and knew immediately what it was. Her ring. He was carrying it with him.

The only thing keeping her heart from jumping out of her chest was the guest cottage door opening and a man coming out, tall and broad like MJ. The same dark, wavy hair. The same self-assured gait as he walked out into the yard with Rachael hanging back a few steps.

Something heavy pressed against Maddie's chest making it hard to breathe. Merrick was the image of an older MJ. It disoriented her, like she'd somehow slipped into the future.

Maddie turned to MJ and studied his face. She didn't want to miss a second. She wanted to know him when he was in his thirties. His forties. All his life.

MJ's eyes were lost, stuck on the man in front of them as he parked the golf cart and sat frozen behind the steering wheel. Maddie still struggled to breathe and hoped Merrick would make the first move.

Tentatively, Rachael approached Merrick and put a hand on his shoulder, urging him forward. Maddie took her cue and squeezed MJ's leg again. "You have to get out," she whispered.

He inhaled sharply and blinked a few times, coming out of whatever thoughts were spinning through his mind.

Slipping one leg out, then the other, he stood tall and strode forward, no hesitation in his step. Times like these, Maddie was thankful for his over-inflated ego that took over. He knew how to handle himself and could flip the all-business side of himself on in an instant, drowning what he was thinking and feeling in the dark depths of his eyes.

Maddie got out of the cart and stood beside it. She'd never been so grateful for anything in her life. After all these years, he was here—MJ's dad was here and they were face-to-face—and she got to be part of it.

She blinked back the wetness in her eyes as a familiar warm band of emotion—she could name it if she let herself—wrapped around her heart.

Merrick, with the sleeves of his white oxford shirt rolled up and the top couple buttons undone, stopped in front of MJ and studied his face with the most amazed and stricken expression Maddie had ever seen on a person. "You're MJ," he said.

"I'm MJ." MJ stood tall in front of his father, though an inch or two shorter. His arms hung at his sides, his chin stiff and tilted up as Merrick took him in.

"I'm…" Merrick glanced over his shoulder to Rachael. She smiled, encouraging him.

"Merrick," MJ said, lifting the tension. Neither of them wanted to use the "D" word.

"It's nice to finally meet you," Merrick said, holding out his hand to shake his son's. "I'm sorry it took so long, but I didn't know you existed."

MJ shook his hand. "I know."

"I'll make it up to you." Merrick had the same dark eyes as MJ. They had the power to hypnotize, to make you believe every word. "Let's go for a walk. We have a lot to talk about."

MJ nodded, his fists clenched and unclenched at his sides, like he was letting something go, something he'd held on to tightly for too many years. His eyes darted to Maddie's, then away again.

She knew in his mind he was merging his past and his present, trying to figure out how all the pieces fit—*if* they would all fit.

Merrick and MJ took a few awkward steps, side-by-side,

attempting a relaxed, friendly stroll. She wanted to tag along and hear every word. She'd played out this moment in her head a thousand times over the years, sometimes with MJ and other times alone in her bed at night. She never once stopped praying for this day to come.

But, as the two of them headed in the direction of the woods, dread seeped into her stomach. They'd visit the grave with the angel on top. The grave that held nothing but secrets and lies.

Twelve

Unease crept over MJ. Not because he was taking a leisurely walk with his dad beside the lake, but because the fact that he was taking a leisurely stroll with Merrick *didn't* make him uneasy.

It should. He should be a nervous wreck, but he wasn't. He couldn't figure out if he was that much of a detached asshole to have no feelings about this at all, or if it just hadn't sunk in enough for his brain to believe it was real.

He pretty much just didn't know what the hell to think.

Beside him, Merrick let out a sharp, disdainful chuckle and shook his head. "Jesus, you're a grown man. I missed everything."

"It's not your fault," MJ said, wondering where the words were coming from. He must have some auto-responder in his brain turned on. God knows he'd thought about this moment enough times. His mouth probably had the words he'd wanted to say memorized.

"I'm sorry," Merrick said. "You shouldn't have had to grow up with him."

The Old Man. Enzo. "Don't worry about it. I survived."

"I need to get you out of here. I don't have any right to make you leave, but I can't stand you being here with him." Merrick reached up and ran his hand briskly over the back of his head, like the thought of Enzo made his skin crawl.

"Turtle Tear?" MJ asked. "Rachael asked me if I wanted to go."

Merrick's head snapped to look at him. "Will you?"

Maddie flashed in MJ's mind. He'd been anxious to get away from her, but now he didn't know if he wanted to. He knew he should. If he stayed, he'd pressure her into being with him just to win her from the other guy. He wouldn't stop until she gave in, and that wasn't how she should make her decision.

But he still wasn't giving the ring back until she asked him for it.

Being at Turtle Tear with Merrick and Rachael—both strangers to him—and his aunt and uncle...Jesus, it would be like a freaking family reunion. Awkward with forced conversation and probably bad food too. But, the alternative wasn't looking so hot either. "Yeah. I'll go."

"Good. I have to wrap up a few legal issues with your grandfather and my lawyer before I join you, but you and Rachael can leave in the morning."

The morning? Nothing like having time to ease into the idea. "I can wait until you've got everything here done."

Merrick shook his head, adamant. "I'd rather have you out from under his nose as soon as possible, if that's okay with you?"

With his housing at school up in the air and Maddie

hounding and haunting his every waking thought—what the hell?—he might as well take off. "Sounds good then."

Merrick nodded to the tree line in front of them. "I used to hide out back here in the cemetery. Morbid, but nobody bothered me. Your aunt was afraid. Wouldn't step foot in these woods."

"My mom's buried in the cemetery. Me and my friend Maddie used to hang out back here too."

Merrick licked his lips and pressed them together tightly. "I'm sorry about your mom."

MJ only nodded. He couldn't talk about it. He'd hated his dad for a long time. Blamed him for his mom being dead. Mostly because he couldn't blame Merrick for not being around himself.

They stopped walking at the cross-shaped path marker on the ground. "Should we visit her?" Merrick asked.

MJ had never thought of this scenario before—not in his wildest dreams. His mom and dad together. Even if one was six feet under. Something about the idea made him queasy, but he swallowed it down. "Yeah. Probably."

The trail was narrow, so Merrick motioned for him to go first. MJ trudged up the sun-dappled hill, birds singing in the branches overhead. Whatever the weird numbness was that wrapped around him, he hoped it didn't crack when he saw her grave.

Reaching the top of the hill, he stopped and looked down into the cemetery. Merrick stepped up beside him and tucked his hands in his pockets, his chin dropped, gazing at the pink marble grave marker below.

"I picked out the angel," Merrick said.

The hurt and regret in his voice made MJ flinch. "Did she like angels?"

"I don't know. I didn't know her very well."

Neither of them made a move to get closer.

"I used to talk to her when I came here," Merrick said. "I'd sit on the ground and just talk about whatever came to mind." He turned his head slightly toward MJ. "I begged her not to hate me."

MJ closed his eyes. It was rushing in—the emotions—like a hurricane against a seawall. "She doesn't hate you."

"What about you?"

"No."

They stood in silence. Leaves rustled in the wind. "We should get back," Merrick said.

"Yeah." He gestured down to his mom's grave. "I'll catch up." MJ couldn't leave without touching the angel. He had a dumb superstition that it brought him luck. So far, for the past twenty years, he didn't have a lot of proof that it worked, but it was a habit he couldn't break now.

Kind of like Maddie. Just having her sitting in the golf cart beside him on the way to the guest cottage gave him strength. He wasn't sure he would've been able to deal with today without her.

At the bottom of the hill, he picked one of the fat, white

wildflowers that Maddie always loved. She called them Queen Anne's Lace if he remembered right. He stepped up to his mom's headstone and sat it beside the angel, touching her wing.

A small bouquet of Queen Anne's Lace landed beside MJ's foot. He spun to find Merrick at the base of the grave. "I do know she liked these," he said, gesturing to the flowers. "She'd take your aunt Heidi for walks and they'd come back with their hands full of them."

MJ finally knew something about his mom. He'd never known anything but her name and what the Old Man had told him—she was nice, sweet, kind—generic comments that could've been about anyone else in the world.

"Come on," Merrick said. He turned and walked slowly, waiting for MJ to follow.

After a moment, MJ took a few deliberate steps forward. He wasn't used to having someone to follow.

❀

Beside the cottage, Maddie sat beside Rachael, the two of them perched in Adirondack chairs barefooted, sipping iced tea. At the sight of her, MJ could breathe deeper. Having her here was keeping him sane...and making him crazy, but he'd take both if he could always see the smile blooming on her lips as he approached.

Merrick leaned down and kissed Rachael. She reached up and took his hand. Standing beside Maddie, MJ stuck his hands in his pockets. Merrick smiled and nodded at Maddie.

"Oh," MJ said. "Sorry. This is Maddie Simcoe." He felt

stupid not giving context to why she was with him, and he didn't want them thinking she was his girlfriend. "The house manager's daughter."

Merrick reached out and shook her hand. "Merrick Rocha. Nice to meet you."

"You too," Maddie said, beaming. "I've heard a lot about you over the years. I'm happy to say I believed none of it."

Merrick laughed. "I can just imagine."

Really? Was MJ really standing here in the sunshine with Maddie sipping iced tea, laughing with his dad? It was right out of *The Twilight Zone*.

Rachael gave MJ a pointed look. "Before you got here, I was telling Merrick about Enzo's offer to give you Rocha Enterprises."

"You can take my word for it on this one," Merrick said. "I'm making sure it's going to happen with or without your grandfather agreeing to it."

MJ wondered what he meant, but didn't want to get into this conversation right now. Enzo was a poison that he wouldn't let ruin this moment. "So, Turtle Tear," he said, steering them in a new direction, "how long have you had it?"

Merrick's hand tightened around Rachael's and he smiled down at her. "It's Rachael's. She's had it for a few months now. She brought it back to life from ruins."

"We both did," Rachael said, gazing up at Merrick.

Their relationship couldn't be that old. They were still too into each other.

Maddie nudged his foot with hers and smiled her smile

that had held a million promises in the past. How could he trust that smile? Did he even want to?

Who was he kidding? Hell yes he wanted to. He wanted to get inside her and never leave. Physically and mentally. He wanted to know what came between them and why she let it. He needed answers and he'd have them.

Maybe it was his turn to run away and see if she followed.

❀

MJ had been quiet all the way back to the big house. Maddie had the distinct impression that something had happened or been said between him and Merrick on their walk that he was keeping from her.

"How'd it go?" she asked. "On your walk? What did you two talk about?"

He plopped down into a wicker chair on the flagstone patio. "She liked those flowers you like. The white ones. Queen Anne's Lace."

At first, his words threw her, then she realized who he meant. "Your mom?"

He nodded. "It went fine."

Maddie wanted to pry more words out from between his lips, but didn't know if it was her place anymore. She'd taken a big risk two summers ago and crossed the line—leaped over the line—of friendship and they couldn't turn back again.

"He said he was sorry." MJ mindlessly flicked a bug off the arm of the chair. "Asked me if I hated him."

"You never hated him," Maddie said, leaning toward

him over the arm of her chair. She needed to touch him, to make sure he was really okay, but she held herself back.

"No," he said, leaning back in the chair with his hands linked behind his head. His soft T-shirt hugged his chest. "I never hated him. I wanted to sometimes."

"I know."

He slouched down farther in the chair. "Of course you know."

She used to know his every thought. Now it was like their link had been severed. She'd taken a knife to it and slashed it in half. Maddie could only ever guess what he was thinking. What he was feeling. It drove her crazy not knowing what was inside his head and heart. "Do you hate me?" she asked.

MJ lifted his head and gripped the arms of the chair. "I've never hated you. I wanted to sometimes." His dark eyes were heavy with remorse. "I should."

The words were meant to hurt her, and they did. She was immediately sick to her stomach. She was desperate for his forgiveness and he knew it. He played on her emotions to wound her like she'd wounded him.

And it worked. The pain inside her was so distressing, her heart had to be bleeding.

This is what MJ does to you, she told herself.

This is not love.

This is a sickness.

It was good that they weren't together anymore. Just like his grandfather, MJ was playing a game Maddie couldn't win.

"I've made my decision," she said, and instantly knew

that she had. It was the one that had been the only choice all along. "I need the ring back. I'm not marrying Talan. I have to take it back to him."

MJ's eyes narrowed in skepticism. "You're going back to Michigan to give him his ring back?"

She took a deep, steadying breath and nodded. "Yes. In the morning."

He rubbed his finger under his lips, which were pressed together tight. For whatever reason, he wasn't finding her news believable. "I'll give it to you then. In the morning. Before you leave."

Maddie mirrored his shrewd gaze right back at him. "Why not now? What's the point in keeping it?"

"You might change your mind overnight."

"I won't."

They stared at each other, neither of them giving an inch. After a few minutes, MJ stood and stretched. "See you in the morning, Mads." He leaned down and kissed her forehead. "Sleep well."

Times like these, she wanted to smack his face, then kiss him senseless, then smack him again. With her tangle of emotions, it was best that she left in the morning. She'd tell Talan she loved him, but couldn't marry him, and then start the hunt for a job and new roommate before Kara got back from her honeymoon.

It was past time Maddie started her adult life and cutting ties with her past in Sandy Springs was the first step forward.

Thirteen

MJ yawned and hefted his suitcase down the stairs. Why did Rachael have to leave at the ass-crack of dawn?

When he got to the foyer, his suitcase clattered onto the marble floor. The Old Man looked over at him from where he stood near the door. "So, you're leaving."

He wanted to make some sarcastic remark, tell the Old Man not to shed any tears, but he couldn't think of anything worth the time to say. He nodded.

His grandfather approached him with his hand extended to shake. "Tell your aunt and uncle hello and the kids that their granddad says to behave." Enzo chuckled as he shook MJ's hand.

"I will." MJ fiddled with the luggage tag on the suitcase handle. He didn't doubt his grandfather loved his aunt and his cousins, but it reinforced his own black-sheep status in the family hearing Enzo talk about them so fondly. He should be used to it by now, but maybe it wasn't something you ever got used to.

He should at least suck it up. Be a man about it. Not let it get to him.

Rachael strode into the foyer with her hair pinned back in a messy bun, and her heels *click-clack*ing on the marble floor. She looked tired and thrown together, but still beautiful. His dad had good taste in women.

"Do you have everything you need?" Enzo asked her, rubbing her back, still trying to make her an ally. Rachael took a step forward out of his reach.

"I think so," she said, looking around distractedly until she saw him leaning against the newel post. "Are you ready?" she asked him.

"As I'll ever be." He rolled his suitcase over to where she stood. "So, is this place like some kind of tropical paradise, or what?"

Her eyes glazed over and a smile spread on her lips. "I think so."

Jesus, he didn't mean to make her all hot and bothered. "I'm sure it's great." He took her by the elbow, nodded goodbye to his grandfather, and led them out the front door to where Merrick stood waiting beside the black Mercedes sedan.

"Wait," Rachael said, snapping out of her stupor and stopping in the driveway. "We need to tell Maddie goodbye."

Enzo stepped out from the doorway. "Mr. Simcoe said she left early this morning."

Maddie left for Michigan without getting her ring? The thought made MJ's chest clench. How would she explain that to Talan—what a stupid name—unless she decided to keep it?

When she came for her ring, he'd planned on finally getting the truth about why she left him. She wasn't supposed to bolt. What the hell was it with Maddie always running from him?

MJ pulled his phone out of his pocket and dialed her number. It rang once, twice. He scuffed his foot on the concrete. Three times. Her voice mail picked up.

Even though it made him feel uneasy and sick to his stomach, he had to move on without her. She wasn't coming back to him. No going backward, only forward.

He shoved his phone back into his pocket without leaving a message and turned to Rachael. "Let's go."

❀

Merrick took them to breakfast before dropping them off at the airport. The three of them sat in a tight booth in a hole-in-the-wall diner just outside of Sandy Springs. The scenario felt a little too instant family for him. Even though he was coming around to the fact that his dad was here and in his life, being with Merrick and Rachael would take a little time to get used to.

Merrick leaned forward and tapped his fingertips on the table, eyeing MJ. "So, tell me about yourself. What's your favorite food? Favorite movie? Sport? Tell me everything. I know nothing about you."

MJ took a long sip of his orange juice. "Um...I like all food. I guess Italian is my favorite. *The Matrix* is probably my favorite movie, but *Caddyshack* is a close second."

Merrick smiled. "Mine too, right behind the Godfather movies."

"I play baseball. Or, I did. Not anymore." MJ bit the inside of his cheek.

"College ball?" Merrick asked.

"Yeah. GSU."

"What position?"

"Catcher."

"Why don't you play anymore? Injury?" Merrick tilted his head, concerned.

"Fight. Got kicked off the team."

His dad sat back laughing. "Poor kid. You are like me. Stupid and impulsive, aren't you?"

MJ let out a snort of laughter. "You could say that."

Merrick shook his head. "Seems to be an inherited Rocha trait. Sorry you got it."

"It goes with the dimples," Rachael said, placing her fingertip in Merrick's.

"Where did he hide you?" Merrick said, his eyes narrowed on MJ. "My father."

MJ took a deep breath and leaned back in the booth. "As far back as I can remember, I was at a year-round boarding school in Virginia. I remember some woman I called Nona when I was really little. I guess she must've taken care of me. I didn't see her after I started school. I don't have any pictures of her or anything. After third grade, the Old Man let me stay at the estate over the summers. Probably wanted to save himself some cash. God knows he didn't want me there."

"I was away at college," Merrick said. "Jesus, he played us like a game of chess, moving us around the board so we never crossed paths." He sighed, and looking a little lost turned to Rachael.

She stroked her thumb across his creased forehead and cupped his cheek. Merrick smiled and kissed her. "I don't deserve you."

"When did you find out he was coming here?" MJ asked Rachael. He nodded to Merrick. "You didn't say anything."

"I told her the first night she was at the Rocha Estate," Merrick said. "I had some business to wrap up in Miami. I asked her not to mention my plan to you."

"We didn't want you to take off," Rachael said. "I don't know you, MJ. I wasn't sure how you'd react if I told you Merrick was coming."

MJ's knee bobbed under the table.

"I didn't want you to take off before I got there," Merrick said. "I lived the past twenty years not knowing you, believing you'd died. I have a lot of time to make up for."

If words had a size and shape, Merrick's would've been the Grand Canyon. MJ had waited for those words his entire life. Waited for Merrick to be told about him. To come find him.

"I wouldn't have taken off," MJ said. "I have time to make up for too."

Merrick's hands clenched his coffee cup. "Your grandfather will pay for this." His dark granite eyes met MJ's in a silent promise.

Rachael put a hand on Merrick's forearm. "Revenge isn't the answer."

"No," Merrick said, agreeing. "Revenge only brings more loss, more desperation. But men like Enzo always pay in the end. I don't know how it'll happen, but it will. He won't get away with everything he's done."

❀

After breakfast, Merrick dropped them off at the airport. Standing beside the car, he kissed Rachael goodbye. "I don't think I should leave you here," she told him. MJ tried not to listen, but didn't want to walk away without telling Merrick goodbye.

"I didn't want you here in the first place," Merrick told her. There was a harsh edge to his voice that let MJ know he wasn't pleased with Rachael for coming. "I let that discussion go though," Merrick said, "given the fact that you were here for MJ."

"And the fact that you never told me about him," Rachael said, an equal amount of cool reserve in her tone. "I let that go. For now. We'll come back around to it though. Don't worry."

"Two discussions tabled for now." Merrick wove his fingers into Rachael's hair and cupped her head, guiding her in for another kiss. "I'll be home soon."

"You better be." Rachael wrapped her arms around Merrick and held him tightly for a moment before stepping away.

Merrick reached out and shook MJ's hand while patting him on the back. "I'll be there as soon as I can. This shouldn't take more than a few days to finish up."

The sincerity in Merrick's eyes filled MJ with something

he couldn't identify. A feeling he'd never had before. His dad would be there for him. "I'll see you then."

Merrick rounded the car and got in behind the wheel. Rachael and MJ watched him drive away before they turned and began rolling their bags through the parking lot toward the airport terminal.

Leaving Sandy Springs, MJ fingered the ring in his pocket with only one regret: losing his last connection to Maddie.

❀

There was no way the man stalking toward them across the tarmac could fly the helicopter behind him. Not that MJ was judgmental, but he'd believe this guy could lift the helicopter before he could fly it. With his blond ponytail, scruffy face and piercing stare, he might have been the only person MJ would think twice about throwing a fist at.

"Beck!" Rachael grabbed the man in a bear hug. "How's everything on the island?"

"Taken care of. You look good." Beck held her at arm's length and looked her over.

"Thanks," Rachael said.

Rachael took a deep breath and smiled, turning to MJ. "Beck, this is–"

"Jesus," Beck said, chuckling, "you don't have to tell me who this is. Looks like his twin." Beck grabbed MJ's hand and pumped it up and down while patting him on the back. "I didn't know Merrick had a brother."

"He doesn't," MJ said. "I'm his son."

Beck's eyes widened. "Oh. What's your name?"

"MJ. Nice to meet you. Beck, right?"

"That's me."

Rachael stepped forward, standing beside them. "Beck does pretty much everything at Turtle Tear. And he flies that thing." She pointed to the black helicopter. "I don't know what we'd do without him."

Beck smiled and put his hands on his hips. "Job security." He put an arm around her shoulders and squeezed. "And you're like a sister. A sister who hates my girlfriend, but that's normal, right?"

Rachael rolled her eyes at him with an insufferable look on her face. "We get along just fine now that she's spoken for and not after Merrick. So as long as you keep her to yourself—no worries." She smiled, and squeezed Beck's bulky arm.

MJ glanced down at his own bicep and resisted the urge to flex. Without baseball, he'd have to hit the gym more often to keep his muscle. He'd like to work out by lifting Maddie against the wall a few more times.

There went his mind again, wandering off to Maddie and their past. At this rate, he'd need a lobotomy to forget her.

"It's hotter than Hell standing here on this tarmac. Let's get out of here." Beck took Rachael's bag and reached for MJ's.

"I got it, thanks," MJ said. He didn't need a man-servant or whatever this guy probably was to his...to Merrick.

Beck smacked him on the back. "You're a little standoffish, I can tell. Just like your dad was until this one," he pointed to Rachael, "took the stick out of his ass. I expect she'll do the same with you."

Did this guy really just say MJ had a stick up his ass? What-the-fuck-ever. A chip on his shoulder, sure. Of course there was a big fucking chip on his shoulder, but a stick up his ass?

He curbed the urge to plant a fist in Beck's face. The last thing he needed was a ride back to the Old Man's house and more harassment about becoming an MMA fighter, which really wasn't that bad of an idea.

Rachael sat in the front of the helicopter beside Beck, and MJ strapped his harness on in the seat behind her. They wore headsets to talk to one another over the whipping roar of the propellers.

MJ gripped the seat beneath him with sweaty hands. He didn't even like riding roller coasters. The last time he flew, he was drunk. Being in a metal pod with rotating blades keeping them in the air wasn't exactly his preferred method of travel. Guess when you're going to a secluded island there wasn't much of a choice in the method of getting there.

The helicopter lurched up and forward. "Here we go," Beck said, pulling back on the gear stick, or whatever it was that looked like it should be part of an arcade game. MJ's stomach rolled.

Don't puke, he thought over and over in his head. Don't puke. Don't puke. Don't puke. "How long is this flight anyway?" God, the rasp in his voice even sounded like he was going to puke.

"About an hour. You okay back there?" Beck turned his head and glanced back at him. "Uh oh. I think someone's afraid of flying, Rachael."

"I'm not afraid of flying." He was afraid of heights. Deathly afraid of heights. Or the falling from heights to be more accurate.

"You're white as a ghost." Rachael reached back and squeezed his knee. "Just take deep breaths and close your eyes."

"I can't close my eyes. The motion makes me sick if I close my eyes."

"Okay. Okay," she said. "How about looking straight out the window? You can't see down below, just blue. Pretend it's the ocean and you're standing on the beach. The motion you feel is from the waves pulling in and out under your feet."

He nodded his head frantically, blowing out a deep breath. Sweat was beginning to bead on his forehead. God, he hoped this worked.

The beach. Put yourself on the beach. He rolled his shoulders and stretched his neck from side to side, keeping his eyes straight ahead and focused on the clear, baby blue sky.

Blue like Maddie's eyes. She'd look amazing in her bikini beside him on the beach. In the ocean. Laughing in the waves.

Shit. Maddie. Lobotomy.

"Doing okay?" Beck asked through the headphones.

"Fine." As long as he wasn't about to pass out, he guessed thinking about Maddie for an hour would be okay.

Even when she wasn't around she could get inside him and calm him down.

And here he was running away with her ring. Not that he could find her to give it back since she ran too.

Fourteen

MJ could not believe his eyes. He stepped out of the helicopter straight into heaven.

Lush green palm trees and bright flowers lined immaculate, mosaic-paved walkways. Festive music played in the distance. Birds sang, invisible in the trees. The wind blew the humidity away with a soft breeze.

It was paradise.

And his dad had been living here with his perfect girlfriend while MJ was struggling to survive in misery with Old Man Rocha.

He couldn't blame his dad for leaving him at the Rocha Estate when he didn't know he was even alive. At least when he found out, he got him the hell out of there.

When they reached the hotel, a white, stucco hacienda, a curvy blonde came bustling down the walkway. "Beck! Thank God you're back. Riley's being insubordinate again."

MJ wondered how she functioned in heels as high as the ones on her feet.

Beck laughed. "He can't be insubordinate. You're not his boss."

MJ stepped off the pathway out of the blonde's way as she pushed past him to get closer to Beck and Rachael—then she stopped and spun around to face him.

"Oh my God," she said. "Merrick has a brother?"

Beck laughed loudly, stepping between them. "This is MJ," he said. *"Merrick Junior."* She gaped and Beck bent and kissed her. She seemed to relax a little. It made him think of Maddie's body going slack under his while he pressed his lips to hers.

Shit.

Rachael shook her head, stepped around the pair kissing on the sidewalk and hooked her arm through MJ's. "Come on. I'll show you around."

"You okay?" he asked. Her arm felt a little tense where it touched his.

She rolled her neck to one side, then the other. "Fine. Joan likes to get under my skin. It's her favorite pastime. I try to be nice to her, but it's pointless."

"Why is she here then?" MJ glanced back to see Beck and Joan smiling and talking with their hands linked.

"She works for Beck," Rachael pushed her hair back out of her face, "so I deal with it." She laughed. "Funny thing. Beck used to call her Dragon Lady before they started going out. It's a very fitting nickname."

"Why is he with her? I mean, I don't know either of them, but they seem a little mismatched."

Rachael chuckled. "When you can tell me why men do anything they do, then you'll have your answer."

That was an easy one. Sex. Men did everything for sex. But he wasn't going to tell Rachael that.

Approaching the hotel, the bright, early morning sunlight streamed through the palm fronds. MJ put his hand up to shade his eyes, wishing he'd remembered to bring his sunglasses, but he'd left them in his car. The hotel had long, narrow, black-shuttered windows sunk into the white stucco. They were propped open and reminded him of eyelids that would rather be closed until at least noon—like his own.

Orange-red tiles covered the roof and a black wrought-iron fence closed off a courtyard with a mosaic-paved patio to match the pathway. In the middle of the courtyard stood a fountain with a mermaid sitting on a rock in its center holding a conch shell with water spurting out of it. He had the childish urge to throw pennies in and make wishes.

He didn't even know what he'd wish for at this point.

"Heidi and Roger are probably up by now with the kids," Rachael said. "I bet they'll be down for breakfast soon. I'll get you settled in a room, and we can find them in a little while."

"No hurry." MJ's eyes roamed as they walked through a gigantic, sliding wooden door into a lounge area. There was a fireplace built into the corner of the concrete wall. Dark brown leather sofas and chairs sat, scattered around the room, rustic wooden tables between them. Bright red, yellow and aqua blue Mexican rugs lay underneath.

He loved it. He never wanted to leave. Turtle Tear was the most perfect place on Earth, and he hadn't even seen the whole thing.

"What do you think?" Rachael asked, hesitantly. She linked her fingers and rubbed them together.

"It's incredible."

"Thanks." Her smile was amazing. It changed her whole…everything. She was a new person when she smiled like that. MJ wondered how Merrick could ever leave the island with the image of Rachael smiling in his head.

Maddie had a fantastic smile even if it was a little crooked.

Rachael had walked halfway down a hallway in front of him before he realized and started to follow. They came out in the entryway where colorful painted Spanish murals of trees, birds and flowers covered the walls. Raw, wooden beams lined the open three-story ceiling, and a curved staircase with bent wooden rails that looked like tree roots climbed up to the second and third floors. Light streamed in the windows beside and above the great, double hacienda-style front doors.

"You're back." A guy about MJ's age, maybe a few years older, approached Rachael. "Can I get you anything? Have you had breakfast? I'll get Jesse to take your bag up to your room." He glanced at MJ and smiled.

"Thanks, Riley. We'll wait a little while before we have breakfast. This is MJ." She motioned toward him and Riley shook his hand. "He's going to need a room. How about the one on the far end where my friend Shannon was staying? I think you know which I mean."

Riley licked his lips and suppressed a smile. There was a story behind his eyes that MJ thought he might like to hear from the glint flashing there. "I know the one." He headed toward the stairs, beckoning MJ with his hand to follow.

Riley tried to take his bag, but MJ pulled the handle back. "I've got it, thanks."

MJ followed Riley to the end room on the second floor. "If you need anything let me know," Riley told him, "and if you see a blonde that looks like she stole Barbie's wardrobe, stay away. She's crazy as a shithouse rat." He laughed and stepped out into the hall letting MJ close the door.

It seemed Beck was the only one who could stand Joan. MJ would have to stay far away from her. The last thing he needed was trouble with another woman.

Finally alone, MJ rolled his suitcase farther in the room. It was large with windows facing the side and back of the property. A king-size bed sat against the far wall, filled with overstuffed pillows and a puffy, white comforter that MJ figured he'd toss on the floor at night or sweat to death underneath. The hardwood floor was covered with two bright rugs like the ones in the lounge below. The furniture was all rustic, dark oak. At least he thought it was oak, but what did he know about furniture?

He crashed down on the bed and sprawled out, ready for an early morning nap. How long would Rachael leave him up here if he fell asleep? He yawned and sat up, deciding to change from his jeans into shorts.

Laying back down, he flipped through channels settling on a World War II show on the History Channel. These types of programs always put him to sleep. He adjusted the pillow under his head and in five minutes was out cold.

✾

"Gone?" Maddie jumped up from her father's couch and gripped his arm. "What do you mean MJ's gone?"

He looked at her like she was a mental patient. "He went to Turtle Tear with Rachael. I'm sorry he didn't tell you."

Maddie's mind reeled. He left *her* this time. He wanted to hurt her like she'd hurt him.

Her ring! Shit. MJ better not have taken it with him. "I have to call him."

Her dad shook his head, stepped away from her and picked up his car keys. "I'm running some errands. I'd steer clear of the big house today if I were you. Enzo's in a foul mood with Merrick here."

She nodded and watched him leave before dashing to her room and grabbing her phone.

One missed call from MJ from early this morning, but no message. Had he called to tell her goodbye? She dialed his number and bit her fingernail as it rang.

"Mads," he said in a sleepy voice on the third ring. "Back in Michigan already?"

Anger lurched through her veins. "Tell me you didn't take my ring with you."

"I didn't take your ring with me." He chuckled through a yawn. "There, I said it, but it's a lie. I do have it with me."

She kicked one of her flip-flops across the room. "Why the hell would you take it with you?"

"Why the hell did you leave this morning before coming to get it from me?"

"I didn't! I'm standing in my bedroom at my dad's. You're the one who left."

"Enzo said—" MJ groaned. "Never mind. The fact is you can't be trusted to not change your mind. You don't know what you want, Maddie."

If he were there, she'd strangle the life out of him. She gritted her teeth, seething. "I told you my decision. I need the ring to give back."

"Well, I need you to tell me why you left me before I give it back. You need something and so do I, sounds like we have a deal."

Maddie sank onto her bed and let her eyes fall shut. "No deal. Just send the ring back here, MJ."

"Come get it, Mads." He laughed and hung up.

Maddie tossed her phone to the end of her bed. "I hate you," she mumbled, knowing it was far from the truth.

Fifteen

A knock came on MJ's door as he set his phone down, still laughing, imagining how pissed Maddie was.

Slipping off the bed, he stretched, yawned and rubbed his eyes on his way to answer it. Rachael stood on the other side. "Ready to find Heidi and Roger?" she asked, looking refreshed and relaxed in shorts and black bikini top.

He wasn't ready to face his aunt and uncle and meet his cousins, but being stuck in a little island resort with them didn't leave him much of a choice. "Sure."

MJ pulled his GSU baseball cap on backward and met Rachael in the hall. "They're out by the pool," she said, jogging down the stairs in front of him. "Holly and Sam are like fish. You should've seen them with Merrick the other day. He was throwing them up in the air and..." Her face fell. "Sorry."

"For what? My *father* playing around with little kids when he wasn't around for me when I was their age? He thought I was dead, Rachael. I can't blame him for not being there for me."

She tucked her hair behind her ear and nodded.

They were quiet until they stepped outside the lounge doors onto the patio. "Why isn't there anyone here?" he asked.

Rachael twisted her fingers. "It was a private opening

weekend. My mom and aunt and best friend, Shannon, were here, but they left while I was gone. Heidi, Roger and the kids are here for the week though."

They headed down a path to the right of the patio, this one made of large flagstones with big trees clustered on their left. Maddie could never resist climbing the biggest trees in the woods by the lake when they were younger.

It was a miracle she didn't kill him back then; she was always such a tomboy. He followed her around and did everything she did. Jumping out of trees, swimming all the way across the lake, racing their fathers' golf carts. She'd been his entire world.

On some level, she still was. That damn ring up in his room buried in his jeans pocket was killing him, serving as a constant reminder that she didn't belong to him. If she came to get it from him...MJ couldn't even think about hearing those words fall from her lips, the expression on her face as she looked him in the eye and told him why she left him over a year ago.

No. She wouldn't. She'd never tell him.

"Right through here," Rachael said, stepping into a walkway covered by a palm frond tiki roof. The walkway surrounded an open courtyard with a huge pool in the center. A swim-up bar sat on the far side. Two little kids ran side-by-side and jumped over the water, grabbing their knees and splashing down in dual cannonballs.

MJ's aunt was stretched out on a lounge chair in the sun with a book open in front of her face. Roger sat on a stool in the shade of the swim-up bar talking to a dark-haired guy behind it.

Hell with this, MJ thought. He ripped off his shirt and tossed it on the ground with his hat and cell phone, kicked off his flip-flops and took off running for the pool. Just because he wasn't ten years old anymore didn't mean he couldn't do cannonballs with the best of them. Plus, what better way to make an entrance?

He could hear Rachael laughing as he soared through the air, shouted, "Incoming!" and splashed down beside both kids.

MJ surfaced to find the girl and boy sputtering and coughing, trying to stay afloat in the waves he'd caused. "You guys okay?" he asked. "Need help?"

They both shook their heads, eyeing him warily.

"I'm your cousin," he said. Might as well jump right into that too. "MJ."

"We don't have a cousin, MJ," the little girl said. Jesus, she had his dimples.

"You do now," he said. "What's your name?"

"We don't talk to strangers," the little boy said, paddling away toward the wall.

MJ followed. "I just told you, I'm your cousin. MJ. So I'm not a stranger. What's your name?"

"He won't tell you," the girl said right behind MJ, scaring the hell out of him.

"Do you always sneak up on people?" MJ laughed. "What's your name then?"

"Holly. This is Sam."

"You weren't supposed to tell!" Sam screamed.

These two were going to give him a headache in about two more seconds.

"MJ! You're here!" Heidi ran to the pool, knelt and hugged him. Her long, black hair was tied up on top of her head. Everyone in his family looked so much alike—just like the Old Man. "Rachael said you guys got in a couple hours ago. It's so good to see you. We need to catch up."

"Did you introduce yourselves to your cousin, MJ?" she asked her kids who were busy trying to dunk each other underwater.

"We met," he said, hoisting himself up onto the side to sit. Roger was making his way over, holding a drink above his head.

Rachael had taken the lounge chair next to Heidi's and was pretending she wasn't watching the touching reunion. He almost laughed. She might as well come over with them, it wasn't like she'd interrupt a big private family moment. Hell, he was blood to these people, but didn't feel like a family member at all.

MJ raised his hand and motioned for her to come over. She pretended not to see him, but he knew she had.

"MJ," Roger said, propping his elbows on the side next to MJ, "good to see you. How's your grandfather doing?"

"Same evil bastard as always." He kicked his feet, splashing Holly and Sam. They squealed and swam away, shoving each other.

Roger gave him a sideways glance. "He does what's best for you."

MJ turned and looked back over both shoulders with exaggerated movements. "I don't see him anywhere, so you don't have to worry about kissing his ass."

Roger chuckled and took a sip of his drink. "You are just like him."

MJ knew who he meant. His dad.

"That's enough from both of you," Heidi said, sitting and slipping her legs between them to dangle over the side into the pool. "We have enough family drama to deal with without you two creating more."

"Nothing here to deal with." Roger took another sip and waded away from the wall, back toward the bar.

"Sorry," Heidi muttered, "he can be..."

"Merrick will be here soon," MJ said. He scooted his feet out of the water and stood. "I know that's what you were implying."

Roger quickly recovered his shocked expression.

"Yeah," MJ said, "he came to the Rocha Estate. We met. Everything's fine, so you can stop gloating that you have something you're holding over me. You don't. Not anymore."

Roger gave him a calculating smile. "No? I wouldn't be so sure of that. One meeting with Merrick Rocha doesn't reveal all of his secrets."

"Whatever. I'm not playing games with you." MJ ran his fingers through his wet hair and strode over to where Rachael was laying, tanning, with her eyes closed. She'd gathered his shirt, hat and phone and set them on the chair beside her. "Thanks for grabbing my stuff." He stuck his hat on backward and threw himself down on the lounge chair.

"You're welcome. Looks like you're a hit with Sam and Holly."

He snorted a laugh. "Yeah. They love me."

"They're kids. They'll warm up to you fast."

He wasn't too sure about that, but wasn't worried about it either. He'd probably never see them again after this week.

MJ dried his hands with his T-shirt and tapped his phone's screen to see if he'd missed any calls.

His chest constricted. Nothing. Not one call, and Christ, Maddie had to be pissed. Why hadn't she called to argue with him more and call him an asshole?

Then the internal battle began. He wanted to call her. Maybe he shouldn't have pushed so much. Maybe he should've just left the ring and let her go.

Wasn't that what he wanted after all? To be free of Maddie? He was beginning to doubt himself. It rarely happened, but when it did, it was never good.

Sixteen

Maddie had cleaned her dad's apartment from top to bottom—not that it needed it in the first place—and paced a path from the living room to the kitchen and back again at least a hundred times.

All afternoon she'd warred with herself over calling MJ and screaming at him, calling him every name she could think of and telling him she never wanted to see him again.

He brought out the very worst in her.

Maddie winced. Her head ached. She was sick of all the thoughts and feelings torturing her day and night. Ever since Talan pulled that ring out of his pocket her world turned upside down.

No, it was already upside down thanks to the Old Man. She wouldn't even have been with Talan at all if it hadn't been for Enzo Rocha and his secrets and lies.

Maddie wasn't sure how she felt about that. If things could've been different, would she want them to be? If she could turn back time and find an alternate path that didn't have Talan in it, would she?

It didn't matter now.

She'd made her decision.

She slumped down onto the couch, leaned her head back against the soft, worn upholstery and closed her eyes.

Thinking about a past that never was and never could've been was a waste of time. Enzo Rocha *had* run her off and that led her to here and now.

Maddie leaned forward and rubbed her temples, groaning. She needed to erase MJ from her mind, but how could she when so much was left unspoken and unfinished between them.

It wasn't just MJ who had suffered when she left him.

She needed closure. There was no getting around it.

Faced with only one option for getting her life back in order, she slipped her sandals on and jogged down the steps. Once outside, she hopped in the golf cart and headed to the one person who could help her get to Turtle Tear.

❀

Standing outside the guest cottage, Maddie breathed in the sun-warmed scent of honeysuckle that climbed a trellis by the front door. She and MJ used to pick the flowers, sit on the ground and suck out the sweet nectar. But their scent would always bring a flush to her face remembering the taste of honeysuckle mixed with sex on MJ's tongue.

"It's hot," MJ said, stripping his T-shirt off and tossing it on the ground. "Take off your clothes."

Maddie laughed and gave his chest a shove. "I'm not getting undressed out here for the entire world to see."

"No, not the entire world. Just me." He grasped the hem of her baby doll tank and tugged it over her head. It was so hot, she hadn't worn a bra. MJ stepped in to her and closed

his hands over her breasts, kneading while he lowered his lips to her neck.

She let her head fall back and closed her eyes against the sun. It lit up behind her eyelids like fire—like the heat that rushed between her legs. He unbuttoned her shorts and they fell to her feet.

MJ ran the back of his fingers down her sides, his touch so light, it brought chills to her skin. He grabbed her hips and kissed her harder, down her throat, across her collarbone and over the swells of her breasts. If he hadn't been holding on to her, she would've crumpled to the grass.

When his lips left her skin and he stepped back, she whimpered. "Keep your eyes closed," he said. "Don't move."

A moment later, she heard him return to her. He didn't touch her, but she felt the heat of his body, so close, but never close enough. Not even when he was inside her.

A light, fluttering tickle ran over her nipple. Her eyes popped open to find him teasing her with a silky honeysuckle stamen, leaving behind dewy nectar droplets. MJ flicked the stamen over her shoulder and lowered his mouth to the peak of her breast, his lusty, dark eyes locked on hers. His tongue circled her nipple before he took it in his mouth and sucked, making her moan with pleasure.

MJ lowered her to the ground and opened his hand revealing a palm-full of yellow and white flowers. "Honey-suckle never tasted so sweet," he said, trailing another sta-men down between her breasts to her belly button.

Maddie was intoxicated by the lush scent of nectar, the

wet tip of MJ's tongue sliding down her body, his hands slipping her underwear down her thighs. Being with him like this was more than she ever dreamed it would be. He set her on fire, melted every thought in her mind and had her begging and panting underneath him every time they were together.

She'd never get used to it. Never get enough. She was addicted to the taste of his kiss, the sound of his husky voice whispering all the dirty things he wanted to do to her. Addicted to running her hands and lips over his firm, sculpted body, the sensation when he pushed inside her and she knew she was on the verge of losing control.

MJ lazily traced a honeysuckle stamen down from her belly button. Spreading her legs apart with his shoulders, he continued the path, brushing her very center with the silky strand.

Maddie arched her back at the sensation. Too light, too soft, too torturously erotic to handle. "MJ," she whispered. "Please."

"Please what, Mads?" He nibbled and kissed the inside of her thigh.

"I need more," she begged. "Touch me."

"I am touching you." He swirled the stamen through her folds.

"You know what I mean," she said, desperate to have his fingers rubbing and circling.

"Tell me."

She groaned, hating this game. He knew she wasn't good

at asking. Instead, she reached down, ready to show him. He caught her hand before she touched herself. "No. This is just for me."

MJ gripped her wrist and licked her center, collecting honeysuckle nectar and her own dewy wetness on his tongue. Maddie jolted and lifted her hips for more. She needed relief, needed him to take her over the edge.

❀

"Maddie?"

Startled from her memory, she jumped and spun toward the lake and Merrick's voice. He sat on the bank with khaki pants rolled up to his knees and a gray T-shirt that hugged his chest. If this was what MJ would look like in his early thirties, Maddie might never get the closure she wanted.

Internally, she rolled her eyes at herself. She needed to calm her overactive hormones. No more strolls down memory lane straight into MJ's arms. That had to end right now.

Which brought her to why she was standing there in the first place. "I need your help."

Merrick patted the ground beside him. "What's going on?"

She strolled over to him and sat on the bank. The breeze rippled the water. Cattails swayed. "I need to get to Turtle Tear. MJ has something of mine, and I need to get it back."

He frowned. "What does he have?"

Suddenly, she felt like a tattletale. This was MJ's dad and she'd never had anyone to run to when they were little to tell on him when he was being a bully to her. "A ring."

"A ring? Why do I get the feeling there's more to this than just a ring?" Merrick bent his knees, crossed his ankles and sat back resting on his hands.

Maddie cringed. "It's an engagement ring."

"MJ gave it to you?" Merrick was surprised. Probably because yesterday MJ gave no indication that he wanted anything more than friendship with Maddie.

"No. He took it from me."

Merrick shook his head. "You're engaged? And MJ took your ring? Why would he do that?"

This was all more complicated than she wanted it to be, and explaining it made her sound like a nutcase who couldn't get her head on straight. "I'm not engaged. I have a boyfriend in Michigan, where I live. He proposed. I told him I had to think about it. We're taking a break until I figure it out."

Merrick lifted his chin with a knowing smirk. "And MJ thought he'd make the decision for you."

"Something like that." The image of MJ hovering over her while she was bare-chested and sprawled across the kitchen table flashed through her mind. The way his eyes blazed and he held the ring in his fist like he wanted to shove it down her throat. "He and I used to—"

"I get it," Merrick said. "I wasn't buying the whole friendship thing between you two. Any idiot can see there's more."

"There's not," she said. "Not anymore. That's why I need to get my ring back and get him out of my mind." She took a shaky breath. "I need to tell him it's over and make sure he knows I mean it."

Merrick stretched out his long legs. "Are you going to rip his heart out? Because I can't help you do that."

Maddie let out a sad, incredulous laugh. "I did that over a year ago. He doesn't expect anything else from me." She met his eyes, so much like MJ's, and prepared to plead with him if she had to.

He sighed. "I know that desperation. It makes you do crazy things." He scratched the thick stubble on his chin. "Sometimes crazy things work though. Be at the airport in two hours. I'll have a helicopter waiting to take you to Turtle Tear."

A zing of hope rushed through her. She tried to trample it down by reminding herself this was a mission for closure. "Thank you. This is...thanks."

"You're welcome."

She jumped up and brushed off the back of her shorts before spinning around and taking a step toward the golf cart.

"Maddie?"

She glanced back at Merrick. His lips were pressed firm, his eyes thoughtful. "Don't force anything." He chuckled. "Take it from someone who's forced his way into everything his entire life. Don't make it hard on yourself."

She nodded. "Okay."

A few hours later, a helicopter was at the airport waiting to take Maddie to Turtle Tear.

A man with dishwater blond hair pulled back and muscles the size of a professional wrestler stood at the gate holding a sign with her name on it. She rolled her suitcase up to him and held out her hand. "I'm Maddie Simcoe."

He took her hand and shook it. "Beck Tanner. I hear you have some ass to kick on the island." His chuckle was followed up by an amused whistle. "Junior's got it coming for swiping your ring. I take it there's history between you two?"

She blinked a few times, wondering how much he knew and who had told him. "We grew up together."

Beck grabbed her suitcase and began walking toward the tarmac where a black helicopter sat. "Let me give you some insight on how a man's mind works. You don't steal a woman's engagement ring unless you mean to replace it with one of your own."

He was full of it. MJ was paying her back. Taking the ring was revenge. And pride. His ego got the best of him. "And you have first-hand experience with this?"

He laughed. "Hell no. I'd never do something so stupid. Junior's dad on the other hand…" He shook his head putting her bag behind the passenger's seat. "There's a man who would take a woman's engagement ring if he wanted her back." Beck winked at Maddie. "Like father like son."

"You don't know what you're talking about," she said, but she couldn't ignore the pang of anxiety that started to spread through her like wildfire.

It made sense. What if MJ wasn't just bribing her with the ring? What if he did want her back?

Even if he did, it was too late. She was determined to find closure with him.

"Watch your head," Beck said, helping her up into her seat, "and get your fists warmed up. We'll be landing in about an hour."

An hour and she'd face MJ. Her stomach fluttered and her breath caught in her throat. Maybe this wasn't such a good idea after all.

Seventeen

$\mathcal{R}$achael had been acting strangely all day. Merrick had called just before they'd gone back to the hotel with his aunt and her perfectly annoying family to have lunch, and Rachael disappeared before they even ate.

Now she was jittery and kept looking up in the sky like she expected someone to drop down out of it at any moment.

The sun was setting, throwing an orange glare into his eyes.

"MJ, come make a wish." Holly sat on the edge of the fountain holding a penny out to him. "The mermaid grants all wishes. Rachael said so."

"Did she?" He scooted his chair out from the patio table and sauntered over to the fountain. "Thanks." She dropped the penny in his hand, and MJ closed his fingers around it, but didn't know what to wish for.

"You have to blow on it before you throw it in," Sam said, swirling his hand through the water.

He wished his dad...

He wished Maddie...

He took a deep breath and blew on the penny sitting in his palm. He wished for once in his life he'd find somewhere to belong.

The coin plunked down into the water and sunk to the bottom, and that was when he heard it. The *whomp, whomp, whomp* of helicopter blades.

Sam and Holly shot to their feet, shielding their eyes with their hands to watch it fly over the hotel. "Is Uncle Merrick back?"

"No," Rachael said from where she sat at the table with Heidi and Roger. "It's a friend of mine and MJ's." She gave him a pointed look.

No. It couldn't be.

Still, his stomach tightened in anticipation. Rachael stood and tipped her head toward the shelter beside the tree line where a few golf carts sat. "Why don't you ride to the landing pad with me?"

His heart lunged forward, but his feet stayed rooted to the patio. Maddie was going to murder him first and ask questions later.

Sam reached out with his foot and pushed the back of MJ's leg making his knee pop. MJ jolted forward and darted a look back at the two kids who were now laughing like cracked-out monkeys.

Hell, if he stayed here, he'd probably end up getting wrestled into the fountain by his crazy little cousins. "Yeah, I'm coming."

He followed Rachael across the lawn and slid into the passenger side of the first golf cart. She turned the key and pulled out from under the awning. "What's going on with you and Maddie?" she asked.

"Nothing." It might not have been entirely true, but it wasn't exactly a lie either.

"MJ," Rachael put a hand on his arm, "Merrick told me you took her engagement ring. Something's going on."

"Maddie told him? It's..." He bounced his knee and tapped his fingertips together. "We used to be together, okay? Now we're not. That's it."

She put her hand back on the wheel to navigate a curve in the path. "So, you're not a believer in second chances?"

He bobbed his knee up and down. "It's not about chances anymore."

"You took her ring for a reason. You want her to come to you. She's here. What are you going to do?"

MJ pounded his fist on his leg. "Hell, I don't know. This wasn't exactly a well thought out plan. I just took it, okay?"

Rachael swerved around a corner, leaning into him. "If you love her, don't write her off without knowing how she feels."

He held up his hands. "Don't start preaching to me about something you know nothing about."

His thought trailed off as they arrived at the landing sight. The black copter glinted with reflected sunlight, its blades rotating slowly.

Beck and Maddie rounded the side of the helicopter, his hand pushing the top of her head down, protectively. Her wild dark hair blew out around her, and he swore he could see those piercing blue eyes from all the way across the field.

He couldn't deny the rush of warmth in his chest, the

dreamy, gooey feeling flowing through his brain. He was gone over her.

Completely and helplessly gone.

Rachael had hopped out and was waving a hand over her head. He followed suit and stood, straightening his shorts for a distraction.

As they neared, he couldn't help but stare at Maddie's long, tan legs and let his mind wander back to when he had them around his waist as he pinned her against the wall in the stairway. He had to close his eyes for a moment and gather his senses before he went totally insane...and hard thinking about it.

"Hi!" Rachael called.

Beck took his hand from the top of Maddie's head, and they both waved. Her smile faltered for only a second as her eyes locked with MJ's, and she saw right inside him. He felt her there, just like always.

He was so transparent to her.

She gave Rachael a hug. "Thanks for letting me come and sending Beck to get me."

"Anytime! You're welcome here whenever you want to come."

Beck whacked MJ on the back and leaned in to whisper in his ear. "Lucky for you I'm taken."

MJ bristled. What was with this guy? Every time he opened his mouth, MJ got the urge to smash his face in.

Maddie took slow, deliberate steps toward MJ, her eyes hard enough to cut glass.

He didn't know what to do with his hands. He wanted to reach out and pull her to him, but couldn't, so they just hung like dead fish against his legs.

"Give me my ring so Beck can take me back."

He leaned in close, drilling his eyes into hers. "Tell me why you left and I'll give it back."

Her eyebrow quirked. "Give. It. To. Me. Now."

He stood straight and smiled. "Those aren't the magic words."

Maddie lunged forward and shoved him as hard as she could, which only made him take half a step back. "Give it to me!"

MJ laughed. "We're not little kids anymore, Mads. You can't yell and push me around to get what you want."

She fisted her hands, jabbed them to her hips and MJ swore it sounded like she growled at him. "I'm trying so hard not to kill you right now," she said.

The lethal tone of her voice made MJ cringe a little.

"Are we going to stand out here all afternoon, or can we go back to the hotel?" Beck asked. "I'm starving." He tossed Maddie's suitcase in the golf cart and got behind the wheel. "Bus is leaving. If you want a ride, get in. If not, you're walking back."

Rachael climbed in the front passenger's seat and left MJ and Maddie to hop in the back. She folded her arms and angled her knees away from him.

As the cart bumped down the path, he couldn't help watching her from the corner of his eyes. He could sense her excitement in the way her fingers tapped against the seat beside him and from the way she darted her eyes from side to side. Her breath came in short bursts and she smiled despite her anger.

"It's beautiful," she said, gazing around at the lilies and water. "I can't wait to see the hotel."

"It's great," MJ said, then looked down and coughed.

"I wasn't talking to you," she said, but she relaxed against the seat and shifted her body, not toward him, but at least not away either. "It smells good, like flowers and warm grass," she said, turning to look at him. "Like back at the lake." Her eyes widened. He was surprised how easily she fell back into talking about their past. Apparently, it surprised her, too.

"It does smell like back at the lake." He wanted this ease with Maddie. He'd missed it. He'd missed her, for so, so long.

She smiled, and her eyes glassed over. She blinked a few times and turned away. He wondered if she was crying. He wanted to tell her he was sorry for treating her the way he had.

Maddie dared a sideways glance and met his eyes. They held for a long moment, then she looked away. "Why didn't you tell me you were leaving to come here?" she whispered.

"I just..." He didn't know what to say. Instead, he rested his hand on her thigh and squeezed gently.

Maddie sucked her lips in, and a tear slipped down her cheek as she lowered her head to his shoulder. He took a careful breath and held it, not wanting to break the trance they were in—the bubble of Turtle Tear where they could pretend nothing had ever come between them. Gingerly, he lowered his cheek against her hair and felt its soft, silkiness press against his face.

She was shaking and even though he didn't know what the future held for them, he put his arm around her shoulders. "Don't cry," he whispered.

What did he tell Rachael about chances?

He had no willpower when it came to Maddie. He had to have her back. No other man could have her. She was his and always had been.

As they reached the hotel, the aroma of grilled steak and chicken filled the air. MJ's stomach growled, making Maddie laugh. "It smells incredible," she said, brushing her fingers under her eyes. He could barely tell she'd shed a tear.

The four of them left the cart under the awning and made their way across the lawn to the hotel. "Wow." Maddie's eyes wandered, taking in the exposed beams, tile roof and mosaic patio.

"Pretty nice, huh?" His hand brushed against hers, and he fought the urge to grasp her fingers and thread his own between them. His mind couldn't keep up with the constant push and pull of their relationship, and his heart just wanted to give in.

"I'll send someone out to bring your suitcase in," Rachael told Maddie. "Sit down and relax. I'll bring you a drink."

"Is that Maddie?" Heidi jumped up and scurried over to

them, embracing Maddie in a quick hug. "I haven't seen you for such a long time. How've you been?"

Maddie beamed. Heidi had been like an older sister to her when they were growing up. Whenever Maddie wasn't with MJ, he knew he'd find her with Heidi. "Good! How are you? Look how the kids have grown!"

MJ's grandfather had always made sure his cousins came to visit when he was away at school. Maddie got to know them, but he never did.

He stood there while they chatted, wondering if he should sit down or wait for them to finish their catch-up session. Rachael and Beck went inside. Maybe he'd go in, too, and help get drinks.

One step toward the door and Maddie caught his arm, breaking off her conversation with Heidi. "Show me around inside?"

He had a powerful urge to take her up to his room and show her a lot of things. "Sure."

She kept her hand on his arm as they strolled through the door into the lounge. "This is where guests would hang out," he said, sounding stupid, but it wasn't like he was a Turtle Tear expert.

"Are Rachael and your... is Rachael going to open it to the public?" She held on a little tighter, like she was afraid her almost slip of mentioning the D-word would make him pull away. MJ hated putting her on edge like this, making her feel like she was on eggshells around him. It had never been this way between them.

It wasn't his fault they were apart, and he wouldn't feel guilty for the strain in their relationship. What did she think would happen when she left?

The mental tug-of-war was killing him.

Was there something wrong with him that he couldn't let go of the anger? He hated the grudge he kept between them, like a big box packed with memories he held pressed between his chest and hers, keeping them apart.

If he'd packed their memories away in that box, why couldn't he move on?

"MJ?" Maddie tilted her head looking up at him with curiosity, probably wondering where she'd lost him.

"Sorry." He rubbed the back of his head. "I'm not sure what Rachael's plans are."

He led her down the hallway to the grand entryway. She spun in half a circle, gazing up at the mural-covered walls and high, beamed ceiling, still hanging on to him. "This is amazing."

He loved the way her eyes lit up as they darted around trying to take in as much as they could. He loved the look of awe on her face, and the clean, soapy scent of her hair as it swung toward him. He loved *her*, even if he didn't want to.

He did want to.

More than anything.

Rachael's laughter made MJ and Maddie turn their heads toward the kitchen.

"I'm telling you," Beck said, out of sight, talking to

Rachael, "he's gone over that chick. He's trying to play it cool, but Junior can't hide how pussy-whipped he is."

Son of a bitch. MJ was going to kick that guy's ass.

Beck and Rachael, who was flushed from laughing at Beck's comment, stopped abruptly under the large archway separating the entryway from the kitchen. MJ met Beck's eyes, and Beck couldn't possibly miss how pissed he was.

Beck smirked and lifted his chin.

Rachael glanced from one to the other, then stepped between them, breaking the tension. "Here's your drink, Maddie." She handed Maddie a tall glass filled with something clear, a lime wedge stuck on the rim. "Dinner's almost ready. I'm starving. Let's go back out and sit down."

"Good idea," Maddie said, steering MJ back down the hallway by his arm. "Are you okay?" she whispered in his ear.

"That guy's an ass," he whispered back, his nose brushing her cheek. He wanted to keep it there and nuzzle her neck.

She stifled a laugh by putting her fingers to her lips.

"What's so funny?"

She glanced up at him smiling her beautiful Maddie smile. "You." She squeezed his arm, pressing her chest against him in a hug.

They pulled two round patio tables together, and MJ held a chair out for Maddie to sit. The chef, Carlos, brought out baskets of tortilla chips, strips of steak and chicken sizzling on cast-iron skillets, and painted ceramic bowls filled with grilled peppers and onions, guacamole, shredded cheese and every topping a person could want on a fajita.

As they ate, Maddie's thigh rested against his. Once she reached for the salsa and her breast brushed his arm. He wanted to pull her body against his and keep her there for the rest of the evening. All through the night.

"How's your father, Maddie?" Heidi asked between bites. "It's been too long since I've visited."

Maddie drew the tines of her fork through her rice, contemplating something. It wasn't the first time MJ wished he could read her mind. He put his hand on her knee, and she flinched at his unexpected touch.

"He's good," she said. "I wish I could spend more time with him. Wish he'd retire."

Heidi took a sip of her water. "I don't know what my father would ever do without him. Those two are like Sherlock Holmes and Dr. Watson."

"More like Jekyll and Hyde," MJ muttered and shoved a chip in his mouth.

Beside MJ, Rachael let out a small laugh that she tried to hide with a cough. Across from him, Roger scooted his chair back and joggled his empty beer bottle back and forth. "I'm going in for another. Anyone need anything?"

Rachael jolted up from her seat. "I'll get it for you. I should've kept the staff here for the entire week."

Roger waved a hand. "No, no. I've got it. Sit and relax. Enjoy your dinner."

MJ wondered what Beck and Joan's job descriptions were. Obviously not the waitstaff.

"I'm stuffed," Maddie said, tossing her linen napkin on the table. "I need to go for a walk or something."

Rachael glanced over from MJ to Maddie. "Neither of you have seen the entire island. Let me grab something. I'll be right back."

MJ watched Rachael dash into the hotel. In less than a minute she was back and handing him a key. "You go with her," she told him. "She shouldn't be out walking alone. Gators come out at night."

He wasn't sure if he should believe Rachael or not, but then he didn't want to risk Maddie becoming gator food. Not that he could fight one off if it came after them. "Okay. What's with the key?"

"There's a little house that way." She pointed over his shoulder. "You'll know it when you see it. Merrick built it for me. It's incredible. You have to see it." The corners of her mouth turned up into a sly smile as her eyes darted between him and Maddie.

MJ didn't know why, but he had the distinct impression Rachael was up to something.

Eighteen

You'll know it when you see it, Rachael had said. Maddie replayed those words in her head as she gaped at the enormous tree house perched in the tall cloister of trees in front of them.

"They must be on timers," MJ said, confusing her.

"What are on timers?"

"The lights." He nodded toward the wall of windows beyond the wraparound front porch, brightly lit with a warm, yellow glow.

It was the first he'd spoken since dinner, and Maddie was dying to tap into his thoughts. "Merrick had this place built for Rachael? Wow."

He tread onto the first step of the arching staircase, gripping the railing. "Must be for them to have some privacy when other people are here."

She felt her heart speed. She wanted privacy—with him. A jolt of longing shot straight to her center. She couldn't allow herself to feel this way about MJ for one second more. Somehow, she had to purge herself of all of her emotions tied to MJ.

Maddie passed the lit lanterns sitting atop the balusters and followed him up the curved steps to the porch. She knew he was afraid of heights and noted how he stayed close to the house as he jiggled the key in the lock and pushed the door open.

"Whoa," he said, stopping on the threshold.

She peered around him and inhaled sharply. It was beautiful. The definition of love nest. A sunken hot tub sat in the center of the room with a wet bar to one side, plush white carpeting and a soft, white sofa and chairs against the opposite wall.

MJ stepped inside and she followed. "This looks like the only room down here," he said. "Bedroom must be upstairs."

Maddie's eyes roamed up a spiral, wrought-iron staircase to where it disappeared into the second floor. "Must be." She shivered.

"Are you cold?"

"No." The shiver was anticipation of what could happen between them if they climbed those spiral stairs to the bedroom.

MJ's eyes followed hers to the staircase before darkening with need. She knew that look so well, had seen it hundreds of times. Had loved how she could make him want her so badly.

He started toward her, and she backed up, bumping into the railing. MJ gripped the balusters on either side of her waist, trapping her. He lowered his head and pressed his lips to the curve of her neck. All of the tension ran out of her body at his touch. "MJ," she warned, but wasn't sure if the warning was meant for her or for him. She gripped the hem of her shorts, willing herself not to touch him back.

He touched her nose with his and very slowly turned his head from side to side. "Do you want me to stop?"

She couldn't stand it. She'd never wanted something so badly in her life—something she knew in her heart belonged to her—that she couldn't have.

MJ took her hands, threaded their fingers and raised them above her head, pinning them against the railing that climbed above her. He angled his head, his lips only an inch from hers. "Mads," he breathed, "you belong to me."

"I know," she whispered back. "But I can't have you."

"Like hell you can't." He pressed his lips to hers, and hunger for him consumed her. She squeezed his hands, pressed her body against his and parted her lips, savoring every soft, wet inch of his mouth.

He tasted of lost memories, hope, anguish, home. He tasted so familiar, it brought tears to her eyes. Her MJ.

God, she'd missed the feel of his hands on her skin, his body pressed against hers, his ragged whispers against her flesh promising his love forever.

One moment being in the wrong place at the wrong time, and she'd let fate tear them apart? How could she ever walk away from him? How would she do it again?

Deepening their kiss even more, MJ let go of her hands and wrapped his arms around her waist. Picking her up, he headed toward the couch.

Maddie broke away from him. "No. I can't," she said, her breath heaving, and head spinning.

"Yes," he insisted, gently biting her bottom lip.

"MJ..."

"Shh...It's just you and me. Here. Now. Don't think, just feel." He lowered her onto her back on the couch and knelt between her knees. "I'm not giving you up without a fight. You can't leave me this time unless you swim back."

He leaned toward her and she braced her hands against his chest. Her resolve was weak. She couldn't even collect her thoughts to utter a protest.

MJ took her hands and placed them on either side of her head. His eyes roamed from the top of her head down to her collarbone, then back up to her eyes. She saw the pain shoot through them and felt it echo in her chest.

"What did I do wrong?" he whispered. "What made you leave me?"

She felt the slow burn behind her eyes and couldn't stop it. Tears gathered, blurring her vision. She blinked hard and his finger traced one down her cheek.

"Tell me," he urged.

She closed her eyes, squeezing out even more tears, and he kissed her. It was gentle and patient. He loved her. She'd never questioned it, but his kiss conveyed just how much she meant to him. The feelings she'd held back for so long surfaced and overwhelmed her, coming out in a heaving sob against his lips.

"Mads?" He stroked her cheeks with his thumbs. "Talk to me."

"I can't." She shifted underneath him and sniffled while she wiped her eyes. "Please. Not right now." He wasn't in any state of mind to hear the truth.

He slammed his hand into the back of the couch, making her flinch. "Then when?" he shouted. "You never said goodbye. You were just gone. You tore my fucking life apart, Maddie! And you can't tell me why?"

He clenched his jaw and lowered his forehead against her chest. "Do you know how absolutely destroyed I was?" He looked up with a scornful smile on his face. "I still am. I can't get over you. I can't stop wanting you. It's a fucking nightmare I live every single day. Then you come back with that fucking ring."

He shot up onto his knees, grabbed his shirt and tore it over his head. Grabbing her hand, he pressed her fingernails into his chest. "Why don't you rip me open and tear my heart out. That's what you're doing, so quit dragging it out and end me."

Maddie had never seen the desperate, crazed look in his eyes. She did this to him. She'd caused him this pain he couldn't hide from her anymore.

His arms dropped to his sides, his chin to his chest. "Do you know the complete fucking horror of watching the only person you ever trusted walk away from you?"

Maddie couldn't stand it one more second. She had to take his pain away. Now was not the time to tell him why she left. She couldn't tell him she loved him, and saying I'm sorry wouldn't be good enough. So, she'd show him in the only way that mattered.

She got to her knees on the couch in front of him and took his face in her hands. "MJ," she whispered, and waited until he brought his dark, distant eyes to hers before repeating his words back to him. "Here. Now. Don't think, just feel."

Maddie brushed her lips against his, testing his response. He took a deep, jerky breath, then pulled her to him, crushing his lips against hers. His tongue pushed into her mouth demanding more. His hands ran up the back of her shirt, then around to the front. His fingers slipped inside her bra while he trailed kisses across her jaw to her neck.

She let her head fall back and thanked God for giving her this time with him. She'd pay whatever the price was to make MJ forget his pain for as long as she could—to make her forget how long it had felt like she was missing a limb, a vital organ, without MJ in her life.

She ran her fingers through his dark, wavy hair, nuzzled her nose in it, breathing him in. He tugged down the V-neck of her T-shirt and found her breast, licked and sucked her nipple sending waves of heat on a path leading straight between her legs.

Her chest heaved, her back arched, giving him more. He could have all of her, even if it could never happen again. She'd remember this moment for the rest of her life. She'd think of this night and feel these feelings that were stronger than anything she'd ever felt. At least she'd have this memory to keep with her and know she'd once been able to love this much. She'd once been loved by him in return.

Tears streamed down her cheeks again, landing in his hair. He glanced up with a flurry of emotion in his eyes. "Stop?" he asked.

She shook her head. "No," she sobbed.

He rose on his knees and kissed her cheeks, her nose, her eyes, her forehead. Then he eased her back down onto the couch, turning them so she lay on top.

She loved lying on him, feeling him breathing underneath her, resting her head on his chest and listening to his heartbeat. She never thought she'd find herself here again.

MJ gathered her hair behind her head with one hand and kissed her while hitching her knee up beside his hip with the other. He clutched the back of her thigh, tracing his fingers up under the leg of her shorts.

Maddie was so lost to his kiss and his touch, she could barely catch her breath. She pulled her lips from his and kissed her way down his neck to his chest. She couldn't fight her desire and didn't want to. This was MJ. She shouldn't have to fight it. She ground her hips against his, and felt his erection press between her legs. The sensation made them both groan.

MJ grabbed her other leg and pulled it up by his hip so her legs were open to him and thrust against her.

"God," she whispered against his chest, tracing his pecs with her tongue. "I've wanted this for so long."

"You should've come back to me." He thrust again, and she wished they didn't have clothes between them.

"I couldn't," she panted, teasing his nipple with her teeth.

He grabbed her chin between his thumb and forefinger and pulled her head up. "You don't say anything I understand, so stop talking before you piss me off again." To make sure she did, he lifted his head and kissed her, sucking her bottom lip, then her top before closing his mouth over hers and claiming her with his tongue.

His slow, rhythmic thrusts urged her to rock against him. She couldn't help herself, or the tickling, burn of desire that had to be sated between her legs. She was so wet, she could feel the dampness as she slid against him.

Their kiss broke, and she rested her forehead against his as they panted and she rode him. He ran his hands up the back of her thighs not stopping when his fingers traveled under the legs of her shorts and reached the edge of her panties.

Maddie was dying for his touch. She whimpered when his fingers stopped their progression. MJ groaned and ran his fingertips over the thin material. "Fuck, you're dripping wet."

She gazed into his eyes, silently begging. He pressed his lips together, and she saw him battling with himself. Then his mouth took hers as he pulled back the scrap of material between her legs and his fingers plunged inside her.

She bucked her hips and moaned against his mouth. He

could always make her come so easily. She was so close. She felt his other hand wiggle under her panties and his finger ran between her buttocks. He teased her opening while the fingers inside her circled and stroked.

He'd never done this to her before. Nobody had ever touched her like this. She melted against his chest, arching her back, giving him access to take more, give more. "God, MJ, that feels so good," she said.

She closed her eyes and let him take her under. She was all feeling and sensation. There was nothing to her but the places he stroked and teased.

A knot tightened in her belly and grew until she was crazed with the need for release. She held on to MJ's shoulders, almost afraid, knowing when it hit, she'd shatter.

His thumb found her clit, circled once and she was gone. Blackness spiraled behind her eyes, her blood rushed like thunder in her ears, her body spasmed and quaked.

MJ slowed his fingers as she came down from her orgasm. She realized she'd been biting his shoulder and kissed him where she'd left teeth marks before collapsing back down on his chest.

He rubbed her back and kissed the top of her head.

A calm came over her that she hadn't felt for over a year since she'd been away from him. Her soul was at ease. It latched onto his and quieted. Without MJ there was a constant clawing and gnawing inside her to find something to fill what was missing. Whatever she did, however she tried to fill the void, it wasn't enough.

MJ silenced the part of her that was always aching for more. It was a blinding truth that she couldn't deny. A blinding truth she'd have to live without.

He tucked her hair behind her ear. "Do you love him?" he asked.

She closed her eyes against the assault his words released on her heart. She'd told him she wasn't marrying Talan. Why was he asking her this? "MJ, I—"

"More than me?" he said, tilting his head to try and see her face.

She tucked her chin to her chest, unwilling to look him in the eye.

"I know you must love him," he continued. "You wouldn't even consider marrying him if you didn't."

Maddie had aimed to ease his pain, and all she'd done was open the floodgates. She pushed up and held herself above him. "Don't." She kissed him. "Don't."

Determined to finish what she started, she eased down his body, kissing and caressing his chest, resting her hand on his key tattoo that marked him forever as hers. She trailed her lips down across his abs, pausing at the defined V that led down into his shorts. She knew he liked it when she glided her tongue along the ridges.

MJ sucked in air through his teeth in a hiss and wove his fingers through her hair. Maddie unfastened his button and zipper and freed his hard length from his boxers. She kissed the tip before wetting it with her tongue.

Squeezing his thighs, she took him deep in her mouth,

silently begging for his forgiveness. Not only for the past, but for the future when she wouldn't ever be his again.

She asked herself for forgiveness as she bobbed her head up and down his shaft. She hurt herself as much as him. More. She sacrificed her entire life to make sure his heart was protected from the awful secret his grandfather kept.

It wasn't fair to either of them.

He was the one she'd planned to marry. He was the one she'd planned to have babies with. He was the one... always the one.

Her desperation to please him had him thrusting into her mouth. He couldn't help himself, and she loved when she made him lose control. She felt his muscles clench and tremor and knew he was close.

"Jesus, Mads," he groaned, and spilled himself into her mouth.

She licked her lips and crawled back up his body to lie in the crook of his arm. "Spend the night with me here. Just hold me and don't let go until morning."

MJ lifted her chin and kissed her. "I won't let you go for the rest of your life if that's what you decide. All you have to do is ask."

Nineteen

He couldn't believe he had her here like this. Those ice blue eyes of hers had cracked him open. His soul had seeped out and now lay bleeding on the couch downstairs. Or maybe she'd devoured it along with his heart. In either case, they no longer resided inside of him.

God, he hoped this was the right thing to do.

He couldn't live in fear of getting hurt again.

He couldn't live without his Maddie.

Entwined on the big bed upstairs, a warm breeze blew over MJ's bare chest. He twisted a piece of Maddie's hair at the back of her neck around his finger. He watched her chest rise and fall as she slept, her skin a silky shimmer in the moonlight.

Above them, he could barely make out the etchings in the wooden beam that ran the length of the room. Two hearts with two different sets of initials inside. M.R. + R.D in one. A.W. + I.B. in the other. Even if he didn't know Rachael's last name, who the first set was in reference to was obvious, Merrick and Rachael, but he had no clue about the second set.

Maddie murmured in her sleep and rolled over to her side. She'd been out cold for a couple hours, but MJ couldn't sleep. He couldn't believe she was here beside him again. He couldn't stop the fear he kept swallowing back. Fear that this was only one night and she'd leave him again.

MJ rubbed his eyes trying to clear his mind. He couldn't lie there awake any longer with his thoughts running rampant. He needed air. Slipping out of bed, a flash of light outside caught his eye.

It was a round orb deep in the trees, like a flashlight in the distance. MJ moved close to the window and pressed his palms against the pane. The circle of light was moving, getting closer, making a jagged path through the brush.

He padded silently across the room, down the spiral staircase and out the front door. Under his feet, the wooden deck was still warm from the sun even though the moon cast long, obscure black shadows across it.

At the side of the deck, he pushed his fear of heights aside in favor of curiosity and leaned over the railing. His mind kept yelling, *curiosity killed the cat,* and giving him visions of lying on the ground below with a broken neck for being so stupid. He told his mind to shut the fuck up and tracked his eyes through the trees, straining to find the light.

There it was, even closer, but completely still.

Abruptly, it was gone, but MJ caught the sound of branches snapping underfoot and a flash of long, dark hair in the moonlight.

"Hello?" he called. "Rachael, is that you?"

He had no idea why Rachael would be walking through

the trees, alone, in the middle of the night with a flashlight. If she had such an inclination, she'd stick to the path.

Against his better judgment, or maybe because of poor judgment, he jogged down the tree house stairs to the ground below and trod across the dew-damp grass to the tree line. "Hello?" he said, too low for anyone too far in the trees to actually hear.

A rustle in the brush a few yards in and to his right prodded his curiosity. With measured, deliberate steps, MJ followed the noises hoping to catch a glimpse of light or the mystery woman again.

Reaching the spot where he thought he'd heard the noise, he bent and leaned forward to peer through a grouping of saplings.

Two wide dark eyes stared back at him.

The woman gasped and bolted through the trees.

"Wait!" he yelled. "Who are you?"

She didn't answer, and he chased after her, sticks and rocks prodding and poking the soles of his bare feet. She wasn't far ahead. MJ wove his way through the trees and ducked under low limbs. Brambles scratched his legs and snagged his shorts. He heard her panting as she ran, each of her footfalls cracking branches on the forest floor.

Sweat glazed his face and chest. Gnats buzzed around his head. Why the hell did she keep running? Who was she and why was she hiding?

There was a loud snap under his feet and his ankle twisted. He fell with an *oomph* of air being knocked from his lungs. He rolled through two dense bushes into a clearing and stopped flat on his back on the ground. The woman scrambled to the far side and backed against a tree. In the shadows of the moon, she appeared like some wraith-like being his imagination dreamed up. Her long hair snarled around her face, a white dress torn along the hem from traipsing through the woods.

"I'm not going to hurt you," he said holding his hands up in front of him. "Who are you? Are you supposed to be here?" He didn't think so, or she wouldn't be running around in the dark hiding in the woods.

"You can't trust her," she whispered, her voice deep and raspy. "Everything she says is a lie. Don't believe what she tells you."

Her words were a wrecking ball crashing through his mind. "Maddie?"

The woman's hands moved along the tree bark behind her like she was looking for a secret trapdoor to make her escape. "Don't believe her," she said again, and disappeared around the tree into the darkness.

❀

MJ's ankle throbbed but it wasn't swollen. He could walk on it just fine, if a little slowly as he made his way back to the tree house and up the stairs. At least it was a distraction from his fear of heights.

A distraction from the mutterings of a stranger—who might have been a delusion conjured by an emotional breakdown—in the woods. God knew the past few days had taken their toll on his mental stability. Not that he was all that stable to begin with.

Why the hell would some lady in the woods on a remote island be here to warn him against Maddie?

Christ, he was losing his mind.

"What are you doing out here?" Maddie's voice startled him. He jumped back with his hand to his chest.

"Jesus. Don't do that."

She laughed and rested her hand over his pressed against his heart. "Sorry. I didn't mean to scare you."

Her hair was tousled from sleep, her lips were red and puffy from being kissed. "Why are you awake?" he asked, brushing thoughts of mistrust from his mind.

She wrapped her arms around herself. "I got cold."

He knew she meant she woke because he wasn't there. It was hot and muggy, there was no way she was actually cold.

"So why are you out here?" she asked.

He gestured behind him. "I thought I saw a woman in the woods with a flashlight." He'd skip the embarrassing details of chasing a woman whom he was ninety-nine percent certain was imaginary, tripping and twisting his ankle.

She furrowed her brow, skeptical. "Who would be out here in the woods at..." she glanced at her wrist where she habitually wore her watch, but wasn't wearing it. "At whatever time it is right now?" She gave him a playful smile. "You're seeing things."

He shrugged. "Probably."

Maddie stepped past him and leaned against the railing gazing out into the trees. "A flashlight, huh?" She glanced over her shoulder at him. "Like a glowing orb of light?" She spun around. "Are you sure it wasn't a ghost?" She launched at him, grabbing his hips to try to scare him.

Maddie had always been addicted to everything paranormal. She read books and watched TV shows about vampires, werewolves and ghosts. For the longest time when they were little, she was even convinced that there was a ghost living in the west wing of the Rocha Estate.

She probably still believed it. "No," he said, pulling her in close, "it wasn't a ghost."

She kissed his chin and trailed her lips along his jaw, standing on tip toe to reach his ear. "Whoever it was, she's gone now. Come back inside with me."

At her sultry voice, a flame of lust licked low in his groin. He swept an arm behind her knees and scooped her up, parting her lips in a deep kiss. Whatever his subconscious was warning him against could wait until morning.

❀

When Maddie opened her eyes to MJ's mass of tussled hair and dark stubble on his jaw, she had to fight back bittersweet tears.

More than a year had passed, wasted, and still Maddie knew she couldn't have a future with him.

She gazed at MJ's beautiful, sleeping face again. This

would be the very last time she lay next to him while he slept. The last time she'd be exactly where she belonged. Her life would always be off-kilter without him, but she didn't have a choice. She couldn't hurt him like her mother had hurt her all those years ago. Maddie knew first-hand that a wound that deep never completely healed. She would be the last person on Earth to inflict that upon MJ.

She'd sacrificed his love. There was no turning back now no matter how much it tortured her. After seeing MJ tear his shirt off last night and tell her how much she'd hurt him, she knew she'd keep Enzo's secret until she died. Maddie would never hand over the huge amount of pain and hurt she held back from MJ. Not ever.

Maddie ran her fingers through his hair. He stretched and a smile sprawled across his lips before his eyes slowly opened. "Morning."

She touched his sleep-puffy lips with her fingers, and he kissed them. "Morning," she said.

Maddie knew he wouldn't take her if she didn't belong to him. No matter how much she wanted MJ to make love to her last night, she didn't dare ask. She couldn't do that to him.

"What are you thinking?" MJ asked.

She turned her head and gazed up at the twin hearts etched in the beam that ran across the ceiling. "Nothing."

"I don't know what came between us, Mads," he said, stroking her arm with the back of his fingers. "You used to tell me everything."

Maddie wanted to bury her head under her pillow and hide from him. She didn't have an answer, not one she could give that would satisfy him.

A knock on the door made Maddie jump. "Get the hell up you two!" a man shouted.

"Is that Beck?" She sat up and shimmied out from under the blanket. "I think it is."

"Fucking Beck," MJ muttered, tossing back the blanket and standing. He strode toward the open window. "What do you want?" he yelled out.

"Get your asses down here. I'll take you back before you miss brunch."

"We're not hung–"

"Good. I'm starving!" Maddie hopped out of bed even though leaving the tree house was the last thing she wanted to do. She wished time would stop and she could stay here alone with MJ for all eternity, but when he started talking about why she left him, why she wouldn't tell him the reason, she needed an escape.

"We'll be right down," MJ called to Beck, then rubbed the back of his head. "I will get answers," he told her. "Before I let you leave this island."

"Before you *let* me?" she said, surprised at his demanding tone.

He nodded, his expression severe. "You're not the only one with everything at stake here. I let you walk away last time and didn't chase you down. I won't make that mistake again."

Twenty

$\mathcal{B}$eck was waiting at the bottom of the deck stairs in a golf cart when they finally made it outside. " 'Bout time," he said, grinning. "I was seconds from coming in and dragging you out."

MJ scowled, and Maddie elbowed him. "What's for brunch?" she asked as they piled into the cart.

"Not what Junior was hoping for from the sound of it." Beck chuckled as he sped off from the tree house, and Maddie squeezed MJ's arm to keep him from a smart-ass retort. "Among other things, Carlos made one of his specialties, huevos rancheros, and Rachael made one of hers. Burnt bacon." He laughed. "The first time I met her, she made the whole crew breakfast."

Beck nudged MJ's shoulder. "Pissed your dad off. He didn't think us peons should get special treatment," Beck went on. "He was a real dickhead back then. I don't know what Rachael did to him, but he's a changed man."

None of them spoke for a minute. Maddie grew anxious. "So, Rachael burned the bacon that day?" she said.

"Yeah, she did," Beck said, his smile returning. "Nobody said a word about it though." He drummed his fingers on the wheel. "Listen, Junior. I know the news of you had to come as a pretty big blow to your dad. He'll be calling me any day now to come haul his ass back here so he can catch up on the past twenty years he's missed with you. I hope you give him a chance."

MJ rubbed his hands together, frowning. "It's all good."

Maddie reached back and took his hand, rubbing her thumb over the top in circles trying to soothe him. It was all good. He and Merrick had taken the initial step toward getting to know each other and Maddie had no doubt they'd continue to bond. But, she could only imagine how he was feeling after meeting Merrick for the first time. All the anticipation. How his insides must be twisted in knots thinking about a future and wondering how much Merrick would be a part of it.

Beck pulled the golf cart under the awning where the others were parked. "I'm going to take a shower," MJ said. He raised Maddie's hand to his lips and kissed it before they got out of the cart.

"Okay," she said, spotting Rachael sitting alone at one of the patio tables with books and what looked to be maps in front of her. "I'll keep Rachael company."

They walked to the gate and through to the patio. "Morning," MJ said to Rachael, who looked up and cast a knowing smile on them.

"Good morning," Rachael said.

MJ kept walking into the hotel.

Rachael pushed out the chair beside her for Maddie. "Sit down. Have a good night?"

Maddie eyed a glass pitcher of orange juice sitting on a

sideboard by the door and poured herself some before joining Rachael at the table. "It was nice. Thanks."

Rachael grabbed Maddie's left hand. "I see you still aren't wearing a ring."

"No. I didn't manage to get it back." She took a small sip of OJ.

Rachael squeezed her hand. "Are you sure you want it back?"

Maddie nodded, yawning, exhausted from her late night with MJ. "I'm not accepting the proposal. I need to give the ring back."

A smile broke on Rachael's face. "You and MJ?"

"No. I'm staying single for a while. I have to get my head on straight, find a job and a place to live when I get back to Michigan."

Rachael studied her for a moment. Maddie knew she was wondering what last night was all about if Maddie wasn't back with MJ. The last thing Maddie needed was more guilt.

Maddie rested her chin in her hand and tapped the map on the table in front of them. "What's all this?"

"All of this," Rachael said, straightening a stack of papers, "is the history of this island. The founder, Archibald Weston, and his wife, Ingrid Burkhart, didn't leave much information about their life together, but I did find this."

She pulled out an oversized document, yellowed with age from underneath the map and slid it over to Maddie. A sprawling family tree was drawn in calligraphy on the fragile page with crumbling corners. "It's the ancestry of their family. The Weston's owned a sugarcane plantation northwest of here, up by St. Petersburg. Look," she said, pointing to the limbs branching from where Archibald and Ingrid's joined. "She and Archibald had five kids."

"Wow, that's a big family. Looks like they had…" Maddie ran her eyes over the next set of branches and counted quickly, "seventeen grandkids!"

Rachael spread her arms wide. "And they all would stay here visiting their grandparents. Can you believe that? We're sitting here today where Ingrid and Archibald sat with their kids and grandkids eating their brunch almost one hundred and fifty years ago."

Maddie couldn't quite grasp the level of enthusiasm that Rachael had, but she wasn't the one who renovated the entire property after all. "It's amazing," she said, hoping it conveyed the pride she felt for her new friend.

"It is," Rachael said, then frowned. "Now, if I can just find proof that Ingrid is buried on this island." She returned the family tree to its spot under the map. "I've poured over the topography and I figure if her grave is here, it has to be near the tree house. It's almost the center of the island and the highest spot. She wouldn't be buried where the water level would rise and wash her away." She shivered, then glanced up at Maddie, her eyes still lost in the past. "Does that sound right?"

Maddie rubbed her chin. "Makes sense to me. Maybe you should have one of those ghost hunting teams come out and film for their TV show. They might be able to find her." She was only joking, but her mind slammed back to the night before.

"Oh my God. Rachael!" Maddie reached across the map and grabbed Rachael's arm. "Last night MJ saw a woman with a flashlight in the woods. What if it was Ingrid? You know how they say ghosts always appear as a glowing orb? That's what the flashlight could've been."

Rachael's eyes grew wide. "He's sure he saw a woman out there?"

Maddie nodded. "He was positive. Ask him."

Both of their frozen faces cracked into smiles, and then they fell into a fit of nervous laughter. "It can't be," Maddie said. "I mean, those ghost hunting shows are all a bunch of made-up crap."

"You never know," Rachael said. "Stranger things have happened. This place definitely has a power to it. It keeps you captive. Once you're here, you don't want to ever leave." She ran her eyes over the family tree on the table in front of her and smiled. "Ingrid felt the same connection to this island that I do. It brought her here, like it did me. I wouldn't be surprised if she was still here."

Rachael sat back in her chair and gazed up at the sky. "Either way, I need to find her grave, if just to sit with her for a while." She cut her eyes to Maddie. "I feel like I know her, like I am her. I can't explain it, but I can't give up until I know where she is."

Maddie wasn't sure she understood Rachael's conviction to find Ingrid's grave, but she could tell it was sincere.

Rachael wouldn't give up until she found it. "I'll help however I can," she said, leaning forward and scanning her eyes over the map again.

If there was one thing Maddie loved, it was a good ghost story.

❀

Stuffed from the feast Carlos made for brunch and freshly showered, Maddie and MJ strolled behind Rachael who led them down a path toward the water chattering on and on about Ingrid and Archibald and telling the history of Turtle Tear to Heidi and Roger. Sam and Holly trailed behind, bickering and kicking sand at each other. Every once in a while, Heidi would turn around and yell at them to knock it off, but they never actually stopped.

"Makes you want kids, huh?" MJ whispered in her ear.

The thought of kids someday—with him—was overwhelming and sent a pang of love through her so strong, she almost fell over. "Five," she answered, "like Ingrid and Archibald."

MJ frowned and looked away into the flowers and trees that lined the path. She shouldn't have said that. Any kids she had wouldn't be with MJ. Not like she and he had planned. Back then, she could see their future so clearly, filled with little boys who looked just like him, but that path forked and she'd taken another trail. She wasn't sure where it led, but there was no going back.

"There it is," Rachael said, pointing to a brand-new

white boathouse by the water. "The canoe and fishing gear is inside."

The kids took off running. "Watch where you step!" Rachael called.

"Stay on the path," Roger shouted, jogging after them.

"Huh," Rachael said, tilting her head. "Beck must've brought that speedboat in while I was gone." A small red and white boat sat right off shore. "Probably so Joan can have an easier time getting to town to find a mall."

As Roger and MJ helped Holly and Sam fetch the canoe and fishing gear, Maddie sat with Rachael and Heidi at an umbrella table on a stone patio beside the boathouse. Rachael brushed small seedpods off the glass tabletop. "Those Paperbark Tea Trees are taking over the Everglades." She pointed to a grouping of giant trees with white feathery flowers that looked like bottle brushes. "They drop millions of seeds in each pod."

Rachael brushed her hands together. "Anyway, sorry this place is such a mess. I should've kept the domestic staff on the island all week." She shrugged. "I left in kind of a rush, so..."

Heidi waved a hand in the air. "It's just us. No big deal."

"Yeah," Maddie said, brushing her side of the table clear of the seed pods, "and I invited myself."

The three of them watched MJ and Roger help the kids into the canoe, then climb in themselves and launch off the shore. "Catch me a big one!" Heidi called to them.

Rachael's eyes focused on Heidi with intensity. "You

knew about him all along and never told Merrick." Her accusatory tone made Maddie cringe. Rachael had been waiting until Roger and MJ were out of hearing range with the kids to pounce. "He has a son, and you never told him."

Heidi sucked in her lips. Her red-rimmed eyes shined. "I couldn't. You have no idea what my father is like."

"I *do* know what he's like!" Rachael slammed her hand down on the table. "I don't care. If you loved your brother at all, you would've told him the truth!"

Maddie's throat burned like she'd swallowed hot lava.

There were some things you couldn't tell.

Rachael had no idea the power Enzo Rocha held over them all.

"I *do* love my brother!" Tears rushed down Heidi's cheeks. "I wanted him to know MJ, to raise his son. My father wouldn't allow it. He said it would ruin Merrick's future. He'd never go to college, never become successful. Whatever you think of my father, he only wanted the best for Merrick. He wants the best for MJ, too."

"Well, that's clear." Rachael leaned back and let out a derisive laugh. "He went as far as stealing Merrick's entire life to prove that point."

Heidi wiped her cheeks, anger seeping into her eyes. "My father is making sure MJ gets an inheritance. Merrick can't be trusted to provide for him—for anyone but himself. You should remember that."

Rachael shot out of her chair and leaned across the table toward Heidi. "I don't know what you're implying, but I don't need Merrick to provide for me. I'm not some gold-digging whore, thank you. I love him." Her voice broke on the word love, making Maddie want to stand and wrap her arms around Rachael, to tell her everything would be okay. But would it?

"Then don't imply that I don't love my brother," Heidi said, her voice edged in ice.

Rachael sank back into her chair. "Are there any other secrets about Merrick's past I should know? Let's get everything out in the open."

"None that are mine to tell." Heidi shoved her chair back and eyed Maddie.

Maddie shrank under Heidi's gaze and replayed her last statement. *None that are mine to tell.* Did Heidi know Maddie had been guarding a secret for over a year? It sounded that way.

Heidi stormed off down the path back toward the hotel.

It felt like Maddie had been kicked in the gut.

She gazed out over the sun-sparked water. MJ was a miniature in the far off canoe. She could tell he was laughing and holding a fishing pole. He'd been hidden away for so long from his cousins, from his father, from the truth. Being here had to be affecting him more than she could ever realize. He played it off so well, acted like it was normal to go through a situation like this.

"Your mind is racing," Rachael said.

Maddie cut her eyes from MJ out on the water to the observant, caring brown pair across the table. "I want everything for him. I'd do anything to make him happy."

Rachael brushed a few lingering seed pods from the table. "What about getting back together? Is that what will make him happy?"

Maddie's stomach clenched. She needed space. Needed to breathe and think. "I'm going to take a walk. Be right back."

The tall trunks of the Paperbark trees were shedding, their grainy bark peeling off in long strips. Sunlight dappled through their leaves, lighting on the white, feathery seeds floating down from the canopy.

This island was magical, and Maddie needed magic in her life. Magic or miracles.

She pulled three long strands of bark off a tree and braided them together as she strolled aimlessly over the soft leaves and mulched earth. Her mom always braided her hair when she was little—before her mom left. One long, thick braid down her back. She'd called it Maddie's horsewhip.

Maddie never got to ask her mom what she knew about horses. Probably nothing, but she'd never know for sure now.

Questions needed answers. If she told MJ what she knew, he could get his answers if he wanted them. At least he'd have the choice. Keeping a secret from him didn't give him the opportunity she wished she had.

She tossed the braid on the ground. It would be helpful if she knew her own mind, knew what she wanted—what she would do in his situation. She wavered on everything. Always had. Every single decision. Teaching after she got her education degree, searching for her mom, Talan . . .

She wished she was more like Kara. Like Rachael. They were both so sure of themselves, strong and convicted in what they believed.

Maddie lacked conviction, lacked faith in herself to do what her heart knew was right.

"Leave the island," a woman's voice said from behind her.

She darted around. Off in the distance, a woman stood against a tree, watching her. Maddie gasped. "Who are you?"

"Stay away from him," the woman said, "and leave this place." She turned and disappeared behind the tree she'd been leaning against.

Maddie jogged in her direction. "Wait! Who are you?" She had the strangest impression that she'd seen the woman before.

It was no use. Maddie stopped chasing her. She was gone.

Twenty-One

MJ threaded a worm on Holly's hook and handed the rod back to her to cast. "Watch your brother's head." He figured he better warn her even though he didn't think any hooking of her brother would be accidental. The two had been bickering all morning.

Sam laughed, pulling MJ's attention from Holly. Roger held a worm over his open mouth, pretending he was about to eat it. Sam burst out in fits of giggles watching him. MJ smiled, but it felt bittersweet.

Besides the awkward tension that had always existed between him and Roger over Enzo, MJ felt like he was interfering on personal time between Roger and his kids. There was the sharp edge of jealousy, too. MJ would've done anything to have a father to go fishing with when he was Sam's age.

The only person to ever take him fishing was Maddie's dad. He took them both—MJ and Maddie—just like MJ was his own son. He'd always treated MJ that way.

For a brief summer, MJ thought Mr. Simcoe really would be his father someday.

When Maddie told him on the path earlier that she wanted five kids and then tried to play it off, he knew she wasn't joking. Growing up, she'd always wanted brothers and sisters. He had too. Being alone in the world was one of the reasons they clung together even though they fought all the time, like Sam and Holly. They'd talked about having kids someday, a big family so their kids would always have each other, always have someone to rely on.

Five kids. He could see it now. She'd probably end up with five girls, all with that bushy black hair and fiery blue eyes of hers.

One of the reasons he fought with guys his age, like the idiots on his baseball team—ex-baseball team—was because he couldn't relate to their trivial, bullshit lives. They were all shallow douche bags who probably never had a thought about spending the rest of their lives with a woman who made them feel whole. A woman who was home and family and future.

Yeah, he was young and so were those other guys, but he knew what mattered in life and what he wanted. He wanted what he didn't have growing up. A home. A family. He thought he'd have it with Maddie, but something came between them. He had to know what it was—what to focus his aggression on. What to beat the hell out of to get her back.

He bit the side of his cheek until he drew blood to get his head away from soul-sucking thoughts of Maddie having someone else's kids.

Holly brought her rod back and MJ ducked. She swung it forward over her shoulder and let the line out over the water. "Nice," he told her.

MJ shaded his eyes with his hand and watched Holly's bobber land. His gaze found Maddie, who was lowering herself into a chair across from Rachael at a patio table under a tan umbrella beside the boathouse. Her dark hair blew out behind her with a gentle breeze that shook the saw grass on the bank. There were times, like right then, when he was struck numb by how beautiful she was.

"MJ and Maddie sittin' in a tree K-I-S-S-I-N-G!" Holly sang, watching him stare at Maddie. "First comes love. Next comes marriage. Then comes MJ in a baby carriage!"

Holly laughed like a loon, with no idea how much her words tortured him, and Sam joined in. "You kiss her, don't you?" he asked, making a disgusted face. "I will *never* kiss a girl."

"No. Maddie and I are just friends." MJ ruffled Sam's hair. "But if you never kiss a girl, you have no idea what you're missing. Your mom and dad kiss, right?"

"No!" Holly shouted. "That would be the *grossest thing ever!*"

She'd never seen her parents kiss? MJ glanced at Roger who ignored him and dug another worm out of the bucket. "Well, trust me. It's not gross."

Holly shrieked and Sam made gagging sounds, but kissing was instantly forgotten when Holly got a tug on her line. "A fish!"

She started jerking the line violently, and MJ put his hands over hers to guide her as she reeled it in. "Easy. Just like this."

The fish broke through the water and swung over the canoe like a pendulum. "I got it." Roger grabbed the line and pulled the fish over where he took it off the hook. "How about that?" He held the fish out for Holly to see. "It's small, but it's a keeper."

Holly clapped her hands together, thrilled, and Sam begged Roger to let him hold it.

MJ watched the three of them and glanced back at Maddie. He would have this for himself. It would be his someday. He wouldn't accept any less. He wanted it with her, and he'd find a way to get her back.

❃

MJ didn't have a plan, but he did have a little nugget of leverage over Maddie.

He slid her diamond ring on his pinkie finger and left his room to find her. After they got back from fishing, she went to the pool with everyone else. MJ showered and took some time to gather his wits and steel himself to do whatever he had to do to get her to admit why she'd left him.

At the bottom of the stairs, Beck leaned in the archway from the entrance hall to the kitchen tossing an orange in the air and catching it. "Hey, Junior. I'm taking off to pick up your old man. Want to ride along?"

For a moment it felt like all the air had been knocked out of him, exactly like the night before when he'd tripped and fallen in the woods.

Merrick was coming back.

It wasn't a big deal, they'd already met and talked and everything was good. But, for some reason it felt like it would be their first meeting all over again. On Merrick's turf. Would it be different here on Turtle Tear?

"No," he said. "I'm good."

"You better go if you're going," Joan said, striding around the corner from the kitchen, her blond hair flowing over one shoulder. "There's a tropical storm headed his way. It's supposed to be on top of us by nightfall."

"I'm goin'," Beck said, brushing her off.

Joan frowned and walked between them, down the hallway toward the lounge.

Beck peeled a hunk of skin from his orange. "Some things are easier to get into than out of, if you know what I mean." He winked and handed MJ the piece of peel before following Joan. "Nice ring by the way," Beck called back over his shoulder. "Your boyfriend give you that?"

"Fuck off," MJ muttered as Beck's boisterous laugh echoed off the walls and high ceilings.

Deciding he'd rather avoid Beck and Joan, MJ left the hotel through the hulking hacienda door that led to the front of the property. Beams of sunlight filtered through dark, rolling clouds. Thunder rumbled in the distance. The wind blew and he breathed in the scent of citrus.

An orchard of lime trees stood across from a white, crushed shell courtyard with a cluster of huge, brightly painted clay pots in the center overflowing with flowers and vines.

He made his way across, shells crunching underfoot. The limes smelled so sweet, he had to pick one. Not to eat, just to feel its weight in his hand, hold it under his nose and know this moment was real. He was here. His dad was coming. Maddie was here with him.

A sharp crack of thunder rang out and he glanced up as he reached the orchard. The sky was threatening, the air filled with electricity. The hair on his arms stood on end.

MJ reached up and plucked a leaf from a branch in front of him. He tore it into pieces and tossed it to the wind, watched it swirl and drift over the crushed shells. Turning back to the tree and reaching up for a lime, his eyes fell on the woman from the woods.

She stood far within the trees, hidden in the dark watching him. Her white dress had been exchanged for a long, black one, a halter dress without straps. Maddie used to have a blue one just like it. He loved the easy access he had when she used to wear it. Maybe that's why he was imagining his make-believe woman wearing it.

"Let her go," the woman called out, her voice deep and raspy. "You can't trust her."

"You're not real," he said, pulling a lime off of a branch, closing his eyes and inhaling its scent deeply.

The lime was real. The woman wasn't. She'd be gone when he opened his eyes.

Except she wasn't.

"Let her go," she repeated. "She's a liar."

"Shut up!" he yelled. "I don't know you. I don't trust you."

"You should," she said. "Because I know more than you, and I know you can't be with her. Let her go."

MJ let out a snort of laughter. "You don't know anything." He let the lime roll off his hand and fall to the ground before turning and walking away.

Was she real? Was she a phantom his broken mind kept throwing up in his path? A mythological Fate sent to warn him away from Maddie?

Lightning flashed soundlessly, blinding him from his path for a second, causing him to freeze in his tracks.

Maybe he shouldn't trust Maddie. She refused to talk to him, to tell him what he'd done to make her leave.

Not trust Maddie? The thought was as foreign as...well, as having his father in his life.

He had to get off this island before every last thread of his sanity unraveled.

Twenty-Two

Maddie helped Rachael gather towels, tanning lotion, and rafts. Riley rushed around closing the awnings on the pool bar while Heidi herded Holly and Sam out of the pool. "That was lightning," she yelled to her kids. "Get out now!"

Tucking a pool noodle into a storage closet inside the cloister that surrounded the courtyard, Maddie closed the door and turned to face MJ. He had a strange, almost deranged look on his face. "Where've you been? Everything okay?" she asked.

He ran his hand over his face, transforming it back to normal, or normal with a hint of anxiety. "Yeah. Beck went to pick up Merrick."

"I heard the helicopter leave and Rachael told me he was on his way back."

MJ turned and ambled to a hammock. He fell back into it and closed his eyes, gripping the sides and she caught the flash of the diamond on his pinkie. "My ring," she said, darting forward to retrieve it.

MJ fisted his hand. "You know what you have to do to get it back."

"Why are you wearing it?"

"Because—"

Rachael, Heidi and the kids traipsed into the cloister, and MJ stopped talking.

"You two coming in?" Heidi asked. "You won't want to get stuck in this storm."

"In a minute," Maddie said, eager to get rid of them. This was her chance to get her ring back.

"Where's Dad?" Sam asked.

"He was taking a walk," Heidi said, leading them out onto the path. "He's probably at the hotel already."

Maddie waited for them to get out of earshot. "You're wearing it because..."

He smirked. "Because I can. It's mine until you give me what I want."

She pushed him, sending the hammock swinging. "Why are you doing this to me?"

MJ grabbed her hand and pulled her off her feet. She landed on the hammock half on top of him, half beside him. "I'm not doing anything to you," he said, brushing her hair out of her face. "You're the one who doesn't know what she wants. I know what I want."

He cupped her face and traced his thumb over her bottom lip sending tingles through her body. She touched the tip of his thumb with her tongue, and he pushed it farther into her mouth. Maddie closed her lips around it and closed her eyes. The small, intimate act sent her heart and body reeling.

MJ pulled his thumb from her mouth and she opened her eyes to stare into his. She never knew what she'd find in their depths. They always held a concoction of emotions and if she examined them long enough she could piece them together.

The regret was there, as it had been since she came back. And lust. The lust was easy to spot in MJ's eyes. She thought she saw a flicker of hope, and it made guilt and sadness flare inside her chest.

There was no hope, MJ. He had to know that.

He brushed her cheek with the back of his hand. "Why can't you tell me, Mads?"

The corners of her mouth twitched down and she couldn't fake a smile or stop the frown from forming. A ball of emotion clogged her throat, and her nose burned with unshed tears. "It'll hurt you even more. How can I tell you?"

"Don't be afraid of hurting me. I've already hit bottom without you." He smoothed the creases in her brow with his thumbs.

How could she even think about devastating him while lying here, watching his long, thick lashes brush the top of his cheeks when he blinked, running her fingers through the dark waves at the nape of his neck? She'd give anything for a smile right then, to see those incredible dimples, and the flash of laughter in his eyes.

But there was nothing to laugh about. There were only two parts of one very broken relationship lying in a hammock, one attempting to pick up the pieces and glue them together, and the other holding the knowledge that they could never be whole again.

Thunder echoed. The palm frond roof shook. "We should go in," she said, bracing her hands on his shoulders to get up.

MJ pulled her back down. "Not yet."

She held his eyes again and saw determination. She'd missed it before. "What do you want from me?" she asked.

"I want it all, Mads. I want my life back. You took it away, and I'm taking it back." He balled her hair up behind her head and pulled her to him. His kiss wasn't gentle. It wasn't urgent or rough. It was possessive. Undaunted.

If she hadn't known before, she knew now—MJ wasn't giving her up without a fight.

She broke away from the kiss, breathless and confused. The past year and a half flashed before her eyes. She'd forced herself to move on, but why hadn't he? "MJ, have you been with anyone else since?"

"Since?" He lifted his brows. He wanted to hear her say it.

"Since I left?"

He squeezed her hair tighter, making her lift her chin. "No," he said, narrowing his eyes. "There is nobody else. There never will be. You're mine. We both know it."

It wasn't a question of knowing it. They simply couldn't be together, and it was exhausting. Together and apart, the rush of emotions, the guilt and despair. "I can't do this anymore."

"You don't have to."

The wind howled and whipped through the trees. Rain

broke free of the clouds and fell in sideways sheets, a sprinkle barely reached them and caused Maddie's skin to break out in goose bumps.

MJ's fingertips glided down her neck and across her shoulders. Maddie stood on a cliff and could either turn and walk away or jump. Walking away was safe, it was living a stable, content life. She'd get her life in order and be happy. Even if her soul was always scrambling and searching to fill the emptiness.

Jumping from the cliff was being with MJ. Sometimes he made her feel like she could fly. He had so much love for her, it would carry her like a current of air and never let her fall. He'd been her world for as long as she could remember. He was every good memory, every tragedy, and every moment in between. MJ was her family. He was her past and for a time, he was the promise of her future.

"Do you think," she began, then stopped, not sure how to say what was on her mind.

"Do I think what?" He picked up strands of her hair and let it slide through his fingers.

"Well, in twenty years do you think we'll look back on this and it won't seem so significant? Will all of these feelings dull over time?"

MJ took a minute before answering her. "It depends. If we're together in twenty years and have the life we planned with a home and kids, then this time right now will have been a bump in the road. A big bump, but one we got past."

He lifted her chin with the edge of his fist. "If we aren't

together in twenty years, then right now will still be the most significant time in my life. My last chance to have you. If I fail, the pain of losing you will never dull, never go away."

All Maddie knew was the slow, syncopated rising of her chest and his breathing in and out, her heart beating against MJ's. This moment would last forever for both of them. How they remembered it depended on her.

She couldn't see twenty years into the future. She couldn't see tomorrow with her heart and mind so conflicted.

She let her head fall to his chest and closed her eyes. His warmth and the sharp spatter of rain on the walkway lulled her into a thoughtless daze.

Maddie wasn't certain how long they'd been lying under the cloister roof in the hammock when MJ's body tensed under her. She lifted her head and heard it. Helicopter blades.

The sky was practically black now, the rain relentless. The wind battered the roof of the cloister and bent the trees in half. "This can't be safe to fly in," she said.

"No, I wouldn't think so." MJ helped her sit up and the two of them gazed out into the rain, glistening as it blew through the glow of the outside lampposts.

Beyond the *whomp* of the blades, the engine began to whine, louder and louder as it neared.

"That doesn't sound good," MJ said, taking her hand. His palms were sweaty and cool.

"I'm sure it's fine," she said, but she honestly didn't think the helicopter sounded right either.

The whine of the engine went silent. Maddie squeezed MJ's hand. They waited, listening to the howl and whistle of the vicious wind. Maddie held her breath. Why had the engine stopped? And the blades weren't rotating.

A horrifyingly loud crash of trees cracking and metal grinding echoed across the island.

"Oh God," MJ whispered.

"It's okay," she said instinctively, and pulled him close, holding his head to her chest. "It's okay. Don't worry."

He held her back and studied her face like a light-bulb had just gone off in his head. He shook off whatever thought he had and helped her out of the hammock onto her feet. "We have to get to the hotel."

They ran down the path with the wind and rain whipping at their faces. Drenched and panting for breath, they heard golf carts speeding toward the landing pad. "Come on," MJ said, and tugged her toward one.

He jumped in behind the wheel. Maddie followed as quickly as she could, and hung on as he spun out on the wet pathway. She slid back and forth across the slick seat, grasping the bar that ran up the side for dear life. "How can you see?"

It was dark as midnight with leaves and palms blowing in front of them across the path, and the rain slicing across the windshield in waves. "I can't!" he yelled over the roar of the wind.

He was going to end up driving them right into the water where they'd drown or get eaten. It was a chance she'd have to take, because she wasn't going to tell him to slow down. His dad was in that helicopter. MJ had to get to him and Maddie would carry him across a desert on her back to get him there if she had to.

Two white golf carts came into view up ahead. "There!" She pointed.

"Got it." MJ pulled up alongside them and they jumped out.

The wreckage wasn't hard to find. It smoldered on the ground a few yards inside a dense grouping of Mangroves. "There's Beck," MJ said, and he took off jogging.

She ran to catch up.

Beck limped out of the trees with Riley supporting him on one side and Joan on the other. He held his hand across his chest, gripping his ribs tightly. "We're okay, Junior. You're dad's right behind me."

Maddie stepped up beside MJ. He took her hand. "What happened?" he asked. She felt him shaking.

"Tail got hit by lightning. Controls went out. Engine followed suit." Beck winced in pain. "Hold up," he said, and bent at the waist, panting. "I think I cracked a few ribs. It's hard to take a deep breath."

"I'll bring the cart over," Riley said, and took off running.

Maddie spotted Merrick limping out of the trees with his arm around Rachael. "MJ," she whispered and nodded toward them. "Go."

MJ jogged to Merrick's side. "Are you okay? You're limping."

Merrick put a hand on MJ's shoulder. "I'm fine."

Tears flowed freely down Rachael's face. Merrick brought her hand up to his lips and kissed it. He whispered something in her ear and held her face in his hands for a moment before turning back to MJ.

"Your head's bleeding," MJ said.

Merrick reached up and dabbed his forehead with his fingertips, then examined them. "It is." He shrugged and wiped his hand on his torn pants. "It doesn't hurt."

"Probably a concussion," MJ said. "I'll go bring a golf cart over." He spun Maddie around. "Come with me."

The two of them tread across the landing pad to the golf cart. He was shaking, his face pale. She ran her fingers through the back of his hair. "It scared you."

"I just got him. I don't want to lose him yet." He stopped the cart in front of Merrick and Rachael and got out. Maddie followed.

MJ put a shoulder under Merrick's arm. "Let me help."

Rachael wiped her eyes and fell into step with Maddie behind the father and son. "He could've died," Rachael said, her voice cracking. She sniffled and exhaled a deep breath. "I could've lost him."

"He didn't." Maddie stopped her and wrapped her in a firm hug. "He's fine and he's here now."

"I know," Rachael said. "I guess you don't realize how much someone means to you until you think you've lost them for good."

Her words hit home with Maddie. "You're right. There's

nothing worse than not having someone you love in your life." She watched MJ help Merrick into the passenger seat of the golf cart as she and Rachael approached to get into the back.

God, if it had been MJ in that helicopter. If she'd heard it go down knowing he was inside...She would've hated herself for not being with him for the past year and a half. Hated herself more than she already did. Not being with him, but knowing he was still in the world, hoping and praying he was happy—that was something she could find a way to live with. But, if something happened to MJ... if Maddie woke up tomorrow and found out he was gone from this life...No. She'd never be able to forgive herself for wasting even one day without him.

What the hell had she been thinking all of this time?

Twenty-Three

When they got to the hotel, Beck was already sitting in the lounge in a pair of fresh shorts, shirtless with a bandage wrapped tight around his chest. MJ's feet sloshed in his shoes as he and Rachael helped Merrick upstairs to get cleaned up and changed into dry clothes.

Maddie lumbered up the stairs behind them. He knew the adrenaline rush from the past hour had taken a toll on her. He glanced over his shoulder. Her dark hair dripped water down her arms. Her T-shirt clung to her wet skin, and he'd never once seen her look more beautiful.

She lifted her eyes to his, reached up and placed her hand on his back.

For a moment, huddled close to his father with Maddie's delicate fingers touching him, his world had righted itself. He wasn't the lone, black sheep begging for acceptance in a family that had been saddled with him twenty years ago.

He didn't know this man beside him, but he felt a connection he'd never experienced before. A connection that ran blood-deep. MJ had always wanted to feel this with his grandfather, but could never get beyond the shame and scorn that hung over his head from being the bastard child of the son the Old Man despised.

Merrick patted his shoulder when they reached the second

floor landing. "Did Rachael give you the big room on the end?" He pointed down the hallway.

"Yeah."

"Go ahead and get changed. I can make it to the third floor with Rachael's help."

"Okay." MJ didn't want to let his dad out of his sight, and it made him feel foolish. "I'll see you back downstairs."

Merrick smiled, and it was like looking in a mirror. MJ saw his own dimples in his father's cheeks. "If you don't come down," Merrick said, "I'll come find you this time."

Even though they were only talking about meeting up in the lounge, MJ knew Merrick meant he'd never lose him again. It was a certainty MJ knew by the sincerity in Merrick's voice and the determination set in his eyes.

He watched as Rachael helped Merrick up the next flight of stairs. If he leaned against her, she'd crumble under him. MJ was six foot two and Merrick was a few inches taller and built like a linebacker.

Maddie rubbed her hand across his lower back, stealing his attention away from his dad. She'd never looked at him this way before, with awe and wonder. "I'm so proud of you," she said. "You have everything you've ever wanted."

He turned to her and gathered her wet hair off of her shoulders. "Not everything."

Her eyelids fluttered as she dropped her gaze. MJ brushed a few locks of hair off of her forehead and placed a kiss on her damp skin. "Let's dry off."

He left Maddie outside her room and strode down the

hall toward his own with thunder rumbling overhead and lightning flashing outside the windows.

❀

Maddie came to his room as he was tugging a dry T-shirt over his head. She stood in front of a chest of drawers studying a framed, hand-drawn map of the island hanging on the wall. The paper was yellowed and creased under the glass as if it had been folded in quarters.

MJ walked over and stood behind her. "It's really old. Think it belonged to Archie?"

Maddie laughed. "Archie? I don't know. It could've been his."

He looked closer. The name of the island and the directional markers on all four sides were written in calligraphy inside banners drawn with scrolled edges. "Hey, the hotel's labeled Weston Estate at Turtle Tear."

Maddie stood on tip toe to get a better look. "Must have been when Ingrid and Archibald lived here with their family, before they turned it into a hotel." Her finger darted out, pointing to a huge tree in the center of the island. "Look at the heart with their initials on this tree! This is on a beam in the ceiling of—"

"The tree house bedroom," MJ finished. "I saw it too. I had no idea who A.W. and I.B. were then though."

"I didn't either." Maddie gazed at the map with an intense expression. "By this map, it looks like the tree stood very close to where the tree house is built." She turned and looked at him, her eyes calculating. "Rachael thinks Ingrid's grave is near the tree house. I wonder if she was buried under this tree."

MJ loved the way she held on to uncertainties, mysteries, couldn't let one go until she figured it out. She'd always been that way, and her curiosity had gotten them in plenty of trouble growing up.

"You should tell her," he said, leaning close and breathing in the fresh, rain-soaked scent of her hair.

The windows and walls creaked and groaned from the pressure of the wind blowing against them. The lights flickered and went out.

Maddie turned and poked him in the ribs. "Are you still afraid of ghosts? Remember the time when we were little—I think I was thirteen, so you must've been like nine—when we camped out at the lake and I made you listen to me tell ghost stories, and I held your hands so you couldn't cover your ears?" She laughed.

"How could I forget? You told me there was a ghost living in the west wing of the house. You scarred me for life." He put a hand to his chest. "You won't be satisfied until you've killed me."

She ran her hand down his chest. "No matter what it seems like, I don't want to hurt you," she said, just above a whisper.

MJ wished he could see her face in the dark. He reached for her, but she stepped away from him. "You know," he said, following the sound of her soft inhale of breath, the brush of her hair against her back as she moved, "when we were in the hammock earlier, something happened that I want to talk to you about."

"What?"

His foot bumped into hers, and he took her by the arms to keep her there. "When we heard the helicopter go down, you held me and kept telling me it would be okay."

Her muscles tensed in his hands. "Was that wrong of me?"

"No. But I'm a man, Maddie. You don't have to protect me anymore. You haven't needed to protect me for a long time. I know it's instinct. I'm four years younger and we grew up together like brother and sister, but that all changed a long time ago."

"I—I don't want you hurting. I can't stand to see you in pain."

He pulled her against his chest. "I know, but it's not up to you to shield me from it either. Do you understand?"

She nodded and wrapped her arms around his waist, squeezing him tight. He felt her trembling and when she sniffled, he realized she was crying. "Please, don't," he said, stroking her back. "I didn't mean to upset you."

"You didn't. You freed me."

He pulled her back and lowered his eyes to hers, cursing the blackness of the room that wouldn't let him see her face. "What do you mean, I freed you?"

Maddie laughed through a sob and held his face in her hands before bringing her lips to his. She kissed him like it was the first time. Something inside her had shifted. Had he won her back? He was afraid to ask.

Someone knocked on the door and opened it at the same time. Maddie pulled away from him and in the candle-light that Merrick held inside the door, MJ saw her wipe her mouth with the back of her hand, hiding a smile.

"Sorry," Merrick said. "I should've waited for you to answer. Beck has the only flashlight—guess we know now that we're not prepared for storms—but Rachael had these candles for an anniversary party renting out the hotel in a few weeks." He limped forward and handed them each a few candles and a couple packs of matches.

Merrick had changed into a pair of basketball shorts and a T-shirt. He had a bandage on his forehead and his knee was gouged. The wound looked deep but it was hard to tell how bad it was in the flicker of candlelight. "Knee any better?" MJ asked.

"It's fine. I jammed it into something sharp and twisted it, too. It's not bleeding anymore, so I'm taking that as a good sign." He chuckled. "Come downstairs when you two are ready."

"We're right behind you," Maddie said, hooking her arm through MJ's.

They took a few steps and her phone rang in her pocket. She pulled it out and MJ peered at the screen. If it was the other guy, he'd take the phone out of her hand and toss it out into the storm. The number displayed as unknown. Maddie pushed the answer button and held it to her ear. "Hello?"

MJ lit a candle.

"Yes, this is Maddie Simcoe."

"We'll be right down," MJ told Merrick.

"Northside Hospital?" Maddie said. "What's wrong? Is it my father?"

Merrick stopped in the doorway. Maddie gazed up at MJ. As she listened to whoever was on the phone from the hospital, he saw the world fall apart in her eyes.

"I can't. I'm away at an island resort with no way off because of the storm." Her words broke as sobs began to wrack her body. She dropped the phone and bent over, curling into a ball. "Oh my God. My dad." MJ grabbed her before she fell, and Merrick scooped up her cell phone.

"Hello?" Merrick said. "I'm a close friend of the family. Mr. Simcoe works for my father. What happened?"

MJ lifted Maddie in his arms and carried her to the bed. "He'll be okay. I promise, he'll be okay." He prayed he was right and the news wasn't that Mr. Simcoe had already left this earth.

She reared her head and glared at him like a wild tiger, then beat against his chest with her fists. "This is your fault! If you hadn't stolen my ring, I would've been there! Enzo did this!"

MJ captured her wrists and pinned her to the mattress. "What are you talking about? Why would my grandfather hurt your dad? They're best friends. That doesn't make sense."

"Because I'm here with you!" she yelled, her face contorted with rage. "He's been threatening to fire my father for over a year if I didn't stay away!"

MJ let her go and backed away. He didn't understand—must've heard her wrong—couldn't think because of the freight train rushing through his head. "He was the reason you left me?" It was unreal. His head spun and for a second he thought he might pass out. "Why?"

Maddie jolted up, throwing her feet over the side of the bed. "It doesn't *fucking* matter now! I didn't listen. I *had* to follow you here to get my ring back. *This is your fault!*"

Merrick staggered over, set a candle on the nightstand and handed Maddie her phone back. "They said he fell down a flight of stairs and hit the back of his head pretty hard. He's unconscious, but stable. They'll call with updates."

Maddie fixed her eyes on Merrick's, blue granite to steady brown-black like MJ's own. "Are you saying it was an accident?"

With his hands on his hips, Merrick slowly turned his head from side-to-side like he was trying to hypnotize a snake about to strike. "I heard you say Enzo did this. I wouldn't put anything past my father. Right now those are the only facts we have. Let's focus on what we know and worry about the rest when we can get to him. I'm going to call and have another helicopter on standby for when the storm passes."

Maddie's head fell into her hands. Merrick tightened his lips and stared at MJ, a thousand questions running through his eyes. MJ didn't have any answers.

"I'll leave you two alone," Merrick said. "Let me know if you need anything."

MJ watched him leave and close the door behind him. Between the crashes of thunder, he listened to the soft sobs from behind Maddie's hands. Why hadn't she told him? Why would Enzo want them apart?

A pain stabbed through his chest. Was the woman in the woods right? If the woman was his subconscious telling him not to trust Maddie, had he known all along that she was hiding something from him?

"Mads," he said, twisting his fingers through her hair. "You have to talk to me. I have to have answers."

She didn't budge. He took her hands and pried them away from her face, turning her body to face him. "Now, Maddie. You will tell me now."

"No!" She tore her hands from his, grabbed his pinkie finger and yanked her engagement ring off of it. "I changed my mind. I want to marry Talan," she said, her blue eyes hard as steel. "When I get off this island, I never want to see you again."

The weight of her words slammed into him. His future flashed before his eyes and left a black, gaping hole in its wake as she put the ring on her finger and left him sitting there all alone.

Twenty-Four

God, the absolute anguish in MJ's eyes as she put the ring on her finger was enough to make her heart stop. She'd never forget that look. It would haunt her until the day she died.

She didn't want to marry Talan. Her words to MJ were childish sharp jabs of revenge for making her come here to get her ring back.

That's what MJ did to her. He made her say things she regretted.

If she'd stayed away from him, her father wouldn't be in the hospital. She wouldn't be stuck here without a way to get to him. When would she stop making mistake after mistake when it came to MJ?

Maddie swiped at the hot tears of grief and sorrow streaming one after another down her cheeks.

After her father recovered—and she wouldn't think of any other option—she and her dad could hop on a plane bound for somewhere far, far away and never return. Running away seemed like a very viable option. If only the damn storm would stop.

A sprinkle of water from the window in her room hit her bare legs. She turned to see she'd left it open a few inches. She climbed onto the window seat on her knees and gazed out. The air was charged with electricity. The solar garden lights on the side of the hotel shone in the dark, glittering like Christmas. Two figures moved in the shadows of the lights. A man and a woman holding umbrellas.

Who the hell was outside the hotel in this mess?

She leaned her forehead against the windowpane and squinted, trying to see better. It was Roger and Heidi.

No. That wasn't Heidi, it was the woman Maddie had seen in the woods. The woman who told her to leave the island.

Roger passed her an envelope. "I couldn't get what you wanted. This will have to do." Lightning flashed out over the water. They both turned to watch it crackle and disappear before facing each other.

"Anything less won't do," the woman said. Maddie could barely hear her from all the way up on the second floor with the wind blowing and the rain hitting the window. "I was promised the title to the property and I want it back."

Roger held up his hands. "He couldn't get it. Don't shoot the messenger."

Maddie's door swung open. "You're not marrying him," MJ said, striding toward her. "And you owe me an explanation." His brows sat low over his eyes, a dark, haunted expression lingered on his face.

This day had drained her. She had nothing left inside her to give. "I'm not doing this, MJ. Please leave." She pointed to the open door.

"I'm not leaving." He sat down next to her and leaned against the windowsill, staring at her expectantly.

"Then I will."

She stood and he grabbed her arm. Both of them froze at the sound of the woman outside yelling. "This isn't what we agreed to. I'm not keeping my end of the bargain if he's not."

MJ jerked his head around to look outside. "That's her," he said. "That's the woman I saw in the woods." He glanced back at Maddie. "She told me not to trust you."

Maddie swallowed past the knot in her throat and knelt beside MJ. "Why would she say something like that?"

MJ traced his finger down the glass. "I don't know Maddie. You didn't tell me about the Old Man threatening you, so maybe she's right."

Maddie fisted her hands, and outside, Roger laughed. "What are you going to do about it?" he called after the woman.

She chuckled. "Reveal his secret. What else?"

Unease spread through Maddie's stomach. The secret. Could she mean the same one Maddie had been hiding for a year and a half?

Roger took his glasses off and let his head fall back, looking up at the dark sky like he wished it would suck him up and take him away. He turned and faced the hotel, and Maddie swore he saw her and MJ watching out her window.

She darted back out of the window seat. "Did he see us?"

When MJ faced her, she flinched. She'd never seen him so angry. "I don't know what he's hiding, but I'm in no mood to put up with his bullshit."

He stood and stalked out of her room.

Lightning flashed, followed by a deafening crack, striking somewhere on the island. Tonight she was on the edge of losing everything, all because of one man and his secret. If it came out, Maddie wasn't sure what would be left for her in the light of day.

She followed him downstairs. Her feet hit the entryway as MJ disappeared down the hallway toward the lounge. Someone had set up a candelabra in the corner by the archway into the kitchen. Five flames flickered, sending shadows across the murals on the walls, transforming redbirds into winged demons.

Maybe she was the one who had never grown up and was afraid of ghosts.

She made her way across the tiled floor feeling the air thrum around her, alive with the raging storm.

More candles blazed on the fireplace mantel and hearth in the lounge. The large, wooden sliding door to the patio was open, the air rushing in made the flames sway and dance. Beck, Joan, Heidi, Merrick and Rachael glanced at her when she walked in behind MJ. They sat in the dim light on the leather sofas that lined the walls. It could've been their intense, curious expressions that sent a foreboding sensation through Maddie at the sight of them.

"He won't stand for this!" Roger shouted outside.

Every eye in the lounge darted to the patio door as a woman with long, jet-black hair streaming water down onto her black halter dress stepped over the threshold with Roger standing directly behind her.

The woman scanned the room with wide, ebony eyes, her lips curved into a cunning smile. "My mother, Gina Montgomery, is alive," she announced. "Enzo Rocha is my grandfather." She stepped inside and lowered her eyes at Merrick. "And you're my father."

"My mother's alive?" MJ said, almost choking the words out.

Maddie resisted the urge to run to him and hold him in her arms.

"Gina's alive?" Merrick gripped the arm of the couch and pushed himself up onto his feet. "Who are you? Why should we believe you?"

"You shouldn't," Roger said, stepping inside. "Enzo put her up to this. She's trying to get her hands on a property you own, Merrick."

The woman laughed. "That property was supposed to be my payment for keeping Maddie Simcoe away from MJ so she wouldn't tell him our mother's alive."

Maddie's stomach roiled. In front of her, she watched MJ's back and shoulders stiffen. "Wait," he said, comprehension setting in. He turned to Maddie with so much hurt in his eyes, she knew no explanation, no amount of begging would ever be enough to make this up to him. "You knew my mother was alive and you didn't tell me?"

She opened her mouth and couldn't find her voice.

"I warned you not to trust her," the woman, MJ's sister, said, blinking at Maddie in false sympathy.

"Your grandfather threatened to fire my dad," Maddie said. Standing in front of MJ with the truth out in the open,

Enzo's threat seemed insignificant in comparison to the secret she'd kept from him.

"I can't believe you wouldn't tell me."

Maddie wanted to run from the room, but her feet wouldn't budge. She wanted to fall to the floor and beg him to understand, but her knees wouldn't bend.

His chest expanded with a great breath. His hands rose to his head and he clutched and pulled at his hair. "I have to get the fuck out of here."

Pushing past her, he stormed down the hall to the entryway and threw open the front door. Maddie ran after him. "MJ, stop!" He couldn't run off into the rain and lightning.

She paused at the door for only a second before dashing out after him. She couldn't see him, but heard his footsteps crunching over the path of broken shells. Catching up to him under a tree weighed down with heavy limes and rain-soaked leaves, she grabbed the back of his shirt. "Stop! Please!"

He spun and batted her arm away. "I've never wanted to strangle someone so much in my life. And the fact that you betrayed me terrifies me. It kills me, Maddie. Not you! Anyone else in this fucking world but you."

Desperation overtook her, and she grabbed the front of his shirt. "How could I tell you? She abandoned you. I know exactly how that feels, MJ. I couldn't do that to you. I love you too much to bring that hurt into your life."

He gripped her wrist and tried to tear her hands away, but she held tight. "That's bullshit," he said. "You were afraid your dad would get fired. Like that's anything at all when it comes to telling me my mother's alive."

"My dad's in the hospital! You don't think that's a coincidence do you? Your grandfather did this. I came here and he hurt my dad!"

"You don't know that."

Maddie dropped her hands. "You have more faith in your grandfather than you do in me?"

"You're about equal now in my book."

She sucked in her lips, willing her emotions to steady. Crying wouldn't help her. She had to make him see reason. "Do you remember the first time we got drunk?" she asked.

"What does that have to do with this?" he spat.

Undeterred, she continued. "It was the day before I turned eighteen."

Maddie held the phone receiver tight in her sweaty hand. It had been so long since she'd seen her mom, and now she sat on the couch crushed. "You're not coming home?" she said. To Maddie's ears, her own voice sounded like the same little girl she'd been the day her mom left.

"I can't make it, Angel. I'm sorry. I'm in L.A. and I have an audition tomorrow. I have a good shot at getting this part and then your momma will be on TV! Isn't that great?"

"Yeah. That's great." Maddie tried to smile, tried to sound encouraging. "Good luck."

"You know, now that you'll be eighteen, you can come out here with me! Wouldn't that be fun? Two single women living in L.A.?"

Maddie laughed, but it sounded how she imagined card-board tasted. Dull. Flat. Dry. "I'm going to college, remember?"

"Yes, that's right. You've always been serious and respon-sible." She laughed, but it sounded like mocking laughter to Maddie.

"I have to go, Mom. I'll miss seeing you. Let me know how your audition goes."

"I will, Angel. Have a great birthday." She made kissy noises into the phone.

"Bye," Maddie muttered, and hung up.

Devastated, she ran out the door before the tears burst free and her dad saw her. The last thing she wanted was for him to think another birthday with only him wasn't good enough. It was more than good enough. Her mom was a joke. She couldn't be bothered with Maddie. She wouldn't even call again for another six months.

Maddie was stupid to get her hopes up.

Outside, she leaned against the back of the garage and sobbed. Sliding down onto her bottom, she dropped her head into her hands and let it out.

"Mads? What's wrong?" MJ sat down beside her.

"She's not coming," Maddie said between her fingers. "I don't know why I care."

His arm went around her shoulders. "Because she's your mom. She's supposed to want to be here for your birthday."

He pulled her to him and let her cry against his shoulder for so long, the sky turned dark. Finally, he held her back and lifted one finger. "Be right back."

Maddie tried to pull herself together while he was gone. She dried her eyes and took deep breathes. There was no use crying. She had everything she needed anyway—a home, food to eat and two people she could always rely on, her dad and MJ.

He came back holding a bottle of vodka. "I think we need to celebrate your birthday early. What do you say? Back by the lake?"

She smiled and couldn't hold back her laughter. "I like that idea."

The two of them headed out, not bothering with a golf cart. They took big gulps of vodka that stung the backs of their throats as they walked. By the time they got to the lake, Maddie was already tipsy and couldn't stop giggling.

"I'm sorry your mom sucks," MJ said. "I wish my mom was around for you, like your dad's around for me."

Maddie lowered herself to sit, crashing down on her butt in the grass. "I wonder what she'd be like. I bet she'd believe in ghosts."

MJ chuckled and sat beside her. "Nobody but you believes in ghosts, Mads." He took a big swig of vodka and held the bottle up in the moonlight. "We just about killed it." He handed her the bottle. "Go ahead. You take the last drink."

She did and tossed it aside. "I'm hot." She plucked the front of her T-shirt out, filling it with air and let it go. "I want to swim."

"Swim?" His gaze followed her as she stood and stripped off her shirt.

"Yeah," she said, looking down at him, her head spinning. "Swim." She unbuttoned her shorts and shoved them off.

"Mads. You don't have a bathing suit on." He stood up and she watched his eyes roam her body. Somewhere in the back of her mind she thought she should be embarrassed to be in her underwear in front of him, but she wasn't.

"So. We'll skinny-dip." She ran toward the lake, unhooking her bra and letting it fall behind her. At the bank, she shimmied out of her panties and left them at the edge of the water as she stepped in.

"Vodka does this *to you, huh? I'll have to remember that." He stopped a few feet behind her.*

"I like vodka," she said, laughing so loud, it echoed out over the lake. Maddie looked back over her shoulder. "Why are you still dressed? Aren't you coming in? This is my party, MJ. You have to do what I want."

❀

MJ folded his arms across his chest and rocked from foot to foot. "We drank vodka beside the lake," he said. "You laughed like a crazy person, slurred all the stupid shit you said and talked me into going skinny-dipping. I wanted you so badly it hurt, but you thought of me as a little brother. I held your hair while you puked about ten times under that big willow tree."

She held her breath for a moment. "You wanted me then?"

"I can't think of a time when I haven't wanted you." He let his hands drop to his sides. "Except maybe now."

She squeezed her eyes shut, willing her tears not to fall. "You know, you were stronger and more mature at fourteen than I am at twenty-four. You sat there soaking in all the pain and tears I shed that day. For hours. You never once left my side. I wasn't strong enough to do that for you. I couldn't take seeing you like that. I was too selfish and afraid."

Hesitantly, Maddie rested a hand on his chest. "I'm sorry."

He inhaled a deep, shuddering breath. "I know."

Her insides clenched. "Can you forgive me?"

The minute that passed in silence was excruciating for her to bear. "I don't know," he said, finally. "That's a lot to ask. It's not only that you didn't tell me she was alive, but you let it keep us apart for over a year. Being with me wasn't worth telling me."

"No," she whispered, stroking his wet hair from his eyes, "you're worth everything to me."

MJ pushed her hand away. "Talan's worth everything to you. You decided to marry him, remember? Would you keep a secret this big from him? Would you let it keep you apart?" He took a step closer and loomed over her. "And you had the nerve to blame me for your dad getting hurt. Even if it ends up being the Old Man's fault, you could've avoided all of this by telling me the truth."

Standing so close, Maddie could see the shadow of his jaw clenching and releasing before he pivoted and walked away from her.

Twenty-Five

The phrase *when it rains, it pours* described the past couple days perfectly, and it had nothing to do with the goddamn storm. Needing a few more minutes to calm down, MJ decided to walk around the hotel and go in through the patio gate.

He shook out his arms and rolled his shoulders. The thunder, lightning and rain pelting down on him was a welcome distraction. At least the woman in the woods was real and he hadn't completely lost his mind.

Yet.

Jesus, he had a sister. But that knowledge didn't excite him like it should. It was the way she made her grand entrance, the reason she came to them. If he was Merrick Junior, she was Enzo Junior, and he wasn't sure he wanted to welcome a clone of his grandfather into his life. There were already too many people manipulating him in the name of his own good.

Fucking Maddie. How could she do this to him. The only person he ever trusted completely.

Talan could have her.

Thinking those words and believing them were two different beasts though, and MJ's insides coiled at the idea of her walking down an aisle in a church wearing a white wedding dress if there was someone else waiting at the end.

He didn't know how he'd get past this, but he knew there was no stopping his love for her. It was beyond his control. Always had been.

He rounded the corner and opened the gate. Inside the lounge, Heidi and Beck turned around, watching him approach from where the two of them sat on the sofa. Merrick placed his hands on the back of the couch behind his sister and leaned toward her. "I have two questions," he said. "First, did you know my son was alive?"

She sucked her lips in and nodded, regret and a hint of fear crossing her face.

Merrick stiffened, took a deep breath and swallowed hard. "Did you know Gina Montgomery was alive?"

Her brows furrowed, and she frowned. "Yes," she breathed.

Merrick's hands squeezed into fists, and he closed his eyes. "Get out of my sight. I don't want to see you right now."

Heidi placed her hands over his. "Merrick, please. Dad did it for MJ. You were so young."

"Please!" Merrick shouted. "Just go. I'll find you later."

Beck stood and held out a hand for Heidi. "Come on." He gave Merrick's shoulder a friendly punch before escorting Heidi out of the lounge.

MJ wondered where Roger had gone. The mole must be upstairs with Sam and Holly. MJ knew Roger was too close to Enzo, but he never would've guessed he was doing the Old Man's dirty work.

Joan escorted MJ's sister down the hallway toward them. She'd gotten her dry clothes to change into. His sister plopped down on one of the sofas like she owned the place.

MJ approached her like he would a rabid dog. "What's your name?"

"Nadia. I'm named after our great-grandmother, Nadia Montgomery." She patted the cushion beside her. "Sit."

He almost expected her to tell him she wouldn't bite, not that he'd believe her.

MJ eased down beside her, and Merrick, still standing behind the sofa Heidi had vacated, stared at them like this was all a dream, and not necessarily a good one. The warmth MJ had felt from his father was gone and replaced by skepticism toward this woman beside him.

That made two of them. They really were alike. MJ would laugh if he wasn't so shell-shocked by everything that had happened. Next, the floor would open up and swallow him whole.

Rachael came in carrying a tray of mugs. "Warm cider and rum. I think we could all use some." She set the tray on the rustic, wooden coffee table and eyed Merrick, nodding to the couch for him to take a seat. He did. She sat beside him.

MJ knew the power Rachael had over his father. It was the same Maddie held over him. Or, it had been. Where the hell was she anyway? She better not still be outside or he really would strangle her for being stupid.

Merrick tapped his leg with his fingers, restless. "So, what? You're twins?"

Rachael put her hand over his to still him. He thread their fingers together and held their joined hands to his chest.

"Don't we look alike?" Nadia said, leaning in to MJ and smiling. She had a dimple, just one, but it was there in her left cheek. Did anyone in their family not have those freaking dimples?

"Yeah," Merrick said. "So my father kept you two apart. You've been with your mother?" he asked.

"Yes. Enzo let me stay at the Rocha Estate once when I was little and my mom was out of town, but he wouldn't let me leave the west wing of the house. He didn't think that was a good idea," she said. "He paid my mother to keep me away the rest of the time."

Something clicked inside MJ's brain. The west wing. Ghosts weren't real. Not Ingrid and not Maddie's ghost. Nadia had been both.

"I see," Merrick said.

MJ leaned forward and picked up a mug of hot cider and rum. He downed it in a few gulps, scalding his throat.

"You can have mine, too," Nadia said, watching him like he was her new favorite toy.

"Thanks."

He picked up a second mug and downed it, hoping for enough rum to get even a little buzz.

"I'm sorry I got crazy when you left here to go to Sandy Springs," Merrick said to Rachael. "When it comes to my father, I don't want anyone I love near him." He brushed his thumb over her bottom lip. "He takes everything that's important to me. He can't have you." Merrick looked at MJ. "Or you." His gaze fell to Nadia and held for a moment, but he didn't repeat the sentiment.

Beck walked in, handed Merrick a bottle of double malt scotch and a couple of shot glasses over the back of the couch, patted him on the arm and walked back down the hall without a word.

Merrick smiled and poured himself a shot. "Remind me why I wasn't friends with him sooner," he said to Rachael.

"You don't want me to remind you why," she said, and kissed the tip of his nose. "I could use one of those too."

Merrick downed his shot and handed one to Rachael. "Being your father," he said to MJ and Nadia, "I should know this, but are you twenty-one yet?"

"We have two more months," Nadia said, holding up two fingers.

"Close enough. You're not driving anyway. Help yourself if you'd like." Merrick set the bottle and the glasses on the table.

MJ didn't need to be asked twice.

"Guess I should've asked that question before serving them rum," Rachael said. "Sorry."

"That's okay," Merrick and MJ said in unison.

MJ wasn't used to someone answering for him, telling him he was or wasn't allowed to do things like drink. At school, he'd fought against authority with his fists, getting in fights and getting shown the door. Coach was as close to a father as he had next to Mr. Simcoe, but neither of them ever tried to tell him what he could or couldn't do.

"Where do you and your mother live?" Merrick said, lifting his chin in Nadia's direction.

She lit up like she was in a spotlight. "Mom and I travel overseas a lot. We live in hotels mostly. Mediterranean countries are my favorite. She told me I share your love of olives."

Merrick straightened. "Did she say that?"

"Yeah." Nadia smiled like it was the smoothest comment she could've made, not realizing how awkward the moment was for the rest of them.

"I do love olives."

"What movies to you like?" Rachael prodded, gulping down her cider and rum.

"Actually," she said, simpering, "I love the Godfather movies. *Luca Brasi sleeps with the fishes,*" she quoted, and cracked up laughing. "That line is the best ever in a movie."

God, this girl was whacked. How could she be MJ's sister?

Merrick made a choking sound then laughed, but it was forced.

Rachael hid behind her mug. She'd moved on to drinking Merrick's spiked cider.

"Let's not pretend anymore," Merrick said, his words and penetrating stare sending a shiver up MJ's spine. "Enzo sent you here, correct?" he asked Nadia.

"Yes," she said, wide eyes blinking, trying for innocence.

"Then why on Earth should I believe you're my daughter?"

"Merrick," Rachael whispered.

He turned to her, pressed his lips together tightly and exhaled sharply through his nose. "Fine," he said, turning back to Nadia. "*If* I accept that you're my daughter, then you have to know I won't have a relationship with you if you remain in contact with him. You've already done his bidding here and I'm finding it hard to welcome you with open arms."

MJ watched Nadia's bottom lip tremble. "I had to do what he wanted. He promised he'd get my inheritance back from you."

"Not this again," Rachael mumbled. "What is it with rich people? I don't have an inheritance and it hasn't turned me into a manipulative crazy person."

Merrick licked his lips and smiled. "Want another drink, Rach?"

She shoved his leg. "Shut up."

He winced and held his knee.

"Oh my God, I'm so sorry," Rachael said, realizing she'd shoved his injured leg. She wrapped her arms around his shoulders and nuzzled into his neck.

He tilted her chin up and kissed her. "You can make it up to me later."

MJ felt a hollow emptiness inside where Maddie used to complete him. He needed to find her. "I have to take care of something," he said, standing. "Nice meeting you." He held a hand out to Nadia.

She looked at it like he'd just come from the men's room and not washed his hands. Then she stood and swept him into a bear hug. "I've known about you my entire life. I didn't even have a picture though. It always felt like there was a part of me missing without my twin. Didn't you feel it, too?"

He didn't know what to say. He'd always felt the loneliness of being an only child, but he'd filled that void with Maddie. She was what was missing now. "I didn't know about you. I probably would've felt the same if I'd known."

She pulled back from him. Her face fell. "Oh."

Guilt for wanting to bolt from the room wouldn't stop him from leaving. "I really have to find Maddie. We argued and I left her out in the rain. I'm sure she's up in her room, but I need to make sure she's okay."

Nadia's face morphed into disgust. "Even after knowing she lied to you? Why do you care at all?"

He put a hand on his hip and rubbed his forehead. How could he explain? "Because growing up she was my sister. She protected me. She just didn't realize I don't need her watching out for me anymore. I can take the truth. She lied so I wouldn't get hurt finding out my mother didn't want me."

"She wanted you!" Nadia grabbed his hands. "She's always wanted you. When she got pregnant with us, her family disowned her. She had to take Enzo Rocha's money to survive. He paid her and the family that disowned her to pretend she was dead, to stay away from you and he would've included me if he knew I existed at the time. She had to hand a baby over to him and it was you."

She stroked the back of his hand. "I'm so sorry it was you. I wish it could've been me and you could've grown up with her."

While her words sounded genuine enough, they came twenty years too late to leave him with anything but a slight regret. Regret that his life could've been different if he'd been born the female twin. How did their mom pick? Did she flip a coin, or did he automatically take the sacrifice being born with a penis? Being disowned by your parents and raising a baby on your own that young—Gina Montgomery probably hated men thanks to Merrick and Enzo Rocha.

"Does Gina know you're here?" Merrick asked.

"No," she said, adamantly, but MJ noticed her eye twitch. It was her tell. She was lying.

MJ had enough. "I'm going upstairs." He dodged the table and held his hand out to Merrick.

Merrick took it and pulled him in for a man-hug, back-pat, the kind Coach always gave him. "See you in the morning, kid," Merrick said.

He'd see his dad in the morning. It was surreal. " 'Night," he said, and nodded to Rachael.

Mounting the stairs, MJ couldn't help but feel bad for Nadia. Whatever her motive was for coming here, she wanted a relationship with him and Merrick, but she wouldn't get one with either of them.

MJ found out he'd had what he'd wanted all along. His real sister, if that's who Nadia actually was, felt like a stranger even though she was his twin. There was no magical connection, not even the blood-connection he'd felt with Merrick. But, Maddie was family. The bond they'd made over the years was stronger than anything he'd have with his real family.

MJ found himself racing up the steps to get to her. He'd been too hard on her. He had to fix everything between them before the storm ended and she left the island.

Twenty-Six

Maddie lay on her bed clutching her phone to her chest. She had to call Talan. If she'd learned one single thing from this mess, she'd tell him the truth, and the truth was that she'd always love MJ.

She dialed the number. It rang once before a soft knock sounded at her door. She hung up knowing who it was. She could feel his presence on the other side like an invisible band connected them through her center and his. "Come in," she called.

The lit candle stub sitting on top of the chest of drawers did little to light the room, but she saw fatigue etched on his face, and his eyes always got glassy when he was overly tired.

Without a word, he climbed in bed behind her and wrapped an arm around her waist, snuggling up close. He buried his nose in her hair, and kissed the back of her neck. "No matter who you're with, you'll always be mine, Mads."

She set her phone on the nightstand and laced her fingers with his. She wouldn't argue. Couldn't argue. He was right.

"We'll get past this," he said. "I promise."

Maddie turned her head, leaning it against his. "That's what my dad said."

"He's never wrong." MJ rose up on his elbow and gazed into her eyes.

With anyone else she ended up blinking or looking away after a few seconds, but with MJ, she could spend an entire night looking into the depths of his eyes. She could see right through them, right inside him. It was like being plugged in to the universe and knowing the answers to every question you never thought to ask.

"When we do get past this," he whispered, "and you're mine again, I'm going to make love to you like I never have before."

Overtaken by emotion, her eyes fluttered closed. She felt his nose glide down the bridge of her own. Then his lips brushed against hers, feather-light. "There will never be a day in my life when I don't love you, Madeline Simone Simcoe."

A dam broke inside her, flooding her with relief she hadn't known for over a year. It was finally over. The secret was out.

And MJ said he loved her.

She eased onto her back and welcomed his lips again, pushing her fingers through his hair and pulling him in. Maddie lifted her head off her pillow, deepening their kiss. She had to have MJ in her life. If her dad never woke up...

She couldn't live without her father in her life, let alone both of the men she loved most in the world.

She pulled MJ down on top of her, and wrapped her legs around his hips. She wanted him, needed him to fill the emptiness deep inside.

In this bed far away from home, surrounded by shimmering candlelight and air charged with electricity and desire, she lost herself in his lips, his tongue, his hands gliding down her sides. "I love you, MJ," she said, her voice deep and lusty. "I never stopped."

He answered with a groan, and sat up on his knees, pulling her up with him. He took a deep, shuddering breath and held her left hand between them, watching his fingers stroke her palm. "I understand why you kept the secret and ran from me. When my grandfather says he does things in my best interest, I know it's a lie, but when you do," his gaze rose from her hand to her eyes, making her gasp silently with the intense love she saw in them, "I know you mean it. I know you still thought you had to protect me."

He leaned his forehead against hers. "I know what you've gone through missing your mom all of these years. Not telling me mine was alive and breaking your own heart to save mine—Maddie, I forgive you for not telling me."

Her relief came out in a sob. Her body couldn't hold all of the love she held inside. If she didn't release it, she'd explode.

His eyes fell back to her hand. "There's one thing standing in our way. Did you mean it when you said you wanted to marry him, or were you angry about what happened to your father and taking it out on me?"

She brought her left hand to her right and eased the ring off her finger. "Of course I didn't mean it. You make me a crazy woman. Always have. It should've never gotten to this point. I should've told you about Enzo and your mom. We could've been together this whole time."

"Shh." MJ held out his hand and Maddie placed the ring

in it. He stood and crossed the room to the chest of drawers, opened the top one and set the ring inside.

Maddie watched as he walked back to her, stopped beside the bed and crossed his arms over his chest. "Are you mine?" he asked.

Her heart raced in anticipation of what was next. "I've never not been yours," she answered.

MJ crawled onto the bed and straddled her. His penetrating eyes promised he'd give her what she'd been missing for so, so long. He'd make her whole again.

"I'm taking what's mine," he said, gently nipping her bottom lip with his teeth. "Over and over and over again."

Maddie closed her eyes as he sucked her bottom lip into his mouth and pushed his hands up under her shirt over her bare skin. She'd taken her bra off when she changed into thin cotton pajama shorts and a tank top for bed, and his hands covered her breasts, kneading and rubbing.

"No stopping tonight," she pleaded. "I need you."

"No stopping. Never again."

He lifted her tank top over her head, then got rid of his own shirt, tossing both to the floor. She watched his fingers trail down over her breasts, teasing her taught nipples. The sensation set her on fire. His cherishing expression sent her reeling.

He eased down and flicked his tongue over her nipple before taking it in his mouth. His hands worked their way lower, and pushed her pajama shorts over her hips. "Are you still on the pill?" he whispered against her skin.

"Yes." She pushed his head back to her breast and guided his hand between her legs. "I can't wait another second to have you."

He rubbed her over her panties, sending flames through her center. "Take them off," she begged, grappling with his zipper. She wasn't sure if she meant her underwear or his shorts, but both needed to go.

"We have all night," he said, trailing kisses down her sternum to dip his tongue in her belly button.

"No." Maddie wriggled under his warm fingers, his wet mouth. "I need this right now." She reached inside his boxer briefs and wrapped her hand around his hard, long length to prove her point.

MJ tugged her panties off and ran his hands from her shoulders down over her breasts, stroking her stomach and stopping on her thighs, parting them as he settled his shoulders between them. He paused for a moment. She watched him taking in the sight of the key tattoo on his chest finding it's mate again. The lock beside her hip.

"MJ," she whispered, rocking her hips against his shoulders, tearing his attention away from inked promises.

"I need to make sure you're ready," he said. "It's been a long time for me, Mads, and I won't hold back and be gentle this first time. I don't want to hurt you."

She groaned in frustration. "I know you're big and I know I'm ready to take you. Please put—"

His tongue dove inside her, stopping her words. Her hands flew to his head, her fingers weaving through his hair as he ran a finger through her folds and penetrated her with his tongue.

She felt him moving and heard his shorts fall to the floor. Then both hands were separating the lips between her legs as he suckled and teased her, sliding two fingers in and out of her.

She found his rock-hard erection with her toes and he ground his hips against her foot. His mouth latched on to her clit and sucked hard. A blinding, white heat began to pulse inside her. "Oh, God. MJ." She pushed his head away. "Not yet. I want to come with you inside me. Please." She grasped his shoulders and pulled. "Please."

He rose over her and she gripped him, positioning him at her opening and lifting her hips off the bed, begging. He thrust into her, stretching her and sending sparks flying behind her eyelids.

MJ took her hands, thread his fingers between hers and held them over her head. "You," he said, thrusting hard. "Are." Another hard thrust had her moaning and arching her back. "Mine." Again, he pushed into her deep and hard, hitting the spot that sent her over the edge. She cried out as he rocked his hips with hers and she exploded around him, wet and pulsing with release. It had never been so all-consuming, so raw. She'd split open and couldn't stop trembling.

He stilled and kissed her. She tasted herself on his tongue. He held her head between their joined hands. "Are you okay?" he asked. "You're shaking."

She kissed the corner of his mouth, his cheek, his jaw. "It's never been like that before."

"I know," he said. "You've never let yourself be that open to me before." He nuzzled his nose with hers. "Thank you."

"Thank *you*," she whispered, lifting her hips, urging him to move again as she traced his bottom lip with her tongue.

He lifted her in his arms, rising to his knees and pressing her back against the headboard. He hooked his arms under her knees, spreading her as wide as he could and took her nipple in his mouth as he pounded into her.

Maddie gripped the top of the headboard, let her head fall back against the wall and held on tight. "I love how you take me," she said, feeling a tightening deep inside. "Never stop." MJ knew how to make her body respond to him like he knew how to claim her heart and soul.

A tingling, burning ache circled her opening, rushed through her with his fast, hard thrusts and had her arching and bucking against him, lost to another orgasm ripping through her.

"Fuck, Mads, you're so tight and wet."

His words were a distant murmur against her ear. The waves kept rushing through her, as he plunged into her over and over, seeking his own release. She whimpered and cried out each time he thrust into her. She'd never stop coming.

"Let go," she begged.

He groaned and shoved himself inside her hard. She felt

him pulsing with release as he panted and leaned his head against her chest.

Lowering her down onto the bed, MJ covered her body with his and gripped her chin, gazing down into her eyes with a stern, penetrating stare. "No other man will ever be inside you again. Do you understand?"

His possessiveness was startling, but she wanted his claim on her. Needed it like air and blood. "Yes."

His fingers slid through the wetness between her legs and entered her. "This is mine."

She took a shaky breath, letting her head fall back and digging her shoulders into the mattress as his fingers stimulated her overly sensitive flesh. "Yours," she whispered.

Reaching down, she found him, hot, sticky and semi-hard again already. "Mine," she said.

His chuckle against her neck sent goose bumps down her spine. "Baby, I think we proved it was made just for you."

She laughed until his thumb circled her sensitive bundle of nerves and he had her gasping and writhing again as his fingers worked inside her.

"I love watching you come," he said. "Putting that beautiful expression on your face is what I live for."

Her body quaked and spasmed. MJ kissed her neck, trailing down to her chest before easing his fingers out of her. "I hope you live a long, long time then," she said, licking her lips and catching her breath.

He settled in beside her and pulled the blanket over

them. "I plan to," he said. "Just like I plan to sleep with you in my arms every night from this one on."

Maddie rolled to her side and pressed her cheek to his chest, feeling his heartbeat. "I like the sound of that."

The morning arrived with sunlight streaming through the window, birdsong and feeling MJ's warm skin against hers.

Heaven. She died and went to Heaven. This wasn't her imagination. He was here with her. He was real, and they were together again.

Twenty-Seven

MJ stood on a half-built bandstand on the west end of the island where he'd never been. The groan of cello strings blared through the air around him. Beck sat on the edge of the roughed-in stage with an old, battered cello between his legs and examined the bow like it was the cause of the offensive noise.

"I think you forgot how to play that thing," Merrick said, sitting in a lawn chair in front of the bandstand.

"It's been a long time," Beck said, running the bow across the strings again. The instrument made a nice hum, then squawked. "I just need to warm it up a bit."

"Yeah, that'll make all the difference," MJ said, jumping down and kicking a stone.

Beck pointed his bow at him. "Nobody asked you, Junior."

"What's with the kiss between you and Maddie?" Merrick asked, trying to suppress a grin.

Beck clucked his tongue. "That's dangerous territory there. She came here to get her ring. She's going to crush you like a bug."

"She's not marrying him. We're together like we should've been for the past year and a half."

MJ's defensiveness made Beck lift his hands in surrender. "Hey, I believe you man."

A knowing smile appeared on Merrick's lips. "Rocha men have a way of getting what they want."

Beck tapped the bow on the ground. "I still haven't figured out what Rachael sees in *you*, ya cocky son of a bitch."

Merrick laughed. "If I could get up out of this chair without it feeling like someone was stabbing me in the knee, I'd kick your ass."

Beck snorted. "You could try."

"Why don't you stop murdering that cello and pick up a hammer? This thing isn't going to build itself."

Beck touched the bandage around his chest. "If I didn't know you were joking, I'd pick up a hammer and take it to your head."

"First you wreck my copter, now we're never going to get this bandstand built in time for the anniversary party Rachael scheduled. I don't know why I don't fire your ass."

Beck waved a hand. "Have Riley and Jesse build it. Those two are always fucking around pissing off Joan and not doing anything important anyway."

"Good idea. I'll have her supervise. Within a week, they'll all quit."

"Problem solved," Beck said, swiping his bow across the cello strings making a high-pitched whine.

MJ cringed.

"Don't worry," Merrick said. "I'll have Joan off your hands and on to her new assignment in no time." He glanced at MJ.

"I should've never gotten involved with that one," Beck

said. "I knew she was the Dragon Lady and still fell under her spell."

Merrick shook his head. "Thank God I was always able to resist it."

"There you are!" Nadia said, running up to them, out of breath. "Maddie wants to go back to the mainland," she told Merrick. "I'm taking her in the boat. I'll be back in a little while."

MJ took a couple steps toward her. "Where is she?"

"Like a bug," Beck muttered.

"Shut the fuck up," MJ said, and smacked the back of Beck's head. "She was taking a shower when I came out here."

"She's looking for you," Nadia said, watching them with her brow creased in confusion. "You're coming, right?"

The vise that had tightened itself around MJ's chest loosened. Would he ever stop fearing Maddie taking off on him again?

"Right."

Nadia smiled, but MJ detected zero sincerity in it. The slight curve of her lips coupled with the sharp gleam in her eyes was eerily similar to the expression Enzo wore when he tied another knot around MJ's neck.

MJ shifted his gaze to Merrick. "You have a helicopter coming soon?" He didn't want to leave his dad when they'd just gotten together, but Maddie would always come first.

"Still waiting for confirmation," Merrick said, glancing between MJ and Nadia. He quirked his brow at MJ. MJ took it as a silent apology and a warning to be careful with this girl in Enzo Rocha's pocket who neither of them trusted.

"Come on MJ," Nadia called, jogging to her golf cart. "Be back soon, Dad!"

Merrick looked like he might have a stroke. "I'll check in at the hospital when we get there," he said to MJ. "Take care of Maddie."

"I will." He didn't hesitate to bend down and hug Merrick. "See you soon."

"As soon as I can get there," Merrick said, squeezing his shoulder.

❀

MJ found Maddie sitting in the window seat in her room gazing out at the rain and wind-battered flowers and bushes. She turned to face him when he entered her room. Neither of them said a word.

He took her left hand and rubbed his thumb over her bare ring finger. "Was it hard?"

He hadn't left her to take a shower. He'd left her to call Talan and break the news that she didn't want to marry him.

Her eyes flitted up to his, then down to her hand in his. "Yes and no." She threaded their fingers together and brought his hand to her lips. "Yes, because I hated hurting him. No, because I knew it was the right thing to do."

MJ flattened his palm against her cheek and ran his thumb across her lips.

"I've been in love with you the whole time I was with

him," she said. "He never had all of me. Only a part I let him have…" She looked up at him through her dark lashes, blue eyes blazing. "On loan from you. No part of me ever belonged to him. It was always you."

How could he possibly be this fortunate? A few days ago, there were cracks and craters in him that had been empty for so long, he didn't expect them to ever be filled. Now he had his dad, he had a twin sister that he'd have to find a way to come to accept, and he had Maddie.

Maddie. His soul. His heart.

His home.

MJ thought back to tossing a penny in the fountain out on the patio with Holly and Sam, wishing for somewhere to belong. Funny how quickly wishes could come true.

"It'll always be you," Maddie said, reaching up and stroking the side of his face.

MJ pulled her to her feet and wrapped her in his arms. She smelled like vanilla and spice and he couldn't inhale enough of her. Her soft, silky hair caressed his cheek resting on top of her head, and her soft, full breasts pressed against his chest. "Home," he whispered.

She squeezed him tight. "Home," she said.

Twenty-Eight

Three days later…

The hospital smelled like a sickening mixture of cafeteria food and Lysol, making Maddie's stomach gurgle. She jabbed the elevator button for the second floor and shifted from foot to foot waiting for the doors to close.

MJ was with Merrick and Rachael at an apartment Merrick owned in Atlanta. He'd let them stay there while her dad was in the hospital since it was close. Maddie told MJ she needed some time alone with her dad today and she'd call if he woke up. The roller-coaster ride of the past few days left her feeling claustrophobic and in need of air and space to get her mind wrapped around everything that happened.

She approached room two-eighty-one and peeked inside. The bed closest to the door was empty, and her father's frail frame lay under the white sheet on the far bed beside the windows. He was buried under wires and tubes. Machines blinked and beeped around him.

"Daddy?" she whispered, crossing the room to his bed. "I'm back." She'd spent the better part of the past few days in this room, only leaving when MJ absolutely insisted she come back to the apartment and get some sleep. She bent and kissed the top of her dad's head. His gray, wiry hair prickled her nose. "I'm sorry."

She sat in the chair beside his bed and waited for a nurse to come in and give her an update. When a half hour went by, she turned on the TV to an old movie and let her mind drift to the night before. Exhausted and stressed, MJ had made love to her so gently, so breathtakingly, she'd been shattered and whole at the same time. Needy and complete. Only MJ could make her feel two extremes at once.

Where would they go from here?

She couldn't let her father live alone, and there was no way he was going back to the Rocha Estate. She'd have to find a place for them to live. He'd retire, and she'd find a job to help supplement his Social Security.

MJ would go back to school. She'd see him on weekends. He'd get to know his father.

It would be good.

But it didn't feel good. She wanted his promise of every night in his arms. But, she couldn't do that and live with her dad at the same time. She was twenty-four, but she wouldn't throw her private life in his face.

She and MJ would have their time, but it couldn't be until he was ready for the level of commitment she was. She'd marry him tomorrow if she could, but he needed to focus on graduating and running Rocha Enterprises for now.

If he knew she was making decisions for him, he'd be pissed. He was a man and she didn't need to watch out for him. Or so he said. But, she'd always watch out for him. She loved him. It had nothing to do with age.

A nurse finally came in. She said Maddie's dad's vital signs were all good and they expected him to wake up any time. The swelling in his head had gone down and as soon as he was awake, they would take the oxygen mask off. He had a few bruises and abrasions on his arms and legs, but nothing was broken.

"He hit his head pretty hard for only falling down the stairs, didn't he?" Maddie said.

"We have orders to call the police when he wakes. The doctor alerted a social worker to the case and they want to send over an investigator to speak with him when he's able."

"Good," Maddie said, resting her hand on her father's arm. "Someone did this to him."

The nurse jotted some numbers down on her dad's chart and left the room. Maddie's stomach growled, having not eaten all day. Since her dad was still unconscious, she decided to head down to the ground floor and see what she could find for dinner in the cafeteria. Hopefully, they had a decent cup of coffee. "Be right back," she told him, and patted his hand.

The cafeteria was enormous, with hot food stations, a salad bar, a deli case and dessert counter. She was starving and wanted one of everything.

Maddie put a turkey sandwich and cup of broccoli cheese soup on a tray before filling a paper cup with steaming hot coffee. She paid and made her way back up to the second floor in the elevator.

The doors opened. She stepped out, turned the corner and froze seeing three policemen standing outside her father's room. Rushing forward, she almost dumped her tray. "What happened?" she asked.

"Peach?" she heard from inside the room. "Is that you?"

"Dad." She pushed her way inside.

He was awake. The nurse was checking his blood pressure, and a uniformed officer stood beside his bed with a tablet.

"You're awake," Maddie said, sitting her tray on his side table, and kissing him on the cheek. "What happened?"

He closed his eyes and shook his head in disbelief. "Enzo hit me in the back of the head with something. I didn't see what. I fell down the stairs and that's all I know."

"Will you be pressing assault charges?" the officer asked.

"Yes," she answered for her dad. "Absolutely."

Her dad squeezed her hand. "I'm glad you're here, safe with me Peach."

Twenty-Nine

$\mathcal{M}$ J sat with his dad, Beck, Rachael and Joan on the balcony of his dad's downtown Atlanta studio apartment. The past few days had passed in a blur. He'd spent all of his time at the hospital with Maddie when he wasn't asleep, or feeling guilty for keeping her awake. He couldn't help it. He'd let too many days pass without feeling her naked underneath him. Without making her cry out his name.

Today Maddie asked him for some time alone with her dad at the hospital. He hated leaving her, hated that she needed space, but knew he had to give it to her. He was just glad he had Merrick and Rachael, hell even Beck to keep his mind occupied.

"I'm giving you one hour," Rachael said, wrapping her arms around Merrick's neck from behind his chair. "Then I'm taking you *and you,*" she pointed to Beck, "to the hospital to get checked out. So don't get too comfortable."

Merrick had resisted her urges for the past few days, but this morning when he flew Beck, Joan and Riley in to get some work done, Rachael declared she wouldn't wait any longer and insisted Beck was getting his broken ribs looked at by a doctor, too.

"You're not *my* woman," Beck said, fiddling with his cello strings. "I don't have to do what you say."

"If you want me to let you play that thing for the anniversary party on the island you'll do what I say." Rachael grinned knowing she had him cornered. "On the condition that you actually get it to sound like a musical instrument instead of a dying goose."

With a cigar hanging out of the corner of his mouth, Beck smirked and ran his bow across the strings making the worst sound MJ had ever heard.

MJ laughed. He never imagined hanging out with his dad and his dad's friends like this and feeling so comfortable, like he was one of them.

Beside him at the round, glass-topped table, Joan shuffled some paperwork. "I can't believe you're making me supervise Riley and Jesse on the bandstand build. Those two would be lucky to build a birdhouse, let alone an actual structure."

"Well," Merrick said, "I have some news. You're being reassigned again. The bandstand will be your last project at Turtle Tear."

She dropped her papers and looked up, first at Merrick, then at Beck, finally to Rachael, and her eyes narrowed, accusingly.

"This is news to me too," Rachael said. "I had nothing to do with whatever they have brewing."

"Right," Joan said, propping a forearm on the table. "What will my new assignment be?"

Merrick smiled. "You'll be working for MJ on his first property."

"What?" MJ said, gripping the arms of his chair.

"My exact thought." Joan pushed her chair back and crossed her legs. "I can't wait to hear this."

Merrick took a sip of iced tea. "The first time I spoke to Rachael," he said, "she told me the story of Turtle Tear's founders."

"Archie and Ingrid," MJ said. "She's been going on and on about them."

Merrick laughed and took Rachael's hand. "They're the inspiration behind everything on the island," he said. "When Rachael told me I had a son, I went a little nuts. I didn't know what to do, or where to go. I should've come right to you, but—"

"But, being an idiot is part of your charm," Rachael said, beaming at him.

"I'm glad you find it charming in addition to frustrating." Merrick kissed her and continued. "I ended up calling Max, my lawyer and advisor. As I was talking to him, spilling this insane story of ours, it hit me and I knew what I had to do. I'd given Turtle Tear to Rachael, and I had to give a piece of the same history to you."

Merrick slid a file folder off of the table and passed it to MJ. "The Weston Sugar Plantation, Archibald Weston's family home. It's about a half hour south of St. Petersburg, just outside of Palmetto, and it's all yours."

Shocked, MJ opened the folder with fumbling fingers and took out a photo. He studied the white-columned, antebellum plantation house. It was practically falling down. "It's incredible. Is it safe to go inside?"

"It's safe. Mostly." Merrick pointed to the west wing. "I wouldn't walk around in this section though. I'll train you, teach you everything you need to know."

MJ couldn't stop staring at the pictures, then at Merrick. "I can't believe this. Thanks, um...Dad."

Merrick smiled and rubbed his hand across his stubble-covered chin. Watching him, Rachael laughed. "I think you've left him speechless, MJ."

MJ pressed his palm flat against the file folder. "I'm the one who should be speechless." He handed the file to Joan. "Looks like we better get busy. Restoring this place is going to be practically impossible."

Joan shot him a condescending smirk. "I don't know the word impossible."

"She's a pain in the ass," Beck said, tightening a cello string, "but she'll get it taken care of."

"Riley!" Merrick shouted. "Now!"

After a minute, Riley came out of the sliding glass doors from the kitchen holding a bottle of champagne and a stack of clear plastic cups. He handed them to Merrick. "Am I getting reassigned to Beck now that he doesn't have an assistant?"

"Do you want to work for Beck?" Merrick ask, popping the champagne cork.

"Your sorry ass isn't working for me," Beck said. "I hear you can't even build a birdhouse. If you can string a cello there might be hope for you though."

Merrick patted Riley on the back. "Looks like you're stuck with me."

Riley sat down across from Beck and grabbed a pack of strings from him. "Who said I can't string a cello?"

"I'm that bad to work for?" Merrick asked pouring each of them a little champagne.

MJ laughed. "Maybe you training me isn't such a good idea."

His phone vibrated in his pocket. When he pulled it out and saw Maddie's name on the screen, a surreal feeling passed through him.

They were off the island and she was still his. It hadn't been a dream or his imagination. She came back to him. "Hey, Mads," he said, answering.

"It was Enzo," she said. "My dad's awake. He remembers."

"What?" MJ shot forward in his chair.

"The police have gone to arrest him," she said.

Whoa. MJ knew his grandfather was capable of being cruel, but this was beyond his imagining. "I'm sorry, Mads. Tell your dad I'm sorry."

"It's not your fault. Don't be sorry. He's manipulated you your entire life, too."

Merrick leaned forward in his chair and nudged MJ's arm. "Everything okay?" he mouthed.

MJ shook his head. "I'm coming," he told Maddie. "I'll be there soon."

He ended the call and grit his teeth with his effort to hold back the slur of expletives that wanted to erupt from his mouth. "Mr. Simcoe's awake. He remembers what happened to him. It was Enzo."

Merrick pounded a fist on the table. "They're pressing charges?"

"The police went to arrest him." MJ let his head fall back and groaned. "I can't believe my grandfather did this to her dad."

"She won't hold this against you," Rachael said, coming to stand beside his chair. "I don't know her well, but it's pretty clear how she feels about you."

MJ scooted down in the chair so his head rested against the back. "I just can't believe after everything…this is like the cherry on top, you know?"

"Think they'll find him?" Beck asked. "Enzo? From everything I've heard about him, he doesn't seem like the kind of guy who would sit around waiting for the cops to show up."

"Nope," MJ answered. It hadn't even occurred to him, but now that Beck had said it, he knew Enzo wasn't going to be arrested. "He's the most manipulative bastard there is. He'll surface someday, but not until this blows over."

"Spoken like someone who's suffered under his roof," Merrick said. "I can empathize."

"Let's get to the hospital," Rachael said, taking Merrick's hand and tugging. "I'm sure Maddie could use the support."

"You're lucky you have this as an excuse to get me to the hospital," Merrick said. "I hate being poked and prodded." He pulled her down onto his lap and kissed her cheek and neck playfully.

"That's what she said," Beck muttered and laughed to himself.

Riley gave Beck a few exaggerated blinks. "Really?"

MJ got up and collected the Weston Plantation file from the table. "We'll talk about this soon," he told Joan.

"Can't wait," she said, giving him a thousand-watt smile that was anything but sincere.

"The Dragon Lady has sharp claws, Junior," Beck said, wrapping an arm across his chest and grimacing in pain as he stood up. "Consider yourself warned."

"I sink them in deep too," Joan said, cocking an eyebrow at Beck.

"That's no lie," he said and winked at her.

MJ might never understand what those two had going on between them. Then again, he probably didn't want to.

"Before we leave," Merrick said, raising his cup of the forgotten champagne. "I'd like to make a toast to my son."

MJ couldn't help feeling like he'd reverted to being a six-year-old again when he longed to meet his dad, to hear Merrick call him son.

"I'm already proud of you," Merrick said. "I can see so many qualities of a good man inside you. Determination, loyalty, a fierce protective streak and a heart that will get you into more trouble that you expect." Merrick gave Rachael a knowing look. "But it will also lead you right to where you should always be. So, don't ignore it."

"To Junior," Beck said, tossing back his two-fingers of champagne.

The rest of them swallowed theirs down and MJ let the unfamiliar but warm feeling of belonging sink into his bones.

"Okay," Rachael said, collecting their cups. "To the hospital. Now. No more delays."

MJ followed her and Merrick inside. The studio apartment was modern with high ceilings and exposed metal I-beams. The stark white walls were dotted with bright, abstract paintings. Charcoal gray marble floors spanned the entire space. Ornate, blown glass chandeliers hung from the ceiling and every piece of furniture was made with straight lines and metal legs. It was a culture shock coming here from Turtle Tear.

"Don't screw up my instrument," Beck called to Riley from behind MJ. "Keep your eye on him, Joan."

"She always has her eyes on me," Riley called back, mockingly.

Rachael grabbed her purse and had one hand on the doorknob when Merrick put a hand over his pocket. "Hold on. That's my phone."

Merrick took his phone out and glanced at the screen, frowning. "Hello?" he said. As he listened to whoever was on the other end, he looked over at MJ. "No," Merrick said, "I'm not in contact with my father."

The call was about Enzo. The police? It had to be.

"I'd be happy to answer questions for you. Right now I'm on my way to the hospital to visit Mr. Simcoe." Merrick nodded as he listened. "Yes, my sister and her husband should be on their way home. They've been vacationing this past week with me and my family." Again, Merrick glanced over at MJ, then reached for Rachael's hand. "Nadia

Montgomery, his granddaughter, might be able to locate him. I know for a fact she's been in contact with him as recently as last night, possibly today." Merrick dropped his head. "She's my daughter."

❀

Maddie's dad was incredibly stubborn. He wouldn't let her help him do anything, including walking him to the shower down the hall. "All I have to do is push this IV stand along, Peach. I think I can manage that."

"Fine. I'll wait here." She plopped back down in the chair beside his bed. He'd be released tomorrow and she had no idea where they'd be going. But, Coach knew a lot of people. She'd call him in a little while and see if he had any leads on a cheap place they could rent.

The phone beside Maddie's dad's bed rang. She picked the receiver up and held it to her ear. "Hello?"

"Madeline, it's good to hear your voice." Chills ran over her skin. Enzo Rocha. "The police are looking for you."

"They won't find me. But, I'll always know where you are. The one who pushed and pushed until my secret came out."

"I didn't tell anyone."

"No, but you wouldn't stay away from MJ. You didn't take my warning seriously."

"I'm not listening to another word." She slammed the phone down, grabbed the business card the investigator had left and dialed his number.

After telling him about the call, he suggested hiring private security for her and her father until they could locate Enzo and get him into custody.

She couldn't afford private security. She didn't even have a place to live.

Hopelessness set in. She crawled into a ball in the chair and wept. She couldn't even run away, because her father was in danger because of her.

Thirty

"Don't cry, Mads."

She jerked her chin up to find MJ standing in the doorway. Her heart leapt from her chest to her throat.

He stepped inside the room. "How's your dad? Where is he?"

"Shower," she said. "He's good."

"I know I said I'd see you tonight," he said, walking toward her, "but Merrick and Beck are here getting their wounds from the wreck checked out. Do you mind?"

With fear lacing her veins, she'd never been so happy to see him. "No. I'm glad you're here."

MJ knelt in front of her, scooped her into his arms and kissed her over and over until she couldn't catch her breath.

"MJ," she said, pushing him away. "Enzo just called me. It's not over. He still wants to keep me away from you."

"What? Why?"

"He says I didn't listen. I went to Turtle Tear and it's my fault his secret had to come out."

MJ stood and pulled her to her feet. "Okay. We'll call the police. He can't do this to you."

"I called them. They told me to hire private security. I don't even know where we're going to live. I can't afford to hire security." She wiped her puffy eyes.

Maddie saw the wheels in his head spinning a million miles a minute. "I'll be right back." He pointed to the chair. "Don't leave this room."

He dashed out the door and she sat back down, defeated.

A few minutes later, her dad came back in, dressed in a fresh gown, pushing his IV stand. "I'm back in one piece, Peach, as promised."

"Good, you stubborn old goat." She helped him back into bed and tucked the covers around him.

"Knock, knock," Rachael said from the doorway. MJ stood behind her. "I heard you're the nurses' favorite. Are you flirting with them, Mr. Simcoe?"

He laughed. "All old men flirt with lovely ladies. Come in."

Rachael rounded Maddie's dad's bed and bent to hug her where she sat in the chair. "I have something to ask the two of you." She glanced between Maddie and her dad. "A favor."

"I'm hardly in any position to grant favors," Maddie's dad said, "but you're certainly welcome to ask."

"Well," Rachael said, leaning against the windowsill, "we've had some staffing changes at the hotel. Merrick and I both need some help. I was wondering if the two of you would be willing to come stay at the hotel for a while? Maddie, your dad could relax and recuperate and maybe you could help me organize the fiftieth anniversary party I booked?" She groaned. "And I need help talking Beck out of playing the cello for the couple's big dance."

It was perfect. MJ smiled like he might burst. "Thank

you," she mouthed to him, standing on the other side of her dad's bed.

"It sounds like a grand offer," Mr. Simcoe said. "I'm not sure how much help I'd be to your Merrick though."

Rachael sat on the side of his bed. "You know what he needs more than anything? A man with a level head to guide him, to keep him from being impulsive and doing stupid things." She laughed. "I think you're just the one for that role."

Maddie's dad took her hand. "I've heard a lot about him over the years. I'm ashamed I never gave him the chance to prove himself. Now I know the kind of man Enzo Rocha really is. I'd be honored to help in any way I'm able."

"Fantastic," Rachael said, squeezing Maddie's dad's hand with both of hers. "We'll get you settled in when we spring you out of here."

MJ shook her dad's hand. "I'm relieved to see you doing so well. I'll have you out fishing at Turtle Tear before you know it. I remember a score I have to settle."

"I haven't been fishing in years, but I'm the one who taught you, so don't you go thinking you can land more fish than me."

"As long as I don't have to clean them," Rachael said, sticking out her tongue. "I'll help eat them though."

MJ bent his finger, summoning Maddie to him. "I have something to tell you."

Maddie gave her dad a hesitant glance. He grasped her shirt sleeve and tugged. "Get out of here with your young man. Go do something fun. I'm not going anywhere."

"Merrick wants to come up and say hello when they're done reopening and stitching the wound on his knee," Rachael said, and shivered at the thought.

"See, Peach, I've got company coming. Beat it."

"Okay, okay!" Maddie got up and followed MJ to the elevators. "Are you sure Rachael's okay with this and you didn't twist her arm?"

He pushed the button for the lobby. "Are you kidding? She jumped at the chance to have you stay and bring your dad."

The doors closed and he pulled her against him. She could tell he had something to tell her that he couldn't hold in any longer. "What?" she asked.

"You know Archibald's family home, the Weston Sugar Plantation?"

She prodded his dimples with her fingers and smiled as he grinned. "Yes."

"Mads, I own it. Merrick bought it for me as my first project."

Maddie couldn't believe what he was telling her. "What?"

"Yeah. It's in bad shape, but he's having Joan help me renovate it, and he's going to teach me everything he knows about running the business."

She squeezed him as hard as she could. "I'm so happy for you. So proud." She looked into his eyes, and blinked back tears. "You have your dad, MJ. You're out from under Enzo's thumb."

He kissed her. "So are you. You'll be safe at Turtle Tear."

Maddie's thoughts went to Nadia. She'd been on the island and nobody knew. Anyone else could do the same. But, MJ had given her and her father a place to stay with friends. They wouldn't be alone. "It's going to work out, isn't it?" she asked.

"It already has." He picked her up and pressed his lips against hers, spinning her in a circle. The elevator jolted under them, coming to a stop.

Maddie laughed.

"What?" MJ asked.

"I like it when the ground moves under my feet when you're kissing me."

He spun her around again. "Baby, I promise to always make your world shake."

Epilogue

"I can't believe we're here," Rachael said, holding a map of the 150,000 acres that MJ now owned along with the plantation house and several outbuildings.

Maddie pulled at the strap of the hardhat on her head. It was tight and uncomfortable, but MJ threatened to punish her if she took it off. She wasn't sure what he had in mind, but she was tempted to toss the hardhat to the floor to find out.

He stood with Merrick and Joan at a drafting table, pouring over blueprints. He hadn't told her what he was going to do with the property, but she knew he was making it into a business like Rachael and Merrick had done with Turtle Tear. MJ told her it was a surprise and he wasn't ready to tell her just yet.

It was Maddie's second visit to the plantation, but her father and Rachael's first. MJ and Merrick had lugged a big steamer trunk down out of the attic. Along with some dead bugs, there were photographs, diaries, a few ornate silver pieces, and enough history on Ingrid and Archibald's family to keep Rachael entranced for days.

"Lookie here," Maddie's dad said, shuffling over to them with an old newspaper. "This is from 1974. Read this article." He tapped the side panel of the paper, handing it over to Maddie.

Ghost of Woman Communicates From Beyond

Outside St. Petersburg sits an old antebellum plantation house that used to be home to the Weston family. The Weston Sugar Plantation operated from the 1830s until 1865 when the mill burned down near the end of the Civil War.

Attempts by the current owners to renovate the plantation house have been thwarted at every turn by a ghost they call Ingrid.

Legend has it the woman is Ingrid (Burkhart) Weston, wife of Archibald Weston, son of the original owners of the plantation. The Weston's and the Burkhart's were Florida's Civil War version of the Montague's and Capulet's, making Ingrid and Archibald true star-crossed lovers.

Archibald built a home for his beloved on Turtle Tear Island in the Everglades where they lived and raised their own family. Although Ingrid died while staying at the Weston Plantation, her body is said to be buried on Turtle Tear Island.

"She's not with her body," the current plantation owners say of Ingrid's spirit. "She's here, but she wants to go back."

How do they know Ingrid's wishes? She's told them.

"*Take me back to Turtle Tear* was written in the condensation on the attic window after a storm," they say. "She's written it in the dust on the attic floor too, and every time we bring a crew in to remodel the attic she shows herself, scatters their tools, barricades the stairs and scares them away."

"I feel bad," the current owner says of Ingrid's predicament. "I'd take her to Turtle Tear if I knew how."

For now, she's stuck at the Weston Plantation, desperate to get back to the island home her Romeo built her.

"We have to help her," Rachael said, taking the newspaper out of Maddie's hand. "We have to take her back."

"How? I mean, it's only a legend." Maddie didn't want to discourage Rachael. She knew how tightly Rachael's heart was wrapped up in Turtle Tear's history.

"I don't know," Rachael said. "But the answer is here somewhere." She lifted both hands, palms to the air. "Ingrid's here somewhere. Maybe she can tell us."

"Maybe so," Maddie's dad said, limping away. She couldn't tell if he was serious, or if he thought Rachael was nuts.

Maddie wasn't so sure herself, even if she was a self-proclaimed ghost hunter show addict. MJ had told her the ghost in the west wing of the Rocha Estate had been Nadia. Somehow, she thought she'd known all along that the girl was real, and faced with the possibility of a ghost in real life wasn't something she was prepared to deal with.

"Find anything good?" MJ called, watching her from across the room.

"We found some interesting things." She smiled, wishing everyone would disappear and she could be alone with him.

Since he'd been working on the Weston Plantation, she'd seen a side of him she never knew existed. She saw the man she always knew he'd be emerging.

She was changing too. Trusting him to be strong for both of them. Trusting her instincts. Letting go and opening herself, becoming vulnerable to him.

Their love had grown because of everything they'd been through. They understood it was worth fighting for and wouldn't always come easy, but they knew it was a love that very few people ever found. The once-in-a-lifetime kind.

The Rachael and Merrick kind.

The Archibald and Ingrid kind.

"I'll be right back," MJ told his dad. He took his hardhat off, rounded the drafting table and strode toward Maddie.

Merrick glanced over his shoulder and winked at her. Rachael tried and failed to hide a wide smile, diving into the trunk with both hands. Maddie's dad seemed to be the only one who wasn't in on whatever the others knew.

Grinning, she stepped back as MJ reached her. "What is this? What's going on?"

He grabbed her hands and pulled her to him, taking her hardhat off and kissing her. "Come with me for a minute."

MJ held her hand and they walked out the grand, double front doors onto the wide covered porch with huge white columns running up to the roof. She walked down the brick front steps beside him into the bright afternoon sunlight.

The grass was emerald green, the sky a bright autumn blue. It was her favorite season. They walked down the front path. The breeze blew her hair. "Where are you taking me?" she asked.

He looked back over his shoulder at the house and stopped. "Right here. Turn around."

She spun and took in the tall, sprawling white house. "It's amazing. I can't believe it's yours."

"That's what I wanted to talk to you about." He took her hands and faced her. "When I look at this house, standing right in this spot, do you know what I see?"

"What?"

"I see you in a big, white dress. You're standing right here with your dad. I'm at the bottom of the stairs waiting for you."

Her eyes prickled with tears. He smiled and brushed her hair back over her shoulder.

"Music starts to play—not Beck unless he gets a lot better by then—and your dad escorts you down the front walkway. When the two of you reach where I'm standing, he places your hand in mine."

Maddie couldn't hold her tears back. They flowed freely down over her cheeks.

"Mads, I want this to be our home. Not a business. I want to bring our five kids home from the hospital here. I want to have holidays here. I want to get old with you here."

He knelt down and took her hand. "This is not a proposal. Not yet. The next time I go down on one knee it will be." He took a silver ring out of his pocket and held it up to show her. A tiny, antique heart shaped lock and key were mounted on the filigree ring. It took Maddie's breath away.

"I'm asking for your heart," he said, "before I ask for your hand."

Maddie fell to her knees in front of him. "My heart could only be more yours if I took it out of my chest and handed it to you. I would love to make this a home with you MJ. You've always been my home."

He held her hand and slid the ring in place on her finger. Then he kissed her, the promise between them strong and solid.

Turn this page for a preview of

Taken,

the first in Kelli Maine's
Give & Take series.

One

Three months later...

The club is packed. Bodies grind together on the dance floor. There's barely room to move. You catch my eye.

You're alone.

Bass pounds through my body, rushes from my head to my toes, takes the same path your eyes follow. Your dark-eyed stare is flutter-soft on my skin. It raises goose bumps. Makes me flush. My vodka and cranberry-soaked blood runs hot with need.

You smile. Dimples pierce your cheeks. Your eyes flash. I can't resist.

"Rach!" Shannon grabs my arm. She's sweaty from dancing and pulls her blond hair up off her shoulders. "I'm going." She tilts her head toward Shawn or Shane or Seth— I'm not sure—the guy she met two hours ago.

"How am I supposed to get home?" She drove.

Shannon shoves her car keys in my hand. "See you in the morning." She winks and pushes back through the crowd toward the guy whose name starts with an *S*.

When I turn from watching Shannon go, you're standing right in front of me. "Hi," you say. Familiarity strikes, but I don't think I'd ever forget meeting you.

"Hi." I fall into your dark eyes and can't get out. They're serious and focused on mine. Looking away would be a crime.

You run a hand through your wavy black-brown hair. Are you nervous? I can't tell. "What were you drinking?" You tap my glass, empty except for melting ice.

"Vodka and cranberry." I take in a thick, damp breath. Dancing bodies fog up the air, make it heavy to breathe.

You shake your beer bottle, indicating its emptiness. "I'm headed to the bar. Would you like another?"

I have to drive Shannon's car home, but I don't want to stop talking to you. I nod. "Please." I'll drink slowly. I'll drive even slower.

I follow behind you, taking in the view of your incredible backside in jeans. A black long-sleeved shirt shifts with your strong, wide shoulders and hugs your narrow waist. You work out. *A lot.* The body I'm staring at didn't come from luck and a good gene pool.

You glance back to make sure I'm following. When a group of people push between us, you reach out and take my hand. My fingers curl around yours like they're possessed.

We reach the bar. You squeeze between two men. I stand back to wait while you order. I watch you reach into your pocket. A second later, you turn to me and hand me a glass.

"Thanks." I take a deep drink, ignoring my self-promise to sip and make it last. Looking at you, I need all the courage this vodka is offering.

You sip your beer, watching me. An intense magnetism pulls between us. I'm sweating. I wipe my forehead with the back of my hand. The vodka is kicking in fast. I stumble sideways. You grip my arm.

"Feeling okay?" you ask.

The room spins and tilts. Black spots swim through my vision. "No. I need to sit." My drink slips through my fingers and splatters on my bare leg.

"I've got you." You put an arm around me and lead me toward the door. "You need some air."

I'm blacking out and coming to, over and over again. This has never happened from three and a half vodka and cranberries before. "I need to get home."

"I'll take you," you say.

"No. I..." The words won't come. They buzz around in the darkness inside my mind searching for the light. I watch them break apart and fade.

You usher me through the parking lot. Open the door of a black car. Put me inside. "We'll be home soon," you say, buckling a seatbelt around my waist.

I try to grip the door handle to get out. My arm won't move. My head lulls on my shoulder. The blackness narrows, leaving a small tunnel focused on the dashboard. Then it closes completely.

No more words.

No more light.

No more sound.

Just like that—I'm taken.

**Kelli Maine's Give & Take series
continues with**

No Takebacks…

please turn this page for a preview

One

The sun beats down on us. It's hot. Sauna hot. The kind that makes the air heavy and saturates your skin with a sheen of moisture.

I let my eyes roam over your tan, sculpted chest down to where your fingers thread together resting on your abs.

"Like what you see?" you ask. Smiling, you reach out and trace your finger along my cheek. I wish I could see your eyes behind your black sunglasses.

"You know I do."

You chuckle and link your hands again, relaxing on your lounge chair.

The pool water ripples in the breeze, sunlight glinting off its surface. Pinkish-purple bougainvillea twines up to the palm frond roof of the pool-side bar. How did we get here? Us together? There were so many obstacles between us.

Over the past few months, Turtle Tear has been transformed from ancient ruins to a luxury resort on a private island in the Everglades. In the distance, the work crew bangs and saws, finishing the last few rooms in the hotel.

"Let's cancel tomorrow," you say. "I don't want to share you."

"We've waited too long for this." Even though it's only been about six months for me, you've waited years for this day to come. Tomorrow is the grand opening of Turtle Tear Resort to our friends and family. After that...well, I haven't decided if I want to open it to the public, or keep it private. I guess I'm not ready to share this place or you with anyone else either. "After they're all gone, you can become a hermit."

You take my hand and kiss it. "At least you promised me we could stay in the tree house and not crowd in the hotel with everyone else."

I roll to my side and run a finger down your arm. "I love our little hideaway."

Footsteps sound from the covered walkway. I sit up and turn to see Riley, your new assistant, step out from the shade and into the pool courtyard. "Why are you wearing dress pants and a tie?" I ask him. "Are you insane? It's sweltering out here."

You sit up, and your knees bump against mine. "Riley likes to look professional." You grasp the left side of my red bikini top and tug it closed. "And you're a little too casual. More like falling out."

"No interest in sharing me with this assistant then?" I whisper.

You clench your jaw, but don't reply. I was teasing, but struck a nerve bringing up the reason I left you last time.

"Ms. DeSalvo," Riley interjects, spots of pink on his cheeks from either the heat or from overhearing my comment, "your mother and aunt are scheduled to arrive at ten a.m. tomorrow morning. Do you have a preference of which rooms are reserved for them?"

I shade my eyes and glance up at him, wishing I hadn't forgotten my sunglasses back in the hotel. "No. I'm sure you'll pick very nice rooms for them. I trust your judgment. But can you do me a favor?"

He nods, eager to please. "Of course."

"Call me Rachael."

A sheepish grin spreads across his face. He's young, twenty-two at most, not that I'm much older. But his reserved manner and uncontrollable blushing make him seem a lot younger. "Can I get you another drink from the bar, Rachael?"

I pick up my empty mimosa glass from the small table beside my chair and hold it out to him. "That would be amazing of you. Thanks."

"Mr. Rocha?" he asks, taking my glass.

You pick up your half-full bottle of water and shake it in Riley's direction. "I'm good, thanks. But that reminds me, when's the domestic staff getting in?"

"Three this afternoon."

Riley trots off toward the bar on the opposite side of the pool and courtyard. "Someone has a crush," you say, squeezing my knees between yours.

The stubble on your face has grown to a soft beard that covers your chin, not quite as full as it was when we first met, but soft to the touch and sexy. I can't resist running my fingers over it. "You're right," I say. "But look at him. Those pressed oxford shirts he wears, the flop of dusty blond hair over his forehead and the way he always blushes when he looks at me. How can I not be crushing hard?"

You lower your sunglasses to the end of your nose and arch one brow over your blazing, dark eyes. "You're full of jabs today, aren't you? You know what I meant."

I stand between your legs and take your face between my hands skimming my fingers through your dark, wavy hair. "You know I'm kidding. Look at you." I let my hands run down your neck, across your broad shoulders, down over the bulging muscles of each arm. "Why would I ever want anyone else?"

Your hands find my hips and pull me closer, close enough to rest your cheek against my stomach. "I've already done everything you're just getting to do. I've reached my goals. You could have someone like him—like you. Someone driven, making his way up the ladder. I kicked my ladder down, Rachael."

Why do you think I care that you've decided to retire in your mid-thirties with billions in the bank? Somehow in your head that's a bad thing. "You told me your plan months ago. When we went fishing, remember?"

"The storm that day." You chuckle, sending vibrations through my skin. "I swear, you wrapped your wet little body around my back so tight when I carried you back to the hotel, I had obscene images running wild in my head."

"Every time lightning flashed, I thought we were going to die." I stroke the top of your head, twisting sun-warmed locks of hair around my fingers. "The fish you caught was good though."

You turn your head and rest your chin in my belly button. "Yeah? You hardly touched it."

I bend and kiss the grin off your face. Eating around you leads to kissing you and touching you and meals are quickly shoved aside and forgotten. I've lost eight pounds since I stepped foot on this island. "We need another chocolate raspberry cake."

You growl and lick my stomach sending delicious flesh memories straight to my center. Memories of smeared chocolate frosting devoured with your tongue. "Don't worry. I've got that covered."

"Uh…" Riley stammers, standing at the end of my lounge chair with a fresh mimosa in one hand. "I'll just…" He sets it on the wooden table and shuffles away.

"Thanks!" I call after him. "Think he's a virgin?"

You let out a derisive snort. "Can't imagine why you'd think that."

"I don't know. Maybe he's just modest."

"Hmm. Maybe." With a flick of your fingers, my bikini top falls open. "Glad you're not."

"Not with you." I wrap my arms around your neck and you pull me down on top of you on the lounge chair sucking a nipple into your mouth.

"Ah," I gasp. I'll never get used to the feel of your lips, your tongue. It's too good, too drive-me-insane overwhelming.

I press against your shoulders, releasing my flesh with a drag of your teeth. I have to have your mouth on mine, your tongue sliding over mine drawing moans from deep in my throat.

I devour your lips. No holding back. I held back so long waiting to trust you, but now I need to take and take and never stop until there's nothing left of you. Consume you delicious bite by delicious bite.

Rewarded with a low groan when I nip your bottom lip, I taste my way across your jaw to lap your earlobe and take it in my mouth. Your hands squeeze my ass and slide down between my inner thighs, pulling them apart so I'm straddling you. Your chest is warm under my splayed fingers, salty on the tip of my tongue tasting your hard pecs. You rock your hips into me. I dig my nails into your skin in response making you suck in an airy hiss through your teeth.

The wind blows my hair across your face, cools my bare back damp with heat. You ball my hair in your hands as I trail kisses down your stomach. "I love how you taste."

My hair goes loose around my shoulders and you run both palms down my back. "I never want anyone else here. Just us. Alone."

"Me too," I say, springing your hard length free from your swim trunks. "I'll have you naked whenever and wherever I want."

Your fingers find my nipples and begin pulling, pinching and rolling, sending shocks of clenching arousal through my center. "My sex kitten."

I run my thumb up the thick vein running from the base of your cock to the ridge around the head. A bead of pre-come glistens at the tip. "Mmm, for me?" I tuck my hair behind my ear and lave your slit with my tongue while staring into your deep, dark eyes. "I love giving you that look on your face."

Your heavy-lidded, lust-filled expression shifts for a moment as one side of your mouth hitches into a smile. "What look?"

"Like I'm killing you." I circle my tongue around the underside of your head, flicking and nibbling. "Slowly." I stroke you and let my tongue slide down to trace the seam between your balls. "So slowly."

Your hand cups the back of my head. "God, you're right. You are killing me slowly. Painfully slow. Suck me."

I take you in deep, hollowing my cheeks and moaning along with you. Your hand guides my head, but I know what you like. And I love giving it to you, to that glorious cock that makes me come so hard.

Your breath comes faster as I pick up the pace. I'm wet and throbbing, needy and empty. You have to touch me soon, satiate this ache. Fill me.

Both hands cup my face and pull me off of you, breaking my suction with a wet sucking sound as you free yourself from my mouth. "Take me inside you."

Your fingers sweep my bikini bottoms aside, and you groan finding me wet and swollen, ready to take all of your considerable length. I'm always ready for you.

I angle your tip against my opening and ease down onto you. Both of us sigh in ecstatic relief. Nothing feels as perfect as when you're squeezed tight inside me.

You sit up, shocking me with the way you slide even deeper, and pull my ass into you as close as I'll get. Your mouth finds mine. Our lips barely graze as we breathe the same air, the tip of your tongue teasing mine. At the gentle urging of your hands, I rock my hips torturously slow.

It feels so, so good. You're hitting a spot inside me that sparks tears to my eyes. Our lovemaking is bittersweet with suppressed urgency, denial of clenching muscles begging for a faster release.

Another languid rock into you, and a whimper tumbles out of me. I choke out the word, "God," like a prayer. I'm all senses and longing. I'm going insane.

Your jaw's taught, eyes barely open, brow furrowed in your effort to hold back. "You're...so...tight," you whisper, sounding like you're in pain.

I can only make incoherent noises in response between gasps of pleasure.

You lay back, and I clench around you tighter, desperate to keep you so deep. But when your thumb presses and rubs against my clit, I lean back and brace my hands on your thighs, grinding and bucking. Release is so close. A delicious, tingling burn smolders in my core. "Oh God. Right there."

"That's right, baby. Come for me." Your thumb continues its maddening assault, while the fingers of your other hand pluck and squeeze my nipples.

On the brink of exploding, I raise and lower faster and faster, slamming you deeper inside me. Your hips come off the lounge chair, meeting me thrust for thrust. "Fuck. I'm so close, Rachael."

"Oh! Oh, God!" I throw my head back as the first orgasmic wave crashes over me. "Come, Merrick. Come with me."

Your fingers dig into my hips as you thrust hard twice and groan in release. "Fuck." You throb inside me as you come and I continue to ride you.

My orgasm runs rampant. My fingers take over for your thumb, and I set loose the last pulse of my climax before falling limp on top of you.

We lie panting with the sun beating down on us, the distant buzz of a saw blending with the chirps of birds and rustle of leaves in the gentle island breeze. "I couldn't have dreamt this." I kiss your chest, slick with sweat. "It's too perfect."

You comb your fingers through my hair. "It's more than perfect. Promise me something."

I prop myself up on your chest to look at you. "Anything."

Your face is so serious, so... wide-eyed and wistful. "Never leave."

There's a fear in your eyes I've never seen before. It worries me. "I won't. I promise."

You hold me tight against you and kiss my temple. With your father trying to take everything you own, all of the real estate you've acquired as CEO of Rocha Enterprises, your primal need to grasp on tightly to what's yours is understandable.

But seeing you, confident-to-a-fault Merrick Rocha, falter on your axis, leaves me shaken.

About the Author

USA Today bestselling author of *Taken* and its sequel, *No Takebacks*, Kelli Maine watches entirely too much reality TV, which led to her compulsion to write dramatic romance novels. Blessed with a unique ability to bond with difficult people, she's convinced she could win *Big Brother*. Her deathly fear of heights would keep her from completing half of the detours on *The Amazing Race*, and she's shocked nobody has ever penned *The Survivor Diet Plan: Eat One Cup of Rice for Thirty-Nine Days and Lose Fifty Pounds*!

Kelli lives in northeast Ohio with her family and a crazy cat that broke into their attic and refused to leave. Kelli loves hearing from fans and giving away *Taken* swag on her blog, www.kellimaine.blogspot.com.

You can learn more at: Twitter @KelliMaine

Facebook.com

Don't miss Kelli Maine's Give & Take series

ABDUCTION

He steals her away to a deserted island, to the one place she's dreamed of being—the one place she can't go. He's used to buying whatever he wants, but he can't buy her.

SEDUCTION

How can she resist the magnetism of his body, the longing ache deep inside her? She wants him to take her—on her terms.

DESPERATION

Every attempt he makes to love her only hurts her. How can they go on like this? This is the story of how she was...

TAKEN

Available Now
Includes NEW prologue

HIS PAST MAY DESTROY THEIR FUTURE

The man Rachael DeSalvo loves more than anything is suffering in silence. The grand opening of Turtle Tear Resort should be a time of celebration for Merrick Rocha. But he's suddenly intent on selling off the business he built from the ground up—and Rachael's hell-bent on finding out why. Only one man can give her the answers she seeks, but meeting with him would be the ultimate betrayal to Merrick. Merrick once asked Rachael to trust him against all odds... can he do the same?

NO TAKEBACKS

Available Now